MW00777408

THE HOLE IN THE MOON

AND OTHER TALES

THE HOLE IN THE MOON

AND OTHER TALES BY
MARGARET ST. CLAIR

EDITED AND WITH AN INTRODUCTION BY RAMSEY CAMPBELL

DOVER PUBLICATIONS, INC.
MINEOLA, NEW YORK

Bibliographical Note

This Dover edition, first published in 2019, is a new selection of seventeen stories reprinted from standard texts. A new introduction written by Ramsey Campbell has been specially prepared for this volume.

Library of Congress Cataloging-in-Publication Data

Names: St. Clair, Margaret, author. | Campbell, Ramsey, 1946– editor, writer of introduction.
Title: The hole in the moon : and other tales / by Margaret St. Clair ; edited and with an introduction by Ramsey Campbell.
Description: Mineola, New York : Dover Publications, Inc., 2019.
Identifiers: LCCN 2019014451 | ISBN 9780486805627 | ISBN 048680562X
Subjects: LCSH: Science fiction, American—20th century. | Short stories, American—20th century.
Classification: LCC PS3537.T112 A6 2019 | DDC 813/.54—dc23
LC record available at https://lccn.loc.gov/2019014451

Manufactured in the United States by LSC Communications
80562X01   2019
www.doverpublications.com

Contents

Bibliographical Sources

"Rocket to Limbo." First published in *Fantastic Adventures*, 1946.

"Piety." First published in *Thrilling Wonder Stories*, 1947.

"The Hierophants." First published in *Thrilling Wonder Stories*, 1949.

"The Gardener." First published in *Thrilling Wonder Stories*, 1949.

"Child of Void." First published in *Super Science Stories*, 1949.

"Hathor's Pets." First published in *Startling Stories*, 1950.

"World of Arlesia." First published in *The Magazine of Fantasy and Science Fiction*, 1950.

"The Little Red Owl." First published in *Weird Tales*, 1951.

"The Hole in the Moon." First published in *The Magazine of Fantasy and Science Fiction*, 1952.

"The Causes." First published in *The Magazine of Fantasy and Science Fiction*, 1952.

"The Island of the Hands." First published in *Weird Tales*, 1952.

"Continued Story." First published in *Space Stories*, 1952.

"Brenda." First published in *Weird Tales*, 1954.

"Stawdust." First published in *The Magazine of Fantasy and Science Fiction*, 1956.

"The Invested Libido." First published in *Satellite Science Fiction*, 1958.

"The Autumn After Next." First published in *Worlds of Science Fiction*, 1960.

"The Sorrows of Witches." First published in *Amazons!*, 1979.

Introduction: The Magical Margaret

IN A MEMOIR written in her mid-seventies, Margaret St. Clair mentioned that the critic John Clute described her as elusive. It seems to have been a quality she embraced, keeping much of her early life private, along with her later espousal of Wicca. "Certainly I dislike writing about myself," she declared in the brief memoir, because "I am often uncomfortably aware of not having 'the right attitude,'" and elsewhere "I'd rather write fiction instead of fact." Her literary output—over 100 short stories and eight novels, along with two novels left uncompleted upon her death—can prove elusive, too, spanning all the fields of the fantastic and much of it unreprinted. Let me sketch the lady and acclaim her work.

She was born Eva Margaret Neeley in Hutchinson, Kansas, on February 17, 1911, to Eva Margaret Neeley and George Neeley, a congressman. Her father died when she was seven, and she and her mother moved to Lawrence, Kansas, and in 1928 to Los Angeles. In 1932, she completed her undergraduate degree at Berkeley and married Raymond Earl St. Clair. Two years later she gained a master's degree at Berkeley in Greek classics. After a visit to China the St. Clairs made their home in El Sobrante, California, where they cultivated rare bulbs and raised dachshunds. In 1966, they were initiated into Wicca by Raymond Buckland, the founder of a coven in Bay Shore, New York. After her husband's death in 1986, Margaret spent her last years in a Santa Rosa retirement community, where she died on November 22, 1995.

Her first science fiction story, "Rocket to Limbo," appeared in November 1946. Raymond Palmer, editor of *Fantastic Adventures*, read it in the slush pile and bought it at once. In an essay composed to accompany the tale, St. Clair wrote, "it seems to me that a story about people—their problems, emotions, triumphs, and failures, is a far more interesting story to read—and write [than fiction about the 'battle between worlds']. . . . I like to write about ordinary people of the future, surrounded by gadgetry of super-science, but who, I feel sure, know no more about how the machinery works than a present-day motorist knows of the laws of thermodynamics." This story uses the near future to satirize the present, prefiguring the domestic science fiction of Ray Bradbury and the satirical science fiction of Robert Sheckley, while the twist recalls O. Henry's work.

St. Clair developed this approach in a group of tales about Oona and Jick, a married couple in the future, which (St. Clair wrote in 1981) "were not especially popular with fans, who were—then as now—a rather humorless bunch. The light tone of the stories seemed to offend readers and make them think I was making fun of them." Soon her themes grew weightier, though not necessarily her style. "Piety" (1947) succinctly discusses the haphazard nature of scientific progress in the context of an interplanetary culture shock and reveals the truth behind an alien taboo—a writer's vision of immortality—all in a couple thousand words. "The Hierophants" (1949) fuses science fiction and the Gothic in a way made most famous by Ridley Scott's film *Alien*. In St. Clair's tale too we have a derelict spacecraft that proves to be occupied by an invasive entity, not to mention an unnaturally mobile disintegrating corpse, but the encounter leads to a development both Biblical and magical and ultimately to a sense of mystical loss. Might some yearning of the kind have directed the St. Clairs toward Wicca?

"The Gardener" (1949) is the first of her horror stories and a seminal example of ecological science fiction. Its condemnation of careless tree-felling is just as timely today. The narrative employs the structure of the classic tale of terror as defined by M. R. James: "Let us, then, be introduced to the actors in a placid way; let us see them going about their ordinary business, undisturbed by forebodings, pleased with their surroundings; and into this calm environment let the ominous thing put out its head, unobtrusively at first, and then more insistently, until it holds the stage." St. Clair even uses the Jamesian devices of rhetorical language to convey the uncanny by indirectness ("What were those cracks . . .") and the minor employee who has seen more than the ill-fated protagonist. The tale transfers to outer space the image of an intruder at a window, rendering it eerier still. The Gardener is a genius loci translated into science fiction—an arboreal guardian that draws power from its grove—but its revenge is unusually gruesome and painfully vivid.

"Child of Void" (1949) uses naïve voices—the narrator's and his younger brother's—to throw an alien encounter into sharp relief. The nonchalance with which the narrator contemplates the manifestations in Hidden Valley mirrors how they are apparently accepted by whatever version of the world the characters inhabit. The story implies so much more than it states, not least about the narrator's own physical condition (hinted at but never specified), that it expands in the mind as the alien invaders colonize human consciousness. Their indifference recalls the cosmic disinterest of H. P. Lovecraft's entities, and even their effect on humanity is inadvertent.

"Hathor's Pets" (1950) posits a future in which feminism has been turned back by government sponsorship of brainlessness. This apparently took place in the 1980s, but while nothing dates faster in science fiction than dating, does this ring altogether false? Having established this context, the tale evokes the shock of telepathic contact with an alien and develops into a thoroughgoing tale of terror, where the ending resonates with the satirical theme.

"World of Arlesia" (1950) employs that difficult narrative mode, the second person, although in this case they (we) are addressed by the narrator. The purpose may be to immerse us more deeply in the narrative, just as the characters become submerged in the tale within the tale. The theme of augmented cinema seems unusually prescient, given that the developments we might assume inspired the author—Cinemascope, 3-D, and VistaVision, created to compete with television—had still to come. That said, there's more to the performance, and a paragraph that may initially appear peripheral proves to be nothing of the kind.

"The Little Red Owl" (1951) is one of several supernatural horror stories St. Clair wrote for the long-lived pulp magazine *Weird Tales*. Lovecraft remains the most noted contributor, and his influence was still apparent in its pages, but for some years the editor Dorothy McIlwraith had supported the contemporary style of writers such as Ray Bradbury and Richard Matheson. Under her editorship, Robert Bloch had grown equally modern in his approach, not least with several tales of murderous psychosis, none of which are as ruthlessly dark as St. Clair's tale here. Children as victims were still rare in popular fiction, but she depicts their peril with creative glee as well as sympathy. Decades later, *National Lampoon* ran a comic series by B. K. Taylor called *The Appletons*, where the Appleton children are terrorized by their father with all the magazine's relish for outrageousness, but even this falls short of St. Clair's vision. Her most disturbing insight is that the psychotic Charles believes he loves his victims. As a study of domestic abuse, the tale is well ahead of its time.

By this time, St. Clair had begun developing a short-lived parallel career as Idris Seabright, whose tales displayed an extra stylistic elegance and appeared mostly in *The Magazine of Fantasy and Science Fiction*. Among the earliest is "The Hole in the Moon" (1952), a post-apocalyptic vision of poetic succinctness, a ghost story of the future, an evocation of urban genii loci, a tale of terminal loneliness, an elegy for humanity. In his introduction to it, editor Anthony Boucher commented, "As with so much Seabright, you may find it running through your head like an unforgettable minor melody." Is it also a study of understandable insanity? It has room for that ambiguity as well.

Barroom fantasy is a small but vital subgenre, created by writers such as Arthur C. Clarke (*Tales from the White Hart*) and collaborators L. Sprague de Camp and Fletcher Pratt (*Tales from Gavagan's Bar*). "The Causes" (1952, signed by Idris Seabright) is St. Clair's contribution. It's a tall tale involving Greek gods, not entirely unreminiscent of Thorne Smith's comic novels along those lines, and a similarly witty treatment of a Christian tradition, not to mention a Tantric anecdote and a final narrative flourish. The humor doesn't preclude lyricism—see the description of the trumpet—but it never loses sight of the state of the world. Perhaps that's a joke on the part of the gods, like the resolution of this tale.

In 1952 the occult magazine *Fate* published the first article to define the Bermuda Triangle and associate it with maritime disappearances. Might this have generated St. Clair's "The Island of the Hands" that year? Her mysterious isle seems at first to embody the peril of wishes come true, but the story goes on to explore how human a simulacrum can be, which is to say it examines how humanity can be defined. It's a theme more usually associated with Philip K. Dick, but St. Clair's tale precedes his explorations.

"Continued Story" (1952) is a thoroughly paranoid account of entrapment by the future. The three items that bait the trap may be seen as scientific variations on the enchanted objects whose consequences beset characters in many a fairy tale, and the trap itself is a version of the magic toy shop. Do we as readers share the dark delight with which observers from the future manipulate the people in the story? After all, we're its future now.

Lately we've seen the development of horror stories where the fantastic element is consciously conceived as a metaphor, especially in films—*The Babadook*, for instance, and *Under the Shadow*. In some instances the weight of meaning heaped upon the supernatural may stifle its uncanny power, but this is certainly not the case with St. Clair's 1954 story "Brenda," perhaps because its monstrous symbol of adolescent alienation grows more enigmatic and capacious in its meaning when scrutinized. In horror fiction, mystery can be more potent and satisfying than any explanation, and the final line of "Brenda" is among the most mysterious in the literature.

The space vessel in the 1956 Idris Seabright story "Stawdust" takes its name from a star ("the grape harvestress") in the constellation Virgo, astrologically associated with evil. This hardly explains the surreal fate that overtakes the passengers, but then nothing else does either. If the protagonist is causing it, are they simply conforming to her view of them? How reliable is the viewpoint we're sharing? By this stage of the author's career, we may reflect on how many of her tales focus on abnormal psychological experiences and consider whether this is the key to any of them.

"The Invested Libido" (1958) takes us to Mars. As in Ray Bradbury's Martian fiction, the planet functions as shorthand for the alien rather than a realistic environment, fantastic rather than scientific. Perhaps it may be the source of the depersonalization that the story powerfully portrays before developing dark humor and progressing into lighter comedy—again, not far from Thorne Smith's tales of transmogrification. Indeed, despite the elegance of the depiction, the story ends up smuttier than any jokes Smith published and exemplifies the gradual liberalization of science fiction (previously restricted by various taboos) in that decade.

Like her 1963 novel *Sign of the Labrys*, the last tales here draw upon St. Clair's interest in witchcraft. Science fantasy is a definition that has largely fallen out of use, but in her time it defined the area where science fiction and fantasy overlap, and "The Autumn After Next" (1960) exemplifies the concept, sending a warlock missionary to an alien world to educate the locals in the casting of spells. Like "Piety," it's a comedy of cultural misunderstanding. Despite its hybrid nature, it appeared in a dedicated science fiction magazine, *If*, even though the magic in it by no means conforms to Arthur C. Clarke's rational principle ("Any sufficiently advanced technology is indistinguishable from magic").

"The Sorrows of Witches" (1979) was commissioned by Jessica Amanda Salmonson, who cited St. Clair as a pioneer in writing science fiction about sexuality. In its erotic theme and in some of its imagery—"she had her power from the rotting mummy of a monkey that she fed in abominable ways at the dark of the moon"—it recalls the 1930s fantasies of Clark Ashton Smith and, like his work, would have fit with little or no editing into that decade of *Weird Tales*. One of St. Clair's few pure fantasies, it revives the poetry of that mode and stands as a poignant memorial to her magic—indeed, to the lady herself.

Salmonson was right to celebrate the author as an innovator and, I fear, to suggest that her gender may have earned her some neglect. Even in her lifetime, too many observations made about her bordered on the patronizing and sometimes fell over the edge. The back cover of *Sign of the Labrys* famously declared, "Women are writing science fiction!"—and followed this discovery by observing, "Women are closer to the primitive than men." Still, I'd rather hail her rediscovery than pick at the past, and I hope the present book is just the first stage. Let her magic and her range be celebrated. She enriched the fields in which she worked, and she still can.

Ramsey Campbell
Wallasey, Merseyside, England
February 17, 2019

THE HOLE IN THE MOON

AND OTHER TALES

ROCKET TO LIMBO

MILLIE WAVED TO Herbert, who was getting into the 'copter, and flashed him a wide, insincere smile.

The big chump, she was thinking, don't 'copters ever have wrecks? No, he'll be back at five, safe and sound, and start scolding me about the grocery bills and do I really need another dress and wouldn't I like to have a baby because I'm so restless!

No, I would not like to have a baby, and if a new dress costs too much, how does he think we could afford a baby, anyhow? All he does is complain at me and tell me what to do and get in my way. Nag, nag, nag. He thought the way I acted before we were married was cute, now he fusses at me about the very things he used to like me for.

The big 'copter was out of sight by now. Millie let the corners of her mouth sag; her face took on its normal expression of slight petulance. She prodded for a moment at the intricate spirals of her orchid-tinted hair with her iridescent fingernails and then moved over to the book stand. A good mystery, that was what she needed, something to cheer her up.

She selected two plectoid-covered detective stories, picked out three candy bars, and handed them to the clerk with a dollar bill. Abstractedly—he had been deep in conversation with a customer at the other end of the counter when Millie motioned to him—he punched up the sale on the register and handed her her change and sales slip.

Millie put her purchase in her hand case. She was about to let the sales slip fall on the ground when a word on it caught her eye. She read:

1

"Disposals, neatly and quickly made. Are you HAPPY? Is someone getting in your WAY? DON'T PUT UP WITH IT! We specialize in quiet, safe disposal of human obstacles. No mess, no fuss, no blood. See Smith and Tinkem, 1908 Alamondola, suite three. All inquiries confidential."

It was a very funny thing to find on the back of a sales slip. Millie glanced sharply at the clerk. He had gone back to his conversation and was paying absolutely no attention to her. She turned the slip over two or three times, wondering what it was all about, and finally folded it and put it in her case. What did it mean, anyway?

Is someone getting in your way? . . . No mess, no fuss, no blood. Millie bit her lips. It sounded almost as if—as if someone knew how she felt about Herbert. It must be some kind of joke, some sort of advertising scheme.

She left the 'copter terminal and started out to the parking lot where she had left the family scooterbile. That was another thing, she was crazy for a real car, but Herbert said it would cost too much. Everything she wanted cost too much, and yet, the money he spent on rods and reels, on flies and fishing tackle! She had seen some of the bills last month and had asked him about them. They had had a dreadful quarrel.

Oh, what a nuisance he was!

Perched insecurely on the seat of the scooterbile, threading it deftly in and out of traffic, Millie felt, not for the first time, that she hated him.

She got home early, cleaned the house in an hour, and had a light lunch, with her candy bars for dessert. She ate slowly, turning the pages of the books she had bought and trying to get interested in them. They seemed awfully dull, somehow; she couldn't help thinking about that ad the clerk had given her, and wondering what it meant. After a while she went to her hand case, got the slip out, and studied it again. By two o'clock she was dressed in her black nilofilm, her hair fixed that new way with the sequins, and on her way to 1908 Alamondola.

She drove around the block twice before she parked in front of it. It was a big, old-fashioned building, the kind they had put up forty years ago, of greenish concrete, with many angles and zigzags of metal work. Suite three was on the second floor.

The office girl, though, was thoroughly modern, Millie decided, scrutinizing her. Her forearms had been sprayed with gold dust, and she was wearing slippers with enormous whirlabees.

". . . Is Mr. Smith in?" Millie asked, swallowing.

"You wanted to see him about a disposal?" the girl replied. "Yes. Please be seated." She motioned to a chair. "There's a video in the top of that table there, if you want to look at anything." She watched while Millie seated herself, and then went back to her desk.

Millie looked around the office. She was feeling dreadfully nervous, and the big, old-fashioned room, so sedate and respectable-looking, hardly reassured her. Was it all going to turn out to be a joke? Would she get arrested because she wanted to—to dispose of Herbert?

When, twenty minutes later, the office girl held the little swinging gate open for her and showed her to the inner room where Mr. Smith was sitting, her knees were unsteady and the palms of her hands were damp.

Mr. Smith was a long, lean man. His cheeks were hollow, with a bluish cast, and he wore a small, stringy bow tie. He motioned Millie to a chair with a wave of his left hand.

"Madam was interested in a disposal?" He asked, coming to the point at once.

"D-d-disposal?" Millie echoed. She couldn't help stammering.

"A disposal of some individual whom madam—ah—considers superfluous?" His eyes flickered down over the zircoridium-set wedding band on Millie's left hand. "Madam is married, is she not?"

Millie inclined her neck about three inches to make a stiff nod. It was the best she could manage at the moment.

"We have several excellent disposal services," Mr. Smith said, "but the best and most popular one is our rocket special. It is priced at five hundred dollars, which includes everything. For that sum, we *guarantee* disposal to be absolute, permanent, and complete, with no possibility of an—ah—a kickback. Since disposal is one hundred percent efficient, there is never any unpleasantness for our clients, of a legal nature or otherwise." Mr. Smith paused. He laced his fingers together over his stomach and looked at Millie with a sort of cold benignity.

"But how—I mean—well, how does it work?" Millie asked. She was playing nervously with the clasp of her hand case, snapping it open and shutting it again.

Mr. Smith coughed and cleared his throat. "Let us suppose, for the sake of simplicity," he said, "that the person of whom madam desires to dispose is her husband. Very well. On next Tuesday, between the hours of one and five, if he goes to the fifth floor of Bracey's department store and asks for any one of a list of commodities which I shall indicate to madam, he will become the object of our disposal service. The clerk at Bracey's—who is, of course, a member of our organization—will prepare him properly. When madam's husband awakens, he will be aboard our own privately-owned, especially chartered rocket ship." Mr. Smith halted with an air of finality.

". . . I don't get it," Millie said at last.

"I mean that madam's husband—assuming that he is the person of whom madam desires to dispose—" (for an instant a nasty little light shone at the back of Mr. Smith's eyes) "will be disposed of permanently. No mess, no fuss, no blood. He will merely have taken a long, a very long, rocket trip."

"You mean he gets on a rocket and the rocket never comes back? But where does it go to?" Millie asked. Something about Mr. Smith almost frightened her.

"To limbo, madam. To limbo. That is the best way of explaining it." Mr. Smith made Millie a little bow. "The fee is five hundred dollars," he said somewhat pointedly, "payable in advance."

"Five hundred dollars? That's an awful lot. Herb—" She bit off the word in confusion. She had been about to say that Herbert would never forgive her if she spent that much on something he didn't approve of.

"May I point out to madam." Mr. Smith said, looking down at his fingernails, "that after Tuesday, Herb, whoever he may be, will have no connection with madam whatever. She need have no concern about his reaction to anything she does. He will not be here to react. He will not be anywhere."

Millie opened her hand bag and got out her checkbook. She could always stop payment on it if it turned out to be a fake. "Now about this list you mentioned . . ." she said.

An hour later she was on her way home, the list in her hand case. Mr. Smith had made several helpful suggestions on it. He had pointed out that she must make use of the psychology of the individual of whom she wished to dispose in order to get him to go to Bracey's. (Neither she nor Mr. Smith had ever alluded to Herbert by name.)

One of the items on the list was a counter-weighted, corrosion-resistant, anti-magnetic magnesium all fishing reel; and Mr. Smith had taught her a few conversational gambits and had suggested several tactics to be sure that Herbert went to Bracey's on Tuesday and asked for it. If Herbert failed to respond, she was to go back to 1908 Alamondola Street next week and get a new list. Mr. Smith had assured her that there was no limit to the service his firm was prepared to give in order to make sure that the disposal was consummated and complete. He seemed a nice man, really, but there was something about his eyes . . .

She met Herbert at the 'copter terminal at five. Poor old Herbie, she thought as she kissed him, I almost like him now that I know he's not going to bother me any more. She chattered gaily to him all the way home, and when they got to the house she had him sit down and rest instead of asking him to fix the tap on the kitchen sink, as she had intended to. She even got one of his favorite frozen meals out of the refrigerator to thaw for supper, and sat patiently waiting after their meal while he read the paper and smoked his cigar.

The important thing, Mr. Smith had told her, was to be sure the subject came up naturally. She mustn't seem to push or force the conversation around. Herbert, as he was putting the paper away, gave her a beautiful opening.

"The *Fish Tales* column says local fishermen report record catches of bass," he remarked. "I'll have to see if I can't get out some week end soon."

"Oh? That reminds me, I saw Jim Gardener today." Jim was a fellow-fisherman and long-time rival of her husband's; he always seemed to catch more fish and bigger ones than Herbert did, and Herbert, Millie knew, was jealous.

"You did? What did he have to say?"

"Oh, he talked my arm off about some new kind of reel he got. He says it's the biggest improvement in fishing since the invention of the fly."

"Hm." Herbert was looking interested. "Where'd he get it?"

"At—let me see, now—at Maxwell's. He talked so much about it, I can't help remembering some of the things he said. Counter-weighted, anti-magnetic, and—unh—corrosion-resistant. Made of magnesium, or something. He says there won't be another one in town until next Tuesday."

"Oh." Herbert was looking disappointed. "Will Maxwell's have it in stock then?"

Millie shook her head. She was trying not to show her excitement at how beautifully Mr. Smith's suggestions were working out. "Not Maxwell's. He said something about Bracey's getting in a shipment on Tuesday afternoon. Isn't there a tackle shop on their fifth floor?"

"Yep. You bet there is. I might look in there on Tuesday myself. Jim Gardener doesn't need to think he's the only man in town who can have a new reel."

"Herbert!" Millie forced alarm into her voice. "Oh, don't tell me you're going to spend more money on fishing! Why, Jim said the reel cost so much Nora was still scolding him about it. Herbert! Oh, I wish I'd never mentioned it."

Herbert's lips set in a thin line. "Now, Millie," he said, "after all I earn the living. If I want to buy myself a few little things once in

a while, I guess I have a right to. And I certainly need a new reel."
He got up and folded his paper neatly and put it on top the video.

Millie felt a wild elation. That Mr. Smith certainly knew his stuff. Herbert would go to Bracey's now on Tuesday, she was sure. Wild horses wouldn't be able to keep him away. And after Tuesday, no Herbert. Disposed of neatly. Gone to limbo.

The days moved on toward Tuesday. Millie played six-suit bridge with the girls a couple of afternoons, and she and Beata went shopping on Saturday and Millie got a new hand case and gauntlets.

Herbert blew his top about them, of course; she'd known he would. Ordinarily they'd have had a big fight, but the prospect of disposing of Herbert for good had made Millie more even-tempered than usual. Her attitude seemed to surprise Herbert; she caught him looking at her rather oddly several times during the evening, and he kept talking about criminal extravagance.

He watched her sourly all the time she was undressing for bed, while she took the sequins and bubble pearls out of her hair, and when the light had snapped out and she was lying on her serifroth mattress, he began fussing again.

"The amount you women spend on your hair these days is an outrage," he observed nastily into the darkness. (Millie couldn't see him, but she could imagine how he must look, lying on his back with his arms under his head and a frown over his rather small blue eyes as he addressed the ceiling.) "I saw that old friend of yours today, Jara—what's her name?—Cather, and she was fixed up like a floater in a para review. Everything in her hair but the atomic range."

Millie stiffened on her pillow. She had known Jara Cather all her life, and she had always been envious of her. Jara had always had more of everything than Millie had—more money, more looks, more boy friends, and even, more good marks in school.

"Well, she can afford it, I guess," she answered. "Bob has a wonderful job."

"Not that wonderful. She said her hair cost forty dollars a week the new way she's wearing it."

"What was it like?" Millie asked curiously. She wanted very much to know.

"Oh, all sorts of colors, a regular rainbow, and a big bunch of shiny grapes and vegetables on top. She said it was fluorescent or something. Called it a polaroid-prismatic garnish or something like that."

"Garniture," Millie corrected automatically. Herbert's description of Jara's hair-do sounded like something she'd seen in *Flicker-Facts*.

"Um. Well, anyhow, it looked like the devil on sticks. I don't know what's the matter with women these days."

"Where did she get it fixed, do you know?" Millie queried, trying to keep her interest from appearing in her voice.

"Oh, some blasted beauty shop—Bruxelles', I think she said. She told me it took two women the whole day to do it, and it made such a mess the shop would only arrange hair that way one day out of the whole week. Tuesdays. Why, when I was a boy, my mother got a permanent—that's what they called them then, permanents—at the neighborhood beauty parlor and she fixed her hair at home, with those little straight pins, herself. It looked like a million dollars, too, not like these damned salads the women . . ."

Millie had ceased listening to him. Tuesdays! What a wonderful way to spend Tuesday, while Herbert was being disposed of ! She'd 'phone in for the appointment on Monday, spend all day Tuesday at the shop, having her hair fixed with a garniture like Jara's, and come out in the evening looking really nice and no Herbert to spoil it by scolding her.

What a wonderful time she was going to have—there was over three thousand dollars in the savings account in the bank, even after that check to Mr. Smith, and the stocks and bonds besides. Really the disposal service was cheap at the price, when she considered all she was going to gain by it. A wonderful time, she thought drowsily, and drifted off to sleep.

Monday she called the shop and made the appointment and on Tuesday after she'd kissed Herbert good-bye at the 'copter terminal (a longer kiss than usual, and more affectionate, though she had a hard time to keep from laughing when he said he'd see her that evening) she drove across town in the scooterbile to Bruxelles'.

Bruxelles' was definitely a swank place, out of her price class ordinarily, and she'd never been there before. It took her a moment or two of teetering outside on the pavement before she could get her courage up and go in.

Contrary to her fears, the attendant at the reception desk was extremely polite. "Polaroid-prismatic garniture?" she said. "Yes, Mrs. Stevens. If you will just step this way, please . . ." She led Millie back through a corridor carpeted with softly glowing chromamoss and seated her in the deepest of armchairs in an elegant little room. Millie looked at her watch; it was just ten o'clock.

The first part of the polaroid-prismatic garniture was just like any other hair-do; detergent treatment, scalp and foot massage (only they used an electric vibrator between her toes to help relax the hair follicles in the scalp), egg fluff, and hand brushing. There was an interval at noon during which they brought Millie an assortment of sandwiches (bollo tongue, turken, and caviar) and a shaker of iced tangranate juice, and then the special part began.

Telling her to close her eyes and relax, the two women attendants began stroking a heavy, sparkling oil over her hair. The woman on the right drew up a small machine which began making a deep, soothing drone—it had something to do with the polarity—and the woman on the left began to spray a cloud of pinkish stuff over Millie's scalp. Millie felt delightfully comfortable and relaxed. She opened one eye and looked quickly at her watch. It was just one o'clock.

One o'clock . . . Herbert was probably asking for the fishing reel at Bracey's now. He would probably stop in on his way back to the office after lunch. In a very few moments the disposal process would begin, and here she, Millie, was at Bruxelles', feeling so wonderfully comfortable, getting her hair fixed.

How agreeable getting the polaroid-prismatic garniture was! They had stopped spraying the pink stuff on her hair now, and the woman on the left was swathing Millie's head in lovely warm towels with a delicious violet scent. Millie felt she could go right off to sleep. With her eyes closed, lying there, she felt as if she were drifting slowly down through clouds of soft pink snow, and the snow was falling upward around her. Delightful . . . And in all the upward falling pink snow, all through it, there was no Herbert anywhere.

She looked at her watch. Seven o'clock. Seven o'clock? Why, the shop closed at six. Why hadn't they called her? Millie scrambled to her feet.

Where was she? This wasn't Bruxelles'. Astonished and beginning to be afraid, Millie looked around the little room.

It was a tiny place, about six feet square, with a bunk against one wall and a mirror and wash basin opposite. The light in the ceiling gave off a discouraged, dismal, blue-green glow.

Her polaroid-prismatic garniture still in her mind, Millie crossed over to the mirror and looked at herself.

They had never finished her hair. The oil they had been rubbing in had never been removed, and the pink powder was still dusted on it. What on earth had happened? What was all this?

Feeling really frightened, Millie went to the door and turned the knob. To her intense relief, it opened, and she stepped out into a little hall. There were other doors along it; it seemed to lead into a sort of salon. Nervously, walking with light steps, Millie followed it.

The salon was a room of fair size, lighted by the same ghastly bluish-green. A man was standing at one of the windows, looking out, his back to her. Softly, timidly, Millie walked up.

She must have made some noise, for, when she was about ten feet away, he turned to face her. It was Herbert.

"Well, Millie," he said heavily, "I guess we must have tried the same thing on each other. We're—how d'you say—in the same boat."

Millie looked at him. Her heart was beating with horrible rapidity. Herbert . . . Here . . .

"What—" she said, her tongue feeling thick and stiff, "what—where are we?"

"Why, we're on a rocket ship. Where it is, I don't really know. Maybe not in our universe at all. See, there're no stars." He gestured toward the visiplates through which he had been looking. There was no arcing of stars (Millie had gone by rocket to the moon one year), no planetary discs, no nothing. Nothing at all. Nothing but black.

"But where—where's it going?"

He looked at her under his eyebrows. "To limbo. Just as Mr. Smith said. To limbo, of course."

And Millie sank to the floor, hysterical sobs shaking her.

"I don't see how you do it, Smith," the office girl said. She was sitting on the edge of Mr. Smith's desk, idly swinging her foot so that the whirabees rotated with a soft, musical whirr. "I mean, you're really a genius. That's the second or third couple you've got on the ship, each half of the couple thinking he or she was the only one to want to dispose of the other—! Gosh, it's wonderful."

Mr. Smith (of Smith and Tinkem, disposals) nodded benignly to acknowledge the compliment. He got an emery board out of the drawer in his desk and began to file a fingernail.

"But there's one thing I've always wanted to know," the girl went on. "Where do they go, really? I mean all that stuff about limbo is all very well for the customers, but what really becomes of them?"

Smith filed industriously away at the fingernail for two or three minutes before he raised his eyebrows a little and answered her with a shrug.

"Tinkem takes care of them—after they get to limbo, of course . . ."

PIETY

Frost tossed an avenil wrapper in the space erviser's part reducer.

"These people have found the secret of immortality," he said.

"What a romantic temperament you have," Scott replied softly. "The secret of immortality, it sounds as dated as the philosopher's stone."

"What do you mean? We're not immortal."

"No, we're not—though you may not have noticed that the last report of the committee for India gives the life expectancy there now as seventy years. And because of consistently good medical care, you and I both look a good ten years younger than our actual chronological age."

Scott was in his early thirties; he had the trim body and resilient skin of first maturity.

"That's not immortality."

"No, of course not. That's what I'm driving at. How do we arrest aging and prolong life? With some mysterious serum, by some dark business with a fantastic ray? Hocus–pocus of a sort which would be the equivalent of the philosopher's stone I mentioned?

"We've increased our temporal range to the point where it's not at all unusual to meet active and alert people who've passed the century mark. Society has done that by a system of care which is pre-prenatal, by seeing to it that every human being grows up in the best possible environment and receives the best possible nutrition, and by prophylactic measures of all possible sorts. In a word, we've eliminated from human life all the stresses and strains

12

which can be eliminated. And that's the nearest to immortality we'll ever get."

Frost raised his eyebrows. "You heard what Thor-na'thor said. How do you account for it?"

Scott went over to the viewing plates and turned them to low power. The mass of buildings that was Tarthal leaped into visibility. "I don't account for it," he said, with his back to Frost. "We don't speak his language very well yet; we may have misunderstood. Or he may have been speaking metaphorically."

"Nonsense! You heard him say, 'And you let him die?' when we were telling him about Kynaston's burial. That wasn't metaphor. He sounded deeply and genuinely shocked. In my opinion, Thor-na'thor was shocked because, here on Vardia, among his own people, no one ever dies."

Scott shrugged and did not answer for a moment. "I might believe," he went on after a pause, "that they'd worked out therapeutic techniques which are more successful than ours in prolonging life, if the Vardians weren't obviously at a low level of scientific progress. Their vehicles are steam-powered, and they light their buildings with carbon-filament electric lights. Their young men and women dabble in science, yes, but for exactly the same reason that they take an interest in music and painting and the dramatic arts—because it's cultural."

"Got you there!" Frost said in some triumph. He got up and began to pace the cabin's length. "You're assuming that scientific advances occur evenly and are distributed, so to speak, on a plane. Didn't you take any courses in the history of science?"

"One of the most striking features of terrestrial science has been its uneven development. Man knew the diameter of the earth before he was aware of the circulation of the blood, and it was more than two hundred years after the laws of moving bodies were formulated before the science of psychology was born. First the physical sciences, then biology, and at last sociology and the psychology of the depths.

"What reason is there to think that Thor-na'thor's people haven't reversed the progression and developed the life sciences first?"

"The order of development on earth wasn't accidental, but dictated by the nature of things; physics is an easier science than psychology. And leaving that aside, why is Thor-na'thor so reticent about it, assuming you're right? You've tried to pump him a dozen times since he made that remark about Kynaston, and all he does is look embarrassed and change the subject. Supposing he's understood you, and you him, his attitude is more appropriate to a religious matter than a scientific one."

"I've got a theory about that." Frost ruffled up his hair. "I suppose you mean the way he's so careful to keep us away from that building in the north of the city.

"Would it be the first time a scientific discovery has been taken over by religion? Remember those steam engines and assorted gadgets the Alexandrians invented, and how they were used to produce miracles for the devout? Or there may have been a gradual decadence with religion moving slowly in on science. That might explain the general quietism in the atmosphere, though I admit the Vardians don't seem decadent."

"Um."

"You don't believe me?" Frost said.

"Not a bit of it. Nope."

"Will you help me?"

". . . Yes."

Thor-na'thor was a good dinner guest. He held his liquor well, he laughed in the places where laughter was appropriate, he even essayed a mild jest or two of his own. He was genuinely friendly and amiable.

Nevertheless, Frost and Scott were not pleased. They were too tense and excited to enjoy their guest's social qualities, and his ability to soak up liquor without being affected by it was nothing less than catastrophic. They were both a good deal drunker than Thor-na'thor was, and it was not their tongues the evening had been designed to loosen.

Scott twitched an eyelid in signal to Frost. "Got a Venusian liquor," the latter said feebly to Thor-na'thor. "Like your opinion on it." He got a bottle from the buffet.

"Certainly," Thor-na'thor replied, smiling and holding out his glass. "Delighted, my boy. What generous hosts you terrestrials are!"

"Thanks." With inebriated precision, Frost poured a huge snort of phyteumah into the Vardian's glass, and portions as much smaller as was consistent with decency into Scott's and his own.

"I especially appreciate your invitation," Thor-na'thor went on, sipping at his drink, "since I have been distressed—absurdly, I suppose, but there it is—over the death a few days ago of a pet of mine. This evening has been a welcome distraction for me." He sipped again.

Frost and Scott exchanged quick glances. Was this going to be easier than they had thought?

"That's too bad," Scott said. "What was it, a dog?"

"An animal very similar to a dog. I had reared Lilil from shortly after her birth. One grows attached to them."

Still sipping, Thor-na'thor launched on an anecdote designed to illustrate Lilil's cleverness and quasi-human abilities. It grew into a biography, and still he sipped phyteumah from his glass. When the glass was empty, Frost poured more in it unobtrusively while Thor-na'thor talked on. The glass was refilled twice before the Vardian paused. "I regret her death," he finished.

Scott decided to plunge. "How fortunate you are spared such losses with your own people!" he said, tripping over the consonants. "You Vardians don't die, do you?"

"No." The answer was immediate.

Frost cast a glance of triumph at Scott. The latter scarcely perceived it; Thor-na'thor's open admission had nonplussed him. He halted and tried to cudgel his foggy mind into deciding what to say next.

"What is the cause of that?" he got out at last; he had had too much to drink.

"What boys you terrestrials are!" the Vardian answered, smilingly. He got to his feet. "Thank you for a delightful evening. Good night." He halted at the top of the companionway. "I believe we shall have rain before morning," he said, and was gone.

"The blamed old buzzard!" Scott said. He took a sip of water and another Sobrior pill. "Leading us on, guzzling our food, guzzling our drink, and finally laughing at us! He told us that yarn about that dog of his just so we'd bite and ask him if the Vardians were immortal! The blamed old ape!"

"Yes, but never mind that," Frost replied. He had taken two Sobrior pills and was quite himself again. "The important thing is that he admitted it."

"He only said that to make us look like fools."

"What does he care whether we're fools or not? There's really something there, or he wouldn't be so coy about it!"

"I'll find out what he's up to if it's the last thing I do!"

"Listen, let's try—"

Thor-na'thor said, "Yes, this machine would be most useful to my people. We have dramatic entertainments, but nothing like that." He indicated the tiny stereo projector Scott was holding out to him. "We Vardians are a happy folk, but I believe your machine would make us a little happier."

"You could make a lot of money with it," Scott said.

Thor-na'thor gave a slight shrug. "Money—that is not so important on Vardia. But it is true that I should be the object of a great deal of gratitude from my people if I introduced it to them."

"You'd like that?" Scott asked. "You Vardians value that?"

"We value it greatly. I should like it very much."

"It's yours," Scott said, holding out the stereo projector.

An expression of extreme pleasure came over Thor-na'thor's face. "Thank you!" he said, extending his hand. "You are very generous."

"If," Scott hurried on, "you'll tell us why the Vardians don't die."

Thor-na'thor pulled his hand back. "I beg your pardon," he said quietly. "I had thought it was a gift."

Scott's cheeks began to burn. "Oh, heck," he said brusquely, "take the th—"

"Shut up, Scott," Frost broke in. And then, to Thor-na'thor, "We'll give it to you, and gladly—and a lot of other stuff, too—if you'll do what Scott said. How can it hurt you to tell us? Why don't you want us to know?"

"You are joking. You terrestrials are always joking. There are things of which one does not speak."

"Then take us to the building we've never been allowed inside."

"You mean the library? No, it would do you no good. I am sorry, my boy." Thor-na'thor always addressed the two earth men as "my boy" though only heaven knew what the temporal relationship between them was. "It is impossible."

"You can have this too if you'll only tell us the secret," Frost said. He brought out a power generator, a model of compactness, less than thirty centimeters on a side, with a sealed-in permanent power source, and added it to the stereo projector.

Thor-na'thor listened politely while Frost explained the generator's working and use, and at the end shook his head once more. "No. I am sorry, there is no secret. No." He nodded good-by to both of them, and started toward the airlock.

"Hey!" Scott shouted after him. And then, when he turned, "take the projector with you!"

"But—"

"It's okay. We want you to have it. It's a gift."

When Thor-na'thor, holding the projector carefully between his hands, had departed, Frost turned on Scott.

"What the heck did you do that for?" he demanded. "Are you crazy? He wanted that projector; it's possible we might have been able to make a deal with him after all."

"You know we wouldn't. And—oh, he made me feel so cussed small when he said that about having thought it was a gift. I could've hidden underneath one of those little blue Martian geckos. And besides, the old buzzard's pretty decent. Likeable."

"Hunh! You'd better get into a different frame of mind before tonight, then. Maybe I'd better try it by myself."

"No. I'll back you up."

Scott whispered to Frost, "Funny sort of library. People go in and people come out, but none of them is carrying anything. Of course, it could be the books don't circulate."

"It could be Thor-na'thor was lying, you mean." Frost whispered back. "It's not a library, it's the place where the Vardians go for their shots or what. Thor-na'thor must think we're awful fools."

Scott made no reply. He was shivering. The nights on Vardia in this latitude had a penetrating chill, and they had been waiting behind the gelid marble of the monument for Thor-na'thor for several hours. The Vardians were addicted to routine, but Scott was beginning to wonder if something had prevented their official host from taking his regular evening stroll. Scott wished he had worn a heated suit.

"I think—" Frost said at last. "Yes, here he comes. And he's by himself."

As the Vardian moved past the base of the monument to Trj Doteon, the two earthmen fell in on either side of him.

"We've got you centered," Frost said into the Vardian's ear.

"What do you want me to do?" Thor-na'thor answered placidly.

"Go with us to the ship."

When they were inside the *Alceste*'s cabin again, Frost said, "You forced this on us. I hope you'll decide to be reasonable. Do you know what a sliver gun is?"

"I have not that honor," Thor-na'thor replied. His expression was peculiar; whatever it expressed, he did not appear to be alarmed.

Still centering the Vardian in his bolter, Frost got out a sliver gun from a locker and pointed it at the Vardian.

"Little but mighty," he said. "Thor-na'thor, this is it. Being shot by a sliver gun is rarely fatal, unless you're hit in a nerve center. But a wound from it produces tonic spasms of all the voluntary muscles. I was shot by one once; I'd rather have a major burn without anesthesia.

"Scott, hold out his hand."

Scott locked the Vardian's wrist in a tight grip and held the member out to Frost.

"Now," Frost said. "Why don't you Vardians die?"

Thor-na'thor laughed. "Torture, my boy?" he said. "It is too bad, I am afraid I shall look ridiculous. But there is no secret. You are too young to understand."

Frost drew a deep breath. His finger wavered on the lever of the sliver gun. Then he tossed the gun down on the cover of the locker and turned bitterly on his heel.

Scott released the Vardian's wrist. "As I thought," he said. "You'd better go, Thor-na'thor. I imagine we'll be starting back to Terra in a few hours."

"So soon?" the Vardian asked courteously. "We Vardians should like an opportunity to say farewell properly to our guests."

"I'm afraid so. I wish—"

"Would you like me to give you the projector back? You do not need to be ashamed; it is a very valuable thing."

"No, not that. I was wishing that the all-earth Central Committee would decide to send a commission to Vardia to investigate this business about Vardians never dying. But it's impossible; the committee has a great respect for local autonmy."

Handshakes, at Thor-na'thor's request, were exchanged. Their parting was friendly. As the *Alceste* took off on the first leg of the long return, Frost said: "I wonder what it was?"

Scott shook his head. "There might have been something. But we'll never know."

Thor-na'thor walked up the broad low steps of the library. He tipped back his head to look at the inscription over the big door; it was in the long-obsolete non-phonetic Vardian script, but he knew what it said.

At the threshold an attendant smiled at him and held out a basin for him to wash his hands. The attendants knew him well by sight, since his visits to the library always exceeded the daily minimum prescribed by law; Thor-na'thor was a pious man.

When he was clean, he passed into the enormous adytum. He paused at the entrance to enjoy the deep pleasure which the sight of the vast room always roused in him.

From ceiling to floor it was lined with books; the biographies, lovingly, piously compiled, of every man, woman and child who had ever lived on Vardia since the enormously distant time when the art of writing had come to the race. Two balconies zoned the room, and everywhere were reading desks.

Thor-na'thor approached one of the librarians. He walked slowly, for he was thinking of what he had read above the door, "No one who ever lived deserves to die" and feeling for the thousandth time its deep truth.

The librarian greeted him courteously. "Will you have one of your friends," she asked, "or shall it be a stranger?"

"A stranger," Thor-na'thor replied without hesitation. It was considered far more pious to peruse a stranger's life than that of one of one's friends.

She went to a shelf, handed him a book. "No one has had this for a long time."

Thor-na'thor went over with it to a reading desk. He opened it, savoring to the full his grateful task of rescuing from oblivion one of the honored Vardian dead.

"Habor-binhabor," he read in the second chapter, "was inordinately fond of the old-fashioned game of matzor. On the ninth of Satatius, 20034, he stayed up until after midnight playing it, and on another occasion."

Thor-na'thor closed the volume over his forefinger. How strange the earth people were, he thought, how violent, how crude, how young! Heartless, too—witness how they had let their comrade Kynaston die utterly. There had been not the slightest attempt to write his biography. Perhaps, as their race grew older, they would learn that the whole purpose of man on earth is to keep alive the memory of the honored dead. Perhaps they would learn then that no one who is remembered ever dies.

THE HIEROPHANTS

It was an emergency landing. The asteroid was a bubble of lava, honeycombed with passages, as light as pumice, as brittle and dry and dead as the craters of the moon. Somebody had landed on it once before; the nose of a space cruiser, thirty years out of date, projected incuriously from one of the lava caves.

"But what if the parts don't fit?" the girl asked. She was not worried—they had plenty of oxygen and food—only a little tense.

"Some things don't change," the man answered abstractedly. "As long as ships fly at all, they've got Omega power. And the axis in that hasn't changed in the last fifty years. You're sure you understand what you're to get? I'd go myself, only—" He leaned with all his weight against a wrench.

"Oh, yes." The girl began hanging tools from the belt of her suit. "The main axis assemblage and the top lateral coils."

"That's it. Don't forget your torch—you may have to burn your way in. Hurry back, kid. I'll be missing you." He bent to his work.

Nais nodded. She pulled the visor of her helmet into place. Outside the *Lyra,* she switched on her suit's arti-gravs. With Earth's normal gravity tugging at her heels she walked across the curving surface of the little moon.

The name on the snout of the derelict was *Star Rover;* its owner must have had a romantic temperament. There was no provision for exterior opening of its ports. Nais, striking arcs for her torch, sighed. She could look forward to a long, slow job burning through the tough metal of the hull. Even thirty years ago metal had been pretty tough. But she had plenty of time (plenty of oxygen, plenty of food) and if her hands had the faintest possible tendency to tremble, why, it was because there was always something disturbing about a derelict.

The oblong she was burning out turned slowly red. It began to bulge from the pressure of air inside. Nais stepped hastily away. Even on the tiniest of asteroids, an asteroid like a lava bubble floating in space, mass remains mass. She had no desire to be hit by a section of beryllium hull.

The oblong of metal came out like the cork from a bottle of champagne. The edges of the aperture it left slowly cooled. When enough heat had been dissipated to make entrance possible, Nais put her hands on the sides and clambered in, her helmet light sending long shafts stabbing into the ship's dark interior.

Abruptly she bit back a cry. A man in a space suit sat in the circle of white light. He was nodding at her. After a moment she smiled shakily. He was dead, of course, had been dead for thirty years. And his nodding was caused by the air's flowing past him as it went through the opening in the hull.

She went up to him and touched him on the shoulder as he sat at the desk. He floated slowly away from her, his face crumbling as he moved. Repressing a shudder, Nais looked down at what he had been writing when he died.

The earlier pages of the book were a log, a not unmoving chronicle of defective instruments and the bad fortune which had brought the *Star Rover* by imperceptible stages to the asteroid and the lava cave. He had attempted repairs. There was, he had written, no cause for anxiety—he had plenty of oxygen and food. Then there was a break in the record. A page was left blank. And then at the top of the last page he had written:

The apple tree, the singing, and the gold.

That was all. Nais caught her lower lip between her teeth. She realized incredulously that she was afraid. For a moment the emotion was so strong that her hand jerked on the suit's radio, her lips parted to call to Anseln for help. Then common sense reasserted itself.

The *Star Rover*'s owner had died a natural death. (From what? He had written, "Plenty of oxygen, plenty of food." Why, from a sudden heart attack.) Isolation—the terrible isolation of the black, unanswering void, the isolation the earth-bound could never comprehend, had driven him mad before his death. He had died dreaming of the golden trees of earth. But he was dead, and she, Nais, could not afford the luxury of fear. Plenty of oxygen, plenty of food! But there was always danger, and quite apart from danger, she and Anseln were due in Aphrodition on the 17th. She had a job to do.

She turned up her helmet light. The touch of the tools hanging from her belt reassured her. She found the Omega power unit and got down beside it on her knees. The cover had to come off first, and then there was the complicated job of freeing the main axis assemblage. Most of the bolts were stiff.

Gradually Nais became absorbed in her task. As always when she worked with a ship's Omega, the marvelous simplicity of the thing's heart soothed and delighted her. Everything was in good shape. It was a pleasure to handle it. Once when a tendril of her hair caught on her helmet—it must have been a tendril of hair—and sent a sharp pain through the base of her skull, she ignored it. She was almost done with the main axis assemblage now.

She lifted it out, set it carefully on the deck. She began on the top lateral coils. The coils were strong enough, but exceedingly brittle; one had to use great care in handling them. From time to time as she worked, Nais stopped and listened. Once she shook her head for quite two seconds, to clear a noise from it.

She had got the right top coil out and was well along with the left center one when she put down her wrench. For a moment she hesitated. Then she walked slowly toward the stern exit port. Her face was as smooth, as bland, as innocent, as cream. . . .

Afterwards Nais was not quite certain how her initiation began. Was the pain at the base of her skull the beginning, or had that been really nothing but the pull of a wisp of hair? Had it begun when she heard the faint, far-off singing coming through the beryllium walls of the ship? Or had it been earlier, when she stood beside the *Star Rover*'s owner and felt the awful twinge of fear? But she had left the *Star Rover*'s stern exit and walked out mindlessly into the black.

The asteroid was a bubble of lava, honeycombed with tunnels like a rotten apple with worm tracks, brittle, dry and dead. There was no sense to any of it. But Nais, standing there in the darkness, so deeply meshed in abstraction that she hardly knew who Nais was, saw a golden haze come into being. She saw a miracle. She saw Eden being born.

It was born very slowly. Bemused as she was, Nais yet felt that time itself had somehow thickened and become gelatinous, and that she walked forward through this resistant medium toward Eden as if she walked under water through a heavy sea. The uncreated paradise was on the other side of a barrier of hours; and minutes came between the pulsations of her heart.

The tranced, hypnotic calm she had worn at first was deserting her. There were moments, in this slow and tremendous birth from blackness, when blackness seemed to spread over the new earth. Eden hovered tremulously between being and not-being. And Nais strained toward it through glassy gulfs of time, sick with longing and anxiety.

It came at last, soundlessly, like a great thunderclap of light. Eden delivered, Eden triumphant, Eden reborn. There was a brook at Nais' feet that flowed in a bed paved with emerald grass and tiny flowers. Kneeling, she pulled her helmet's visor up and stripped off her gloves. She scooped up the water in her hand to drink—she knew with a conviction as strong as instinct that she must drink of it.

It was very cold and burned her hand almost like fire. For an instant she watched its odd, half-alive sparkle in her hand. Then she set her lips to it and drank. She stepped across the brook.

She stood now in a meadow where there were no shadows, where everything seemed to burn in a faint radiance of living gold. The grass under her feet was starred with flowers whose colors were gently luminous. The arch of heaven was a deep, lovely apple-green, and the wind that blew across her cheek and ruffled the hair within her helmet seemed to trail with it light lambent corpuscles of gold.

Ahead of her were the trees. The faint, aureate haze was thicker about them and wound in delicate tendrils around their trunks. They lifted their branches above it in ardor, in challenge, in triumphant life. The leaves that clothed them were flame made gem-like and frozen into the shape of a leaf, ecstasy made green and visible. In the midst of the trees was one tree taller than the others, and this tree, and this tree only, bore fruit.

Nais licked her lips. Desire had dried them and made them parched. She began to run toward the trees as fast as she could, stumbling in her space suit and hating, as she ran, her body for its clumsy humanity. Yet here in Eden even desire and pursuit became richness, almost joy.

The trees were a long way off. Nais had to stop more than once to rest, and these halts increased her feverish impatience. She wanted to run until her heart burst or until she got to the trees. She had forgotten—from the instant the chilling water of the brook touched her lips she had forgotten—Anseln, the ship, everything. There was in her mind awareness of nothing save the supernal Eden in which she stood.

The voices that had been in her ears since—she could not remember—since before, grew louder. She was almost at the edge of the marvelous grove. But even in her wild haste she had realized that the ground over which she ran was not like the soil of Earth—a base, gross element—but ethereal, glorious, mixed with light. And now, almost under the branches of the trees, she halted, knowing that the ground before her was holy, was literally holy ground.

She might be sick with longing, her whole being turned toward the trees as urgently as the compass needle turns to the north, yet she could not, she dared not, go further. She must have a guide. There must be someone to reveal the mysteries to her, a hierophant.

In the J. J. Rikstoff Museum in Aphrodition there is a bas-relief which critics have called the finest work of art ever executed by a humanoid race. It comes from a temple which the Sanders Expedition excavated twenty or thirty years ago, and it enjoys, in a quiet way, a considerable fame. It represents a man and woman in the scanty, handsome costume of Old Venus standing before a blossoming tree. From one of the branches someone—something (whatever that radiant shape is, it is certainly not human) is handing them a barely ripened fruit.

A daring archeologist has hazarded the guess that the sculpture represents the supreme moment in the long-lasting mystery cult which contented Venusian minds and hearts for so many centuries, but this hypothesis has met with little approval from the academic world. No one has ever conjectured what the dart-shaped object at the lower left of the relief may be. At any rate, there the stone slab stands, whatever it may mean, and people come from all over the system to look at it. Nais might have remembered that stone, had she been capable of remembering anything.

She waited under the trees. And though waiting was painful, she bore it patiently. Overlying her eagerness was the knowledge that waiting was a part of Eden's law, not to be rebelled against. The golden singing within her brain was growing stronger. She must wait.

The aureate haze about the trees began to thicken, to glow more brightly. In its center was what was like a cocoon of ardent, ever more burning filaments. Nais watched, tremulous with expectancy.

The choiring voices soared up and up. The chrysalis of light split soared up and up. Was it one chrysalis or a hundred? There was a dazzle among the trees.

Nais' hands went up in homage. Out of the valves of light had stepped . . . one cannot describe the indescribable. Philologists tell us that the word "angel" meant nothing more originally than messenger.

"Do you come with clean hands?" the voice of the hierophant said within her brain.

"My hands are clean," Nais answered humbly.

"Are you pure in heart?"

"My heart is pure."

"What do you most desire?"

"To taste of the fruit."

"Enter, then," the hierophant said. "Enter and taste."

Nais stepped forward. Her heart was like a bell ringing joy, joy, joy, within her breast. As her feet touched the ambrosial soil of the grove she felt a surge of joy through all her limbs. In all her life she had never been alive until now. Glory, glory, glory, glory and joy, sang her heart.

At the foot of the tree the hierophant was waiting for her. Gravely he reached up and plucked from the bough one of the glowing globes. He gave it into Nais' hand. She raised to her lips the divine fruit. . . .

★ ★ ★ ★ ★

"Are you all right, darling?" Anseln begged. "Nais, say you're all right!"

Nais looked at him remotely. She had been plucked back so abruptly from Eden's deathless world, plucked back through such cold gulfs of distance and time, that she felt herself permeated with a mortal difference. The cabin of the *Lyra,* the whole world of humanity, seemed dim, wasted and unreal. Perhaps it always would.

Anseln was chafing her hand. "You're all right, honey, aren't you? Nais, I can't stand it if—if I was too late."

With a great effort Nais lifted one hand and placed it on her husband's head. His tense face relaxed a little.

"Baby," he said almost brokenly. "What would I have done if I'd been too late? You were standing there in the lava cave with that white thing coiled all around you, burning you, sucking the life from you. I had to drive it off with my stun gun. It was a horror. It didn't want to leave. Nais, how could I let you go into such danger? I'll never forgive myself."

"I'm all right," Nais said. She spoke through lips that hardly seemed to be her own.

"You—you've got to be," Anseln said. "I'm going to hurry with the repairs and get the ship away from here just as fast as I can. Get you to doctors, a hospital. And then I'm coming back here and blast that white thing, that devil, into Hell."

"No!" Nais said.

When he, after many anxious inquiries, had gone back to his work on the main axis assemblage, Nais half-turned on her side so that she lay looking up at the wall. Her thoughts came slowly, and they were long, icy thoughts.

There had been Eden, and a divine grove, and a hierophant. She had thought she stood in Eden; Anseln had seen her standing wrapped in a strangling coil of fire. Who had been right? "The apple tree, the singing, and the gold," the *Star Rover*'s owner had written; he too had seen.

There had been a hierophant. Nais' mind went back to the bas-relief in the Rikstoff museum. With a stab of conviction she understood.

Once, millennia upon millennia ago, the asteroid had been a holy place. It had been a place of pilgrimage for the Old Venusians. They had gone there in their ships to be initiated, to penetrate the mysteries, to taste of the divine fruit. Men and women and children, they had seen what Nais had seen.

The race had begun to die out. Fewer and fewer ships had visited the holy place. At last they had stopped going altogether and only the hierophants, long-lived, perhaps immortal creatures of pure energy, had remained. And when Terrestrials, who were like the Old Venusians in so many ways, had landed on the asteroid, the hierophants had remained true to their old function. They had recreated for them the miraculous Eden to which they held the key. They had initiated them.

But human minds and bodies were not like those of Old Venus: that race had been not human, but humanoid. What had spelled sweet consummation for it, an experience which had been the crown of life, could be nothing for a Terrestrial but death. To taste the fruit of the tree was to die of it, as the owner of the *Star Rover* had died. Anseln, by appearing when he had, had saved her life.

He had saved her life. She could go back to Terra now, back to sunny days and laughter and human delights. There was a lifetime to share with Anseln, a home to build, children to give birth to and rear. She would live a long rich human life. And always, whatever happened to her, she would feel empty and cheated. There would always be a corrosive bitterness, an unsatisfied longing, at the core of her. Some part of her would be standing, eternally, with hands outstretched in longing toward the divine tree.

"Almost finished with the repairs!" Anseln called cheerfully from where he was at work. He walked over to where she lay and stood looking solicitously down at her. "Feeling better now, dear?" he asked.

Nais nodded. Dutifully she raised her face for his caress. And as he bent to kiss her, she lowered her eyelids hastily to hide the emptiness in her eyes.

THE GARDENER

Traffic cops have been known to disregard "No Parking" signs. Policemen filch apples from fruit stands under the proprietor's very eye. Even a little authority makes its possessor feel that the rules don't apply to *him*. Thus it was that Tiglath Hobbs, acting chief of the Bureau of Extra-Systemic Plant Conservation, cut down a sacred Butandra tree.

It must have been sheer bravado which impelled him to the act. Certainly the grove where the Butandra trees grow (there are only fifty trees on all Cassid, which means that there are only fifty in the universe) is well protected by signs.

Besides warnings in the principal planetary tongues, there is a full set of the realistic and expressive Cassidan pictographs. These announce, in shapes which even the dullest intellect could not misunderstand, that cutting or mutilating the trees is a crime of the gravest nature. That persons committing it will be punished. And that after punishment full atonement must be made.

All the pictographs in the announcement have a frowning look, and the one for "Atonement" in particular is a threatening thing. The pictographs are all painted in pale leaf green.

But Hobbs had the vinegary insolence of the promoted bureaucrat. He saw that he had shocked Reinald, the little Cassidan major who had been delegated his escort, by even entering the sacred grove. He felt a coldly exhibitionistic wish to shock him further.

Down the aisle of trees Hobbs stalked while the tender green leaves murmured above his head. Then he took hold of the trunk of the youngest of the Butandras, a slender white-barked thing, hardly more than a sapling.

"Too close to the others," Hobbs said sharply. "Needs thinning." While Reinald watched helplessly, he got out the little hand axe which hung suspended by his side. Chop—chop—chop. With a gush of sap the little tree was severed. Hobbs held it in his hand.

"It will make me a nice walking stick," he said.

Reinald's coffee-colored skin turned a wretched nephrite green but he said nothing at all. Rather shakily he scrambled back into the 'copter and waited while Hobbs completed his inspection of the grove. It was not until they had flown almost back to Genlis that he made a remark.

"You should not have done that, sir," he said. He ran a finger around his tunic collar uneasily.

Hobbs snorted. He looked down at the lopped-off stem of the Butandra, resting between his knees. "Why not?" he demanded. "I have full authority to order plantations thinned or pruned."

"Yes, sir. But that was a Butandra tree."

"What has that to do with it?"

"There have always been fifty Butandra trees on Cassid. Always, for all our history. We call them 'Cassid's Luck.'"

Reinald licked his lips. "The tree you cut down will not grow again. I do not know what will happen if there are only forty-nine.

"Besides that, what you did is dangerous. Dangerous, I mean, sir, to you."

Hobbs laughed harshly. "You're forgetting my position," he answered. "Even if they wanted to, the civil authorities couldn't do anything to me."

Reinald gave a very faint smile. "Oh, I don't mean the *civil* authorities, sir," he said in a gentle voice. "They wouldn't be the ones." He seemed, somehow, to have recovered his spirits.

He set the 'copter down neatly on the roof of the Administration Building, and he and his passenger got out. Back in the grove near the stump of the sapling Butandra, something was burrowing up rapidly through the soil.

Hobbs left Cassid the next day on the first leg of the long journey back to earth. In his baggage was the piece of Butandra wood. He was taking particular care of it since one of the room maids at his hotel in Genlis had tried to throw it out. But for the first few days of his trip he was altogether too occupied with filling out forms and drafting reports to do anything with it.

About this same time, on Cassid, a conversation was going on in the Hotel Genlis dining room.

"Tell us what you thought it was when you first saw it," Berta, the room maid for the odd-numbered levels in the hotel, urged, "Go on!"

Marie, the chief room maid, selected a piece of mangosteen torte from the food belt as it went by. "Well," she said, "I was checking the rooms on the level to be sure the robot help had cleaned up properly and when I saw that big brown spot on the floor my first thought was, one of them's spilled something. Robots are such fools.

"Then it moved, and I saw it wasn't a stain at all, but a big brown thing snuffling around on the eutex like a dog after something. Then it stood up. That was when I screamed."

"Yes, but what did it look like? Go on, Marie! You never want to tell this part."

"It was a big, tall lanky thing," Marie said reluctantly, "with a rough brown skin like a potato. It had two little pink mole hands. And it had an awfully, awfully kind face."

"If it had such a kind face I don't see why you were so scared of it," Berta said. She always said that at this point.

Marie took a bite out of her mangosteen torte. She ate it slowly, considering. It was not that the emotion she had experienced at the sight of the face was at all dim in her mind. It was that embodying it in words was difficult.

"Well," she said, "maybe it wasn't really kind. Or—wait now, Berta, I've got it—it was a kind face but not for people. For human beings it wasn't at all a kind face."

"Guess what room this happened in," Berta said, turning to Rose, the even-numbered room maid.

"I don't need to guess, I know," Rose drawled. "One thousand one hundred and eighty-five, the room that Earthman had. The man that didn't leave any tip and gave you such a bawling-out for touching you-know-what."

Berta nodded. "If I'd *known*—" she said with a slight shudder. "If I'd *guessed*! I mean, I'd rather have touched a *snake*! Anyhow, Marie, tell Rose what you think the brown thing was."

"As Rose says, I don't need to guess, I know," Marie replied. She pushed the empty dessert plate away from her. "When a man cuts down one of our Butandra trees—that thing in the room was a Gardener."

The Gardener left the soil of Cassid with a minimum of fuss. Not for it the full thunder of rockets, the formalized pageantry of the spaceport. It gave a slight push with its feet and the soil receded. There was an almost imperceptible jetting of fire. Faster and faster the Gardener went. It left behind first the atmosphere of Cassid and then, much later, that planet's gravitational field. And still it shot on, out into the star-flecked dark.

On his fourth day in space Hobbs got out the Butandra stick. Its heavy, white, close-grained wood pleased him. It would, as he had told Reinald, make a fine walking stick. Hobbs got a knife from his pocket and carefully began to peel off the tough white bark.

The bark came off as neatly as a rabbit's skin. Hobbs pursed his lips in what, for him, was a smile. He studied the contours of the wood and then started to whittle out a knob.

The wood was hard. The work went slowly. Hobbs was almost ready to put it aside and go down to the ship's bar for a nightcap when there came a light tapping at his cabin's exterior viewing pane.

When a ship is in deep space the sense of isolation becomes almost tangible. It seeps into every pore of every passenger. The ship floats in ghostly fashion through an uncreated void in which there is nothing—can be nothing—except the tiny world enclosed by the curving beryllium hull. And now something—something *outside* the ship—was rapping on Hobbs' viewing plane.

For a moment Hobbs sat paralyzed, as near to stone as a man can be and still breathe. Then he dropped the Butandra stick and turned to the viewing pane. There was nothing there, of course—nothing but the black, the black.

Hobbs bit his lips. With slightly unsteady fingers he picked up the stick from the floor and locked it away in his valise. Then he tightened his belt around his paunch, buttoned up his coat, and went down to the bar.

He found the second officer there. McPherson was drinking pomelo juice and eating a bosula tongue sandwich. A plump good-natured man, he always liked a little something to eat before he hit the sack. After his own drink had been brought Hobbs got into conversation with the second officer. A possible explanation for the noise he had heard had come to him.

"Something gone wrong with the ship?" he asked. "Is that why you've got a repair crew out on the hull?"

McPherson looked surprised. "Repair crew?" he echoed. "Why no, nothing's wrong. Captain Thorwald hates making repairs in deep space—always something faulty in them—and he wouldn't order repairs here unless the situation were really emergent. There's no crew out. What makes you ask that?"

"I—thought I heard something rapping on my viewing pane."

The second officer smiled. He decided to make a joke. "Been doing something you shouldn't, sir?" he said.

Hobbs put down his glass. "I beg your pardon?" he said icily.

The second officer grew sober. Hobbs, while not coming under the heading of VIP, was fairly important all the same.

"No offense meant, sir," he said. "Just a little joke. Don't you know how, in the stories spacemen tell, the curse or doom or whatever it is always shows itself to its victim in space by tapping on his viewing pane? When a man's broken a taboo on one of the planets, I mean. That was what I was referring to. Just a little joke."

"Oh." Hobbs swallowed. He held out his glass to the barman. "Another of the same," he said in a rather hoarse voice. "Make it a double."

Tiglath Hobbs was an extremely stubborn man. This quality, in some situations, is hardly to be distinguished from courage. Next wake-period he got out the Butandra stick again. With cold, unsteady fingers he worked on the knob. He had stationed himself close to the viewing plate.

There was no rapping this time. Hobbs did not know what it was that made him look up. Look up at last he did. And there, bobbing about in the tiny spot of light which seeped out through his viewing pane, was the smiling face the room maid in Genlis had seen. Brown and rough, it was regarding Hobbs with incredible, with indescribable benignity.

Hobbs uttered a cry. He pressed the button which sent the pane shutter flying into place. And the next moment he was standing by his cabin door, as far away from the pane as he could get, his fingers pressed over his eyes. When he stopped shuddering he decided to go see Captain Thorwald.

It took him a long time to get to the point. Thorwald listened, drumming with his fingers on his desk, while Hobbs circumlocuted, hesitated, retracted, and corrected himself. What came out eventually was that he wanted Captain Thorwald—just for a moment, just for a fraction of a second—to have the ship's force field turned on.

Thorwald shook his head. "I'm sorry, Mr. Hobbs. It's impossible. Turning on the field would have to go into the log, you know, and there's no reason for it."

Hobbs hesitated. Then he got his wallet out. "I'll make it worth your while. Five hundred I. U.'s?"

"Sorry, no."

"Six hundred? Seven hundred? Money is always useful. You could say you ran into a meteor swarm."

"I—no."

"Eight hundred? Look here, I'll give you a thousand! Surely you could fix the log."

Thorwald's face wore a faint, sour smile but still he hesitated. "Very well," he said abruptly. "Let's say you bet me a thousand I.U.'s that I can't turn the ship's force field on and off again in a sixtieth of a second. Is that it? I warn you, Mr. Hobbs, you're sure to lose your bet."

Hobb's eyelids flickered. If the captain wanted to save his pride this way—

"I don't believe it!" he said with artificial vehemence. "I don't believe a field can be turned on and off that fast. It's a bet. I'll leave the stakes on the table, Captain." From his wallet he drew ten crisp yellow notes.

Thorwald nodded. "Very well," he said without touching the money. "In half an hour, Mr. Hobbs, you shall have your demonstration. Will that be satisfactory?"

"Quite."

Thorwald nodded and picked up the notes with his right hand.

Hobbs went back to his cabin, raised the shutter and sat down by the viewing pane. He had keyed himself up to the pitch where it was almost a disappointment to him that the smiling face did not appear. The moments passed.

Abruptly the ship shook from stem to stern. A billion billion tiny golden needles lanced out into the dark. Then the cascade of glory was gone and the eternal black of space was back.

It had happened so quickly that, except for the pattern of light etched on his retina, Hobbs might have wondered whether he had seen it at all. Thorwald could certainly claim to have won his bet.

But Hobbs was well satisfied with what he had got for his thousand I.U.'s. In the fraction of a second that the force field had been turned on he had seen, crushed and blackened against the field's candent radiance, a dead scorched shapeless thing like a burned spider.

The myriad biting fires of the force field must have charred it instantly to the bone. What Hobbs had seen in that instant of incredible illumination was dead beyond a doubt, as dead as the moon.

By now it must be lying thousands upon thousands of kilos to the side of the ship's course, where the vast impetus of the field had sent it hurtling. Hobbs drew a deep, deep breath. Relief had made him weak.

When he and Thorwald met at the next meal they maintained a cautious cordiality toward each other. Neither of them, then or at any time thereafter, referred again to the bet.

That sleep-period Hobbs rested well. In the next few days he regained most of his usual aplomb. Leisurely he finished carving the Butandra wood into a walking stick. It made a very nice one. By the time the ship docked at Llewellyn, an Earth-type planet but with a third less than Earth's normal gee, he was quite himself again.

In the depths of space, uncounted millions of kilometers away, the blackened husk of the Gardener floated weightlessly. It was quite dry and dead. But did it not stir a little from time to time as though a breeze rustled it? And what were those cracks that slowly appeared in it? Were they not like the cracks in a chrysalis?

Hobbs was well pleased with the state of the plantations on Llewellyn. He told the young man in charge of the local office so and the young man was gratified. By the end of the third day Hobbs was ready to resume his interrupted voyage toward Earth.

Something he saw in a sheet of stereo-press newsprint changed his mind. "Fiend robs, mutilates liner chief!" the big red scarehead bellowed. And then, in smaller type, the paper went on, "Minus finger and 1,000 I.U.'s, Captain unable to name assailant. Police make search."

Hobbs—he was at breakfast—looked at the item incuriously until, in the body of the story, his eye caught a familiar name. Then he read with avid interest.

Eins Thorwald, captain of the luxury space liner *Rhea* (this was inaccurate—the *Rhea* was not a luxury liner but a freighter with fairly comfortable accommodation for five or six passengers) was in hospital today minus one thousand I.U.'s and the index finger of his right hand.

Thorwald, found in a state of collapse in his cabin by second officer Joseph McPherson (see page two for pictures), was unable to give details of the attack on him. He told police he had been robbed of exactly one thousand I.U.'s. Other currency in Thorwald's wallet was untouched.

Thorwald's finger, according to medical officer Dingby of the local police, appears to have been amputated with the help of a chisel or some similar instrument. No trace of the missing digit has been found.

Thorwald himself, after receiving several transfusions, is in Mercy Hospital, where his condition is reported serious. Police are operating on the theory that the attack was the work of some fiend whose hobby is collecting human fingers. A thorough search is being made and they expect an arrest soon.

Hobbs put the newsprint down. His hands were trembling. His florid cheeks had turned white. What he suspected, he told himself, was sheer lunacy.

Hadn't he himself seen the—thing which had rapped at his viewing pane reduced to a blackened cinder by the ravening fires of the force field? But Thorwald had been robbed of exactly one thousand I.U.'s. And he had picked up Hobbs' bribe with his right hand.

Hobbs pushed his plate away and asked the robot for his check. In the lobby he video'd Mercy Hospital and inquired for news of Thorwald. He was told that Thorwald's condition was serious and that he could not possibly see anyone.

Hobbs sat in the lobby for an hour or so and tried to think. At the end of that time he had come to a decision. Tiglath Hobbs was a stubborn man.

He called a 'copter and had it take him to the local office of the Bureau of Extra-Systemic Plant Conservation. Scott, the young man in charge of the office, was out and Hobbs had to wait for him.

It was nearly noon when Scott came in, very brown and erect in his clothing of forest green. He had been supervising the weeding of a plantation of young Tillya trees and there was mud on the knees of his trousers from kneeling beside the seedlings. The knees of his trousers were always a little muddy. He had the green heart of the true forester.

Hobbs came to the point at once. "Scott," he said, "I want you to go to Cassid and supervise the uprooting of the plantation of Butandra trees there."

Scott looked at him for a moment incredulously. "I beg your pardon, sir?" he said at last in a neutral tone.

"I said, I want you to go to Cassid and supervise the uprooting of the plantation of Butandra trees there."

"I—sir, what is the reason for this order?"

"Because I say so."

"But, Mr. Hobbs, the Butandra trees are unique. As you of course know, there is nothing like them anywhere else in the universe. Scientifically it would be criminal to destroy those trees.

"Further than that, they play a considerable role in Cassidan planetary life. To the inhabitants the trees have a large emotional significance. I must ask you, sir, to reconsider your decision."

"You have your orders. Carry them out."

"I'm sorry, sir. I decline to do so."

Hobbs thick neck had turned red. "I'll have your job for this," he said chokingly.

Scott permitted himself a thin smile. "I have civil service tenure, sir," he said.

"You can be removed for cause. Insubordination, in this case."

Scott's smile vanished, but he did not retreat. "Very well," he said. "If it comes to a public hearing we'll see. In any case I can't carry out that order. And I very much doubt, Mr. Hobbs, that you'll find anyone who will. It's not the kind of thing you can ask of a forester."

Hobbs raised his stick of Butandra wood. His expression was murderous. Then his common sense reasserted itself. He gave Scott a nod and left.

He called the travel bureau, canceled his Earthward passage and made reservations for a cabin on the next ship back to Cassid. If he could not find anyone to carry out his orders to destroy the plantation of Butandra trees he would do it himself. Tiglath Hobbs, as has been said before, was a stubborn man.

The trip back to Cassid was unexceptional. Nothing came to rap at Hobbs' viewing pane or to peer in at him. It was so quiet, in fact, that Hobbs had fits of wondering whether he was doing the right thing.

The Butandra trees were, as Scott had said, of considerable scientific interest and Hobbs might be letting himself in for a good deal of unfavorable criticism by destroying them. And the attack on Thorwald might have been only a coincidence.

But by now Hobbs bitterly hated the Butandra trees. Guilt, anxiety, and self-righteousness had coalesced in him to form an emotion of overwhelming intensity. He hated the Butandra trees. How could there be any question about destroying them?

With their repulsive staring white bark and the nasty whispering rustle their long green leaves made they deserved—yes, they positively deserved—to be killed. How could a decent-minded man let the Butandra trees live?

Usually, by the time he got to this point in his thoughts, Hobbs began to pant. He had to make a conscious effort to calm himself.

Hobbs' ship docked at Genlis spaceport late at night. Hobbs was too excited to try to sleep. He paced up and down in the waiting room until day came.

Then he rented a 'copter from a Fly-It-Yourself hangarage and flew to a supply house which specialized in compact power saws. He had decided to fell the trees first and afterwards make arrangements for having the stumps pulled up.

It was still early when he got to the sacred grove. In the tender light of morning the straight, white-barked, green-leaved trees made a pretty, peaceful sight. Hobbs hesitated, though not from any qualms about his contemplated arboricide. What was bothering him was a feeling that entering the grove to cut down the trees, even in daylight, might be dangerous.

On the other hand the best defense was always attack. What had happened to Thorwald had been almost certainly a coincidence. But if it hadn't—Hobbs swallowed—the best way of insuring himself against a similar experience was to cut down the grove.

The grove was, he had decided on Llewellyn, the—the thing's base of operations. It drew power from the grove as surely as the trees of the grove drew nourishment from the soil. Once the grove was destroyed the thing, whether or not the force field had killed it, would have no more power.

Hobbs took the portable saw from the 'copter and slung it over his shoulder. He hesitated a fraction of a second longer. A sudden gust of wind set the long leaves of the Butandras to rustling mockingly. Hobbs felt a nearly blinding surge of hate. His jaw set. He opened the gate and entered the grove.

The power saw was not heavy and he decided to begin his felling operations beside the sapling he had first cut down. He found the stump without difficulty and was pleased to see that it had not put up any shoots. But somebody had dug a deep hole in the ground beside it, and Hobbs frowned over this.

He set the saw down on the turf and knelt to adjust it. He could find out about the hole later. He touched a switch. The saw's motor began to purr.

The Gardener came out from behind a tree and smiled at him.

Hobbs gave a strangled, inarticulate shriek. He scrambled to his knees and started to run. The Gardener stretched out its lanky arms and caught him easily.

With its little pink mole hands it stripped his clothing away. His shoes came off. With ten separate chops of its strong white teeth the Gardener bit away his toes. While Hobbs struggled and shrieked and shrieked and shrieked, the Gardener peeled away the skin on the inner surfaces of his legs and thighs and bound these members together with a length of vine.

It drew scratches all over the surface of his body with its long sharp mole claws and rubbed a gritty grayish powder carefully into each gash. Then it carried Hobbs over to the hole it had made and, still smiling, planted him.

When the Gardener came back an hour or so later from its tasks of cultivation in another part of the grove, a thin crust of bark had already begun to form over Hobbs' human frame. It would not be long, the Gardener knew, before Hobbs would become a quite satisfactory Butandra tree.

The Gardener smiled benignly. It looked with approval at the graft on the trunk of the tree to the right, where what had once been Eins Thorwald's index finger was burgeoning luxuriantly.

The Gardener nodded. "A leaf for a leaf," it said.

CHILD OF VOID

ISCHEENAR IS HIS name, and he lives in the big toe of my left foot. He's fairly quiet during the day, except that now and then he makes my foot twitch. But at night he comes out and sits on my knee and says all sorts of hateful things. Once he suggested—

But I didn't mean to tell about Ischeenar yet. I suppose I got off on him thinking about the fire and all that. It was after the fire that he got into my foot. But I want to tell this in order, the way it happened, and I ought to begin at the beginning. I suppose that means telling about how we happened to go to Hidden Valley to live.

Uncle Albert killed himself and left Hidden Valley to Mom in his will. I didn't want to go there. We had visited Hidden Valley once or twice when I was little, and I hated it. It gave me the creeps. It was the kind of place you see articles about in the Sunday supplement—a place where water flows uphill and half the time the laws of gravity don't work, a place where sometimes a rubber ball will weigh three or four pounds and you can look out the upstairs window and see a big blue lake where the vegetable garden ought to be. You never could depend on things being normal and right.

But Mom wanted to go. She said there was a nice little house we could live in, an artesian well with the best water in the world, and good rich soil for growing our own vegetables. There were even a cow and some chickens. Mom said we could be a lot more comfortable there than in the city, and live better. She said we'd get used to the funny things and they wouldn't bother us. And though she didn't say so, I knew she thought I'd be happier away from people, on a farm.

42

Mom's been awfully good to me. She kept on with the massage and exercises for my back for years after the doctors said it was no use. I wish I could do more for her. Her ideas are usually pretty good, and when I've gone against them I've been sorry. When you think about it, Mom is generally right.

So we went to Hidden Valley, Mom and Donnie (that's my younger brother) and I. It was worse than I had thought it was going to be. The place was still queer enough to scare you purple, but besides that there was something new, a kind of heavy depression in the air.

It was terrible. At first it made you feel like you'd like to put your head up and howl the way a dog does; then you felt too worn out and miserable and unhappy to have energy left for howling.

It got worse with every hour we stayed there. By the time we'd been in Hidden Valley for two days, Mom and I were looking at each other and wondering which of us would be the first to suggest going back to the city. I kept thinking about how sensible Uncle Albert had been to blow himself up with the dynamite. Even Donnie and his kitten felt the depression; they sat huddled up together in a corner and looked miserable.

Finally Mom said, in a kind of desperate way, "Eddie, why don't you see what you can get on your radio set? It might cheer you up." Mom doesn't give up easily.

I thought it was a silly idea. I've been a ham operator ever since I was fifteen, and it's a lot of fun. I enjoy it more than anything. But when you're feeling as bad as I was then, you don't want to talk to anyone. You just want to sit and wonder about dying and things like that.

My stuff had been dumped down all in a corner of the little beaver-boarded living room. I hadn't felt chipper enough to do anything about getting it set up, though Uncle Albert had put in a private power system and there was electricity in the house. After Mom asked me for the second time, though, I got up and hobbled over to my equipment. And here a funny thing happened. I'd hardly started hunting around for a table to put my stuff on when my depression began to lift.

It was wonderful. It was like being lost in the middle of a dark, choking fog and then having the fog blow away and the bright sun shine out.

The others were affected the same way. Donnie got a piece of string and began playing with the kitten, and the kitten sat back and batted at the string with its paws the way cats do when they're playful. Mom stood watching me for a while, smiling, and then she went out in the kitchen and began to get supper. I could smell the bacon frying and hear her whistling "Onward Christian Soldiers." Mom whistles that way when she's feeling good.

We didn't go back to feeling depressed again, either. The funny things about Hidden Valley stopped bothering us, and we all enjoyed ourselves. We had fresh eggs, and milk so rich you could hardly drink it, and lettuce and peas and tomatoes and everything. It was a dry year, but we had plenty of water for irrigation. We lived off the fat of the land; you'd have to have a hundred dollars a week to live like that in the city.

Donnie liked school (he walked about a mile to the school bus) better than he had in the city because the kids were more friendly, and Mom got a big bang out of taking care of the cow and the chickens. I was outside all day long, working in the garden, and I got a fine tan and put on some weight. Mom said I never looked so well. She went into town in the jalopy twice a month to get me books from the county library, and I had all kinds of interesting things to read.

The only thing that bothered me—and it didn't really *bother* me, at that—was that I couldn't contact any other hams with my station. I never got a single signal from anyone. I don't know what the trouble was, really—what it looked like was that radio waves couldn't get into or out of the valley. I did everything I could to soup up my equipment. I had Mom get me a dozen books from the county library, and I stayed up half the night studying them. I tore my equipment down and built it up again eight or ten times and put in all sorts of fancy stuff. Nothing helped. I might as well have held a rock to my ear and listened to it.

But outside of that, as I say, I thought Hidden Valley was wonderful. I was glad Mom had made me and Donnie go there. Everything was doing fine, until Donnie fell in the cave.

It happened when he went out after lunch to hunt for his kitten—it was Saturday—and he didn't come back and he didn't come back. At last Mom, getting worried, sent me out to look for him.

I went to all the usual places first, and then, not finding him, went farther away. At last, high up on a hillside, I found a big, fresh-looking hole. It was about five feet across, and from the look of the grass on the edges, the earth had just recently caved in. It seemed to be six or seven feet deep. Could Donnie be down in there? If there's a hole to fall in, a kid will fall in it.

I put my ear over the edge and listened. I couldn't see anything when I looked. After a moment I heard a sound like sobbing, pretty much muffled.

"Donnie!" I yelled. "Oh, Donnie!" There wasn't any answer, but the sobbing seemed to get louder. I figured if he was down there, he was either hurt or too scared to answer my call.

I hobbled back to the house as quick as I could and got a stepladder. I didn't tell Mom—no use in worrying her any more. I managed to get the ladder to the hole and down inside. Then I went down myself. I've got lots of strength in my arms.

Donnie wasn't at the bottom. Some light was coming in at the top, and I could see that the cave went on sloping down. I listened carefully and heard the crying again.

The slope was pretty steep, about twenty degrees. I went forward carefully, feeling my way along the side and listening. Everything was as dark as the inside of a cow. Now and then I'd yell Donnie's name.

The crying got louder. It did sound like Donnie's voice. Pretty soon I heard a faint "Eddie!" from ahead.

And almost at the same moment I saw a faint gleam.

When I got up to it, Donnie was there. I could just make him out silhouetted against the dim yellowish glow. When I said his name this time, he gulped and swallowed. He crawled up to me as quick as he could and threw his arms around my legs.

"Ooooh, Eddie," he said, "I'm so glad you came! I fell in and hurt myself. I didn't know how to get out. I crawled away down here. I've been awful scared."

I put my arms around him and patted him. I certainly was glad to see him. But my attention wasn't all on him. Part of it was fixed on the egg.

It wasn't really an egg, of course. Even at the time I knew that. But it looked like a reptile's egg, somehow, a huge, big egg. It was about the size of a cardboard packing box, oval-shaped, and it seemed to be covered over with a tough and yet gelatinous skin. It glowed faintly with a pale orange light, as if it were translucent and the light were coming through it from behind. Shadows moved slowly inside.

Donnie was holding onto my legs so tightly I was afraid he'd stop the circulation. I could feel his heart pounding against me, and when I patted him his face was wet with tears. "I'm awful glad you came, Eddie," he said again. "You know that ol' egg there? It's been making me see all sorts of things. I was awful scared."

Donnie never lies. "It's all right now, kid," I said, looking at the egg. "We won't let it show you any more bad things."

"Oh, they weren't bad!" Donnie drew away from me. "The egg's bad, but the things weren't! They were awful nice."

I knew I ought to get him out, but I was curious. I was so curious I couldn't stand it. I said, "What kind of things, Quack-quack?" (That's his pet name, because his name is Donald.)

"Oh . . ." Donnie's voice was dreamy. His heartbeat was calming down. "Books and toys and candy. A great big Erector set. A toy farm and fire truck and a cowboy suit. And ice cream—I wish you could have some of the ice cream, Eddie. I had sodas and malteds and Eskimo bars and Cokes. Oh, and I won first prize in the spelling contest. Mom was awful glad."

"You mean—the egg let you have all these things?" I asked, feeling dazed.

"Naw." Donnie's tone held disgust. "But I could have 'em, all that and a lot more, if I'd do what the egg wanted."

"Oh."

"But I wouldn't do it." Donnie's voice was virtuous. "I said no to 'em. That egg's bad."

"What did the egg want you to do?"

"Aw, they wouldn't tell me." Donnie's tone was full of antagonism. "They never did say. C'mon, let's get out of here. You help me, I don't like it here."

I didn't answer. I didn't move. I couldn't. The egg . . . was showing me things.

What sort of things? The things I wanted most, just as it had with Donnie. Things I wanted so much I wouldn't even admit to wanting them. I saw myself healthy and normal and strong, with a straight back and powerful limbs. I was going to college, I was captain of the football team. I made the touchdown that won the big game. I was graduated with honors while Mom and my girl friend—such a pretty, jolly girl—looked on, their faces bright with pride. I got an important research job in radio. And so on—foolish ambitions, impossible hopes. Crazy dreams.

But they weren't dreams when the egg was showing them to me. They were real, they weren't something I had to hide or laugh at any longer. And all the time a voice inside my brain was saying, "You can have this. You can have all this.

"Won't you help us, won't you please help us? We're harmless, we're trapped and hurt. We came here from our own place to colonize, and we can't get out and we can't get back.

"It would be easy for you to help us. And we'll be grateful. We'll give you all you saw. And more. All you have to do . . ."

I took a step forward. Of course I wanted what they had shown me. I wanted them very much. And besides, I felt sorry for the things, the harmless things imprisoned in the egg. I've known what it is to feel helpless and trapped.

Donnie was beating on my thigh with his fists and screaming. I tried to shake him off so I could go on listening to the other voice. He hung on, pummeling me, and finally, in desperation, grabbed at my hand and bit it hard with his sharp little teeth. "Eddie, Eddie, Eddie! Come out of it, please come out of it!"

That roused me. I looked at him, dazed and resentful. Why wouldn't he let me listen so I could help the poor things in the egg? "Be quiet, Quack-quack," I mumbled to him.

"You gotta listen, Eddie! Don't let them get you! 'Member what happened to Uncle Albert? 'Member how we felt when we first came to the farm?"

The words penetrated. My normal caution was waking up. "But they say they don't mean us any harm," I argued weakly. I was talking to Donnie just like he was grown up.

"Aw, they're big liars. They can't help hurting us. It's something they put into the air, like, by just being alive. They can stop it for a while, if they try hard. But that's the way they really are. Like poison oak or a rattlesnake. 'Sides, I think they like it. They like being the way they are."

Poison oak and rattlers, I translated to myself, aren't consciously evil. They don't will their nature. But it's their nature to be poisonous. If Donnie was right in thinking that the things in the egg gave out, as a part of their metabolism, a vibration which was hostile to human life . . . Uncle Albert had committed suicide by blowing himself up with dynamite.

"We'd better get rid of the egg, Quack-quack," I said.

"Yes, Eddie."

I helped him up the shaft to the mouth of the cave. He'd sprained his ankle. On the way I asked, "What are the things in the egg like, Donnie?" I had an idea, but I wanted to check it with him. I felt his young mind and senses were keener and more reliable in this than mine.

"Like radio. Or 'lectricity."

"Where did they come from?"

"Another—not like where we live. Everything's different. It's not like here. It's right here beside us. An' it's a long way off."

I nodded. I helped him up the ladder and left him sitting on the hillside. Then I went back to the house for my .22 and a can of kerosene.

Donnie watched me anxiously as I went down with them. I don't mind admitting I was pretty nervous myself.

A .22 isn't an elephant gun. Still, at a two-foot range it ought to have some penetrating power. It didn't. The bullets just bounced off from the sides of the egg. I could hear them spatting against the walls of the cave. I used three clips before I gave up.

That left the kerosene. There hadn't been any more attempts to show me pictures or bring me around. In a silence that seemed bitterly hostile I poured kerosene all over the egg. I used plenty. Then I stood back and tossed a match at it.

Heat boiled up. It got so hot I retreated nearly to where Donnie had fallen in. But when it cooled off enough so that I could go back, I found the egg sitting there as good as new. There wasn't even any soot on it.

I was beaten. I couldn't think of anything more to do. I went up the ladder with the empty kerosene can and my gun. Donnie seemed to know I'd failed. He was crying when I came up to him. "Don't tell Mom," I said, and he nodded dutifully.

Would the egg let it go at that? I didn't think so. After supper I said to Mom, "You know, sometimes I think it would be nice to go back to the city for a while."

She looked at me as if she couldn't believe her ears. "Are you crazy, Eddie? We never had it so good before." Her eyes narrowed and she began to get worried. "What's the matter, honey? Aren't you feeling well?"

I couldn't tell her. I knew she'd believe me; that was just the trouble. If she knew there was a chance I could be cured, be made healthy and strong the way she wanted me to be, she'd make a dicker with the things in the egg, come hell or high water. It wouldn't make any difference to her whether they were good or bad, if she thought they could help *me*. Mom's like that.

"Oh, I feel fine," I said as heartily as I could. "It was just an idea. How's for seconds on the strawberry shortcake? It's even better than usual, Mom."

Her face relaxed. But I didn't sleep much that night.

The breakfast Mom cooked next morning was punk. I wasn't hungry, but I couldn't help noticing. The toast was burned, the eggs were leathery and cold, the coffee was the color of tea. There was even a fly in the pitcher of orange juice. I thought she must be worried about Donnie. I had bandaged his foot according to the picture in the first-aid book, but the ankle had swelled up like a balloon, and it looked sore and bad.

After breakfast Mom said, "Eddie, you seem worn out. I think carrying Donnie so far was bad for you. I don't want you to do any work today. You just sit around and rest."

"I don't feel like resting," I objected.

"Well—" Her face brightened. "I know," she said, sounding pleased. "Why don't you see what you can get on your radio set? The cord's long enough you could take it out on the side porch and be out in the fresh air. It's been a long time since you worked with it. Maybe you could get some of the stations you used to get."

She sounded so pleased with herself for having thought of the radio that I didn't have the heart to argue with her. She helped me move the table and the equipment outside, and I sat down and began to fiddle with it. It was nice and cool out on the porch.

I didn't get any signals, of course. Pretty soon Donnie came limping out. He was supposed to stay on the couch in the living room, but it's hard for a kid to keep still.

"What's the matter, Donnie?" I asked, looking at him. He was frowning, and his face was puckered up and serious. "Foot hurt?"

"Oh, some . . . But Eddie . . . you know that old egg?"

I picked up my headphones and turned them a bit. "Um," I said.

"Well, I don't think you should'a built that fire around it. It was a bad thing to do."

I put the headphones down. I wanted to tell Donnie to shut up and not bother me; I know that was because I didn't like what he was saying. "Why was it bad?" I asked.

"Because it stirred the things in the egg up. I kin feel it. It's like you have a station with more juice, you can get farther. The fire gave them more juice."

I didn't know what to say. I figured he was right, and I felt scared. After a minute I made myself laugh. "Nothing to worry about, Quack-quack," I said. "We can lick any old egg."

His face relaxed a little. "I guess so," he said. He sat down in the porch swing.

Mom stuck her head around the edge of the door. "Did you get anything on your radio, Eddie?" she asked.

"No," I said a little shortly.

"That's too bad." She went back in the kitchen and hung her apron up, and then she came out on the porch. She was rubbing her forehead with the back of her hand as if her head ached.

To please her, I put on my headphones and twiddled the dials. No dice, of course. Mom frowned. She went around to the other side of the table and stood looking at the wiring, something I'd never seen her do before. "How would it be if you moved this from here to here?" she said. Her voice was a little high.

I leaned over to see what she was pointing at. "That would just burn out the tubes."

"Oh." She stood there for a moment. Then her hand darted out, and before I could stop her, before I even had any idea what she was up to, she moved the wire she'd been talking about.

"Hey!" I squawked, "Stop that!" I said it too late. There was a crackle and a flash and all the tubes burned out. My station was completely dead.

Mom rubbed her forehead and looked at me. "I don't know what made me do that, Eddie," she said apologetically. "It was just like something moved my hand! I'm awfully sorry, son."

"Oh, that's O.K.," I said. "Don't worry about it. The station wasn't good for anything."

"I know, but . . . My head's been feeling queer all morning. I think it must be the weather. Doesn't the air feel heavy and oppressive to you?"

The air did have a thick, discouraging feel, but I hadn't noticed it before she burned out the radio tubes. I opened my mouth to say something, but before I could say it, Donnie yelled, "Look at Fluffie! She's walking on the air!"

We both jerked around. There Fluffie was, about ten feet up, making motions with her paws as if she were trying to walk. She was mewing a blue streak. Now and then she'd slip down three or four feet and then go up to the former level, just as if a hand had caught at her. Her fur was standing up all over, and her tail was three times its usual size. Finally she went up about twenty feet and then came sailing down in a long curve. She landed on the ground with a thump. And that was the beginning of all the phenomena.

It wasn't so much that we felt depressed at first, though we certainly did. But we could stand it; the depression wasn't as bad as it had been when we first came to Hidden Valley. I guess that was because the things in the egg were more spread out now. Whether that was the reason or not, most of the phenomena were physical.

You could hardly get into the living room. It was like pushing your way through big wet bladders to go into it. If you sat on the sofa you had a sense of being crowded and pushed, and pretty soon you'd find yourself down at the far end of it, squeezed into a corner. When Mom struck matches to make a fire for lunch, the matches were twitched out of her hand and went sailing around the room. We had to eat cold things; she was afraid of burning down the place.

At first Mom tried to pretend there was nothing wrong; after all, you couldn't *see* anything. But I went out in the kitchen at suppertime and found her crying quietly. She said it was because she'd been trying to cut bread for sandwiches and the knife in her hand kept rising up toward her throat. I knew that if Mom was crying it had been pretty bad. So I told her about the egg in the cave and all that.

"They're out of the egg now," she said unhappily when I had finished. "My burning out the tubes this morning let them out. We've got to go back to the city, Eddie It's the only thing to do."

"And leave them loose?" I said sharply. "We can't do that. If it was just a case of deserting the valley and having them stay here, it would be all right. But they won't stay here. They came to Earth to colonize. That means they'll increase and spread out.

"Remember how it was when we came here? Remember how we felt? Suppose it was like that over most of the Earth!"

Mom shook her head till her gray curls bobbed. "This can't be real, Eddie," she said in a sort of wail. "We must be having hallucinations or something. I keep telling myself, this can't be real."

Donnie, outside, gave a sudden horrible shriek. Mom turned as white as a ghost. Then she darted out, with me after her.

Donnie was standing over Fluffie's body, crying with rage. He was so mad and so miserable he could hardly talk. "They killed her! They killed her!" he said at last. "She was way up in the air, and they pushed her down hard and she squashed when she hit the ground. She's all mashed flat."

There wasn't anything to say. I left Mom to try to comfort Donnie, and went off by myself to try to think.

I didn't get anywhere with my thinking. How do you fight anything you can't see or understand? The things from the egg were immaterial but could produce material phenomena; Donnie had said they were like electricity or a radio. Even if that were true, how did it help? I thought up a dozen fragmentary schemes, each with some major flaw, for getting rid of them, and in the end I had to give up.

None of us went to bed that night. We stayed up in the kitchen huddled together for comfort and protection, while the house went crazy around us. The things that happened were ridiculous and horrible. They made you feel mentally outraged. It was like being lowered down into a well filled with craziness.

About three o'clock the light in the kitchen went slowly out. The house calmed down and everything got quiet. I guess the things from the egg had revenged themselves on us enough for having tried to get rid of them, and now they were going about their own business, perhaps beginning to increase. Because from then on the feeling of depression got worse. It was worse than it had ever been before.

It seemed like years and years until four o'clock. I sat there in the dark, holding Mom's and Donnie's hands and wondering how much longer I could stand it. I had a vision of life, then, that people in asylums must have, an expanse filled with unbearable horror and pain and misery.

By the time it was getting light I couldn't stand it any longer. There was a way out; I didn't have to go on seeing Hell opening in front of me. I pulled my hands from Mom's and Donnie's and stood up. I knew where Uncle Albert had kept the dynamite. I was going to kill myself.

Donnie's eyes opened and he looked at me. I'd known he wasn't asleep. "Don't do it, Eddie," he said in a thread of a voice. "It'll only give them more juice."

Part of my mind knew dimly what he meant. The things from the egg weren't driving me to suicide deliberately; they didn't care enough about me for that. But my death—or any human's death—would be a nice little event, a tidbit, for them. Life is electrical. My death would release a little juice.

It didn't matter, it wasn't important. I knew what I was going to do.

Mom hadn't moved or looked at me. Her face was drawn and gray and blotched. I knew, somehow, that what she was enduring was worse than what I had endured. Her vision was darker than mine had been. She was too deep in it to be able to think or speak or move.

The dynamite was in a box in the shed. I hunted around until I found the detonator and the fuse. I stuffed the waxy, candlelike sticks inside the waistband of my trousers and picked up the other things. I was going to kill myself, but part of me felt a certain compunction at the thought of blowing up Mom and Donnie. I went outside and began to walk uphill.

The sun was coming up in a blaze of red and gold and there was a soft little breeze. I could smell wood smoke a long way off. It was going to be a fine day. I looked around me critically for a good place to blow myself up.

They say suicides are often very particular; I know I was. This spot was too open and that one was too enclosed; there was too much grass here and not quite enough at the other place. It wasn't that I had cold feet. I hadn't. But I wanted everything to go off smoothly and well, without any hitches or fuss. I kept wandering around and looking, and pretty soon, without realizing it, I was near the hillside with the cave.

For a moment I thought of going down in the cave to do what I had to do. I decided against it. The explosion, in that confined space, might blow up the whole valley. I moved on. And suddenly I felt a tug at my mind.

It wasn't all around, like the feeling of depression was, something that seemed to be broadcast generally into the air. And it wasn't like the voice inside my head I'd heard in the cave. The best way I can express the feeling is by saying that it was like walking past a furnace with your eyes shut.

I hesitated. I was still feeling suicidal; I never wavered in that. But I felt a faint curiosity and something a lot fainter that you might call, if you exaggerated, the first beginnings of hope.

I went to the mouth of the cave and let myself down through the opening.

The egg, when I reached it, was different from the way I remembered it. It was bigger and the edges were misty. But the chief difference was that it was rotating around its long axis at a really fancy rate of speed. It reminded me of the rotation of a generator. The sensation I felt was coming out from it.

Watching the thing's luminous, mazy whirling, I got the idea that it and the things which had come out of it represented opposite poles. It was as alive as they were, though in an opposite way, and its motion provided the energy for them to operate.

I pulled the sticks of dynamite out of my belt and began setting them up. There really wasn't much danger of blowing up the valley, and as long as I was going to do away with myself, I might as well take the egg with me, or try to. That was the way I looked at it.

No attempt was made to stop me. This may have been because the things from the egg weren't interested in human beings, except spasmodically, but I think it more likely was because they, being polar opposites from the egg, had to keep their distance from it. Anyhow, I got my connections made without interference. I stood back a foot or two.

I closed the switch.

The next thing I knew, my head was on Mom's lap. She was shaking me desperately by the shoulders and crying something about fire.

Now, I don't see how I could have been responsible for the fire. The earthquake, possibly. Apparently when the dynamite exploded, the egg tried to absorb the energy. (That's why I wasn't hurt more.) It got an overload. And the overload, somehow, blew it clean out of our space. I got a glimpse of the space it was blown into, I think, just before my head hit the rock. But anyhow, a thing like that might possibly have caused an earthquake. All the country around Hidden Valley is over a fault.

Anyhow, there'd been earthquakes, several of them. Mom and Donnie had gone out hunting me as soon as the worst shocks were over, and found me lying at the mouth of the cave. They got me up somehow; I don't weigh much. Mom was nearly crazy with worry because I was still unconscious. For the last two hours or so she'd been smelling the smoke and hearing the crackling of the fire.

Some camper up in the mountains, I guess, started it. It was an awfully dry year. Anyhow, by the time I was conscious and on my feet again, it was too late to think about running. We didn't even have time to grab a suitcase. Mom and Donnie and I went down the flume.

That was some trip. When we got to Portsmouth, we found the whole town ready to pick up and leave, the fire was that close. They got it out in time, though. And then we found out that we were refugees.

There were pieces about the three of us in the city papers, with scareheads and everything. The photographers took pictures of all of us, even me, and they tried to make out we were heroes because we'd gone down the flume and hadn't got burned up in the fire. That was a lot of foolishness; there isn't anything heroic in saving your own life. And Mom hated those pictures. She said they made her look like she was in her seventies and heading for the grave.

One of the papers took up a collection for us, and we got a couple of hundred dollars out of it. It was a big help to us, because all we had in the world was the clothes we were standing in. After all, though, we hadn't really expected to live. And we'd got rid of the things from the egg.

As Mom says, we have a lot to be thankful for.

I could be more thankful, though, if I didn't have Ischeenar. I've tried and tried to figure out why he didn't die when the rest of the things did, when the egg was blown into another space. The only thing I can think of is that maybe, having been born here on Earth, he's different from the rest of them. Anyhow, he's here with us. I've managed to keep Mom from finding out, but, as I say, he lives in my big toe.

Sometimes I feel almost sorry for him. He's little and helpless, and alone in a big and hostile world. He's different from everything around him. Like us, he's a refugee.

But I wish I could get rid of him. He's not so bad now while he's young. He's really not dangerous. But I wish to *God* I could get rid of him.

He's going to be a stinker when he grows up.

HATHOR'S PETS

"I WON'T HAVE my baby born here among a lot of lizards!" Vela said passionately. "I just won't! Henry, you've got to help us get out of here!"

Henry Pettit sighed. Would it do any good to try to tell his sister again that Hathor and her fifteen-foot congeners were not lizards? No, it would not. Vela was never very logical and the fact that she had violated the cult of feminine delicacy sufficiently to mention her coming child to him showed how excited she was. Arguing with her in this mood would be wasted breath.

"Why don't you ask your husband to help you?" he said pointedly.

Vela drew herself up. Her small hard face softened momentarily. "Denis doesn't know how to get things out of the Scalies the way you do." she said. "He isn't—Denis has principles. Denis has ideals."

("Denis is too all-fired good and noble to butter up to the lizards in the disgusting way that *you* do," Henry translated silently.)

Aloud, he said, "He's your husband, though. It's his responsibility."

Vela stared at him reproachfully for a moment. Then she burst into tears. Ever since her child had been on the way she had been indulging in orgies of tears. Anything was apt to send her off into a crying jag.

Henry, who was some five years older than his sister, could remember, very dimly, back to the end of the era of feminine freedom, the time when women had been encouraged, nay expected, to be intelligent.

The girls had been in the saddle then—they had ridden high, wide and handsome. But the rise of the government-sponsored cult of feminine modesty, chastity and brainlessness in the late 1980's had put an end to all that. Nowadays a woman was a cross between a dripping sponge and a vegetable.

Mrs. Pettit came waddling up. She had been lingering within earshot behind a tree in the park. "What have you been saying to Vela, son?" she demanded. "The poor girl! I won't have you upsetting her."

"I'm not upsetting her," Henry replied morosely. "She's upsetting herself. Excuse me. I'm going over to the laboratory."

He got up and started rapidly across the grass.

"Henry, *wait!*" his mother shrilled after him. Fortunately he was walking so fast that it was possible for him to pretend that he had not heard.

After lunch his brother-in-law, Denis Hardy, began on him. Denis went over the history of the last few months relentlessly, from the time the strato-liner *Pelican*'s life boat had been trapped in the vortex and whirled into Hathor's universe until the present. He even made a digression to consider whether the vortex had been deliberately created or not.

"Don't you see," he finished, "Vela can't have her baby here. Why, she might—might even have to feed it herself."

"Well, what of it?" Henry replied abstractedly. "Women used to do it all the time." He had had a most interesting morning. He wanted to get back to the laboratory.

Denis turned an angry red. "You're disgusting!" he said sharply. "Can't you keep a civil tongue—" He bit off the words and made an obvious effort at conciliation.

"Why don't you want to go home, Pettit? There's nothing here for a man."

"I like it," Henry answered simply. "Grass, flowers, air—it's a beautiful place."

"That's not the reason," Denis replied nastily. His little ramrod of a back grew straighter. "I know what you're up to in the laboratory. *Forbidden research.*"

"Everything was forbidden at home," Henry answered reasonably. "But we're not home now. It's not forbidden here."

"Right's right and wrong's wrong, no matter where—" Once more Denis controlled himself. The gold braid on his shoulders quivered with effort. "Stay here yourself if you want, then," he snapped. "But the rest of us don't share your peculiar tastes. We want to get back to decency, normality. Is there any reason why you shouldn't use your influence with your scaly friends to have them send us back to Earth?"

There was—but how could he explain it to Denis? Denis had a mind which, even for the second officer of a stratosphere liner, was limited. How could Henry make him understand how horrible mental contact with Hathor was?

It was not that Hathor was malignant or even unkind. Henry had a faint but positive impression of benignity in his dealings with her. But the words with which the human mind bridges gulfs—*when, who, where*—became, when one was in contact with Hathor, the gulfs themselves.

To ask her when something had happened was to reel dizzily into the vastest of all enigmas for humanity—the nature of time itself. The question, "What is it?" forced the questioner to contemplate the cloudy, chilling riddle of his own personal identity. And even, "Where?" brought up a panorama of planes of being stretching out to infinity.

In between times it was not so bad. When Henry had not seen Hathor for several days he was almost able to convince himself that he was not afraid of her. Then he would need something in the laboratory, go to see her to ask for it and come back from the interview sick and shaking, swearing that nothing—*nothing*—would induce him to plunge once more into the vast icy reaches of her inhuman intelligence.

He hunted for a reason Denis would understand. "It's no use asking her," he said finally. "Vela is going to have a child now and so Hathor would never let you go."

"But that's just why we want to go home."

"I know." Henry swallowed. "But Hathor and the others look on us as—you might say—pets. Whether or not they brought us here deliberately—myself, I think it was an accident—that's how they feel about us. And nobody ever turned a pet loose when it was going to have young."

There was no use in telling Denis that Hathor was responsible for Vela's child in the same way that a dog breeder is responsible for the birth of pups. It would only offend Hardy's dignity.

"Pets!" Denis answered, staring. "What are you talking about? They're nothing but lizards. They haven't got stereo, stratoliners, A-bombs, anything. We're their superiors in every way."

"They're *not* lizards," Henry replied. "They're very highly evolved mammals. That crest down the back of their heads is just an accident.

"The reason they don't have those material things is that they don't need them. Haven't you ever seen Hathor materialize things for my laboratory? She does it by moving her hands. She could turn a rubber ball inside out without making a hole in it.

"As far as that goes, if you think they're nothing but lizards, why are you trying to get them to send you back to your own time and space? No lizard I ever heard of could do that sort of thing."

Hathor appeared. One moment the air was empty—the next it thickened and condensed, and there she was. As always when he first saw her Henry was divided between a wild desire to run for cover and an almost equally strong impulse to prostrate himself in awe at her feet.

He glanced about to see how the others were taking it. Denis, for all his bravado, was turning slowly white. And Vela, trying hard to be supercilious, was arranging the folds of her mantilla with shaking hands.

Not that there was anything especially horrible about Hathor to casual viewing. Though she was over fifteen feet tall, and so strong that she could have picked up any of the humans in the park with one hand, her body was slender and well-proportioned.

She looked a good deal smaller than she actually was. The integument that covered her streamlined contours was pearly, pinkish, lustrous. And her tall vermillion crest could hardly be considered a deformity. It was something else that caused the reaction, something in the look of her eyes.

Her impersonal gaze moved slowly over the little group. It slowed and came to rest on Henry. The skies of her mind fixed on him.

"You're Henry," said the glassy, disembodied voice within his brain. "The one—" (not quite one—what Hathor was thinking was more like *semipermeable membrane* or *assemblage of points*) "the one with the laboratory. Yes.

"I'm going to train you—" (a dissolving kaleidoscope of images as thick as snowflakes. From the glittering throng of whirling, evanescent pictures, Henry caught up two which lasted longer than the rest— one of a hawk leaving the falconer's wrist, the other of a slender key turning in a lock.) "Come along." Hathor motioned with her two-thumbed hand.

It was the first time she had ever come after him. Henry felt a premonitory shudder run through his limbs. Nonetheless he got obediently to his feet.

It was nearly supper time when he got back. The smoke of Mrs. Pettit's cooking fire drifted out into the still air and mingled pleasantly with the smell of frying meat.

Henry sank down limply on the grass beside the blaze, shielding his eyes with his hand from the light. It was not until supper had been eaten and the necessary refuse from the meal burned that he could bring himself to speak.

"Vela—Denis," he said, trying to keep his voice from quivering, "Do you still want to get away from here? If you do I'll do all I can to help you. I want to get away myself."

There was a cautious silence. Vela opened her lips and then closed them again. At last Denis spoke.

"Why, yes, we still do. We thought you— Yes, we still want to get away." For a moment the ruddy flicker of the fire lit up the tight lips of his handsome small-featured face.

Whatever had made him decide to be tactful about Henry's abrupt *volte-face,* whether his silence was caused by policy or contempt, Henry was thankful for it. He could not possibly have put into words how hateful Hathor's recent compulsory extension of his senses had made the world where he now was to him.

He had learned too much ever to consider that world beautiful again. And trying to express it verbally would have been almost as bad as the original experience.

"What was Hathor doing with you today?" Vela asked curiously.

"Training me," Henry answered briefly.

"Training you? How?"

"It's something she does with her hands," Henry replied unwillingly. "They disappear. And then I hear what's going on inside the stones."

"Oh." Vela looked rather sick. "Well, are you just going to ask her to send us back to our Earth, or what?"

"Asking her wouldn't be any use. She let me see that today. Anyhow, she knows we want to go home. But I've been thinking." Henry Pettit's voice was getting back its customary tones. "Why do people get rid of their pets? They get rid of them—"

"I don't like 'get rid of,' " Denis cut in sharply. "God knows we aren't here of our own choice and we want to get back to our own time and place. But we're alive here and that's something. We don't want to get killed trying to get back."

"We won't be killed. When people get rid of their pets they don't murder them. They send them to a friend in the country who has more room or turn them over to an animal shelter or something. They don't kill them.

"But as I was saying, why do they get rid of them? Basically for one of two reasons. You get rid of a pet when it's not a good pet—when it sulks, is sullen, uncooperative, disagreeable—or you get rid of it because it makes a nuisance of itself. Like chewing up rugs or howling at the moon. Now if we could only make nuisances of ourselves—"

"How?" Denis asked, frowning. "Hathor isn't around here much, so being noisy won't do any good."

"What about doing something with whatever you're working on in the laboratory, son?" Mrs. Pettit suggested. "Perhaps we could be nuisances with that."

"We can't have anything to do with the laboratory," Denis announced sternly. "Forbidden research is wrong, here or on Earth."

"Oh, be quiet, Denis," Vela said peevishly. Her husband looked as if he could hardly believe his ears. "This is lots too serious for us to be honorable," she went on as if in explanation. "Henry, if you can do anything with your research, do it."

"Well—I might try a matter canker. That's just about the most forbidden research there is. I'd have to be careful not to get a radioactive form of canker, of course."

"Would that annoy Hathor?"

"A matter canker? Yes. A matter canker would annoy anybody quite a lot."

"And if she gets mad enough at us, she'll send us back to our own time and space," Vela said. She yawned. "Let's go to bed early and get lots of sleep. And tomorrow we'll help Henry all we can."

His lab assistants were willing if not very bright. Clad in lead-impregnated coveralls they weighed, stirred, measured, filtered and proved to be so incompetent that on the second day Henry got rid of all of them except Vela.

Her measurements were more accurate than those of the others, and she didn't talk so much. Once or twice before he had suspected that she could be intelligent when it suited her to be.

"Listen, Henry, aren't you afraid Hathor will find out what we're doing before it's ready?" she asked late on the second afternoon. "Then she'd make us stop before we got annoying."

"I doubt it," Henry replied absently. They were engaged with a difficult bit of titration. "There, that's enough— She used to visit the lab a good deal at first but not any more. I don't think she'll be around until it's time for me—for me to have another lesson. I hope we'll be gone before then."

"Well, what about the canker itself? Won't it be dangerous? I should think it would give out a lot of heat."

"No," Henry replied, "there isn't any heat with a canker. Nobody knows why. And they can't find out because it's been ruled forbidden research. About the only direct danger to us would be if the canker got out of control. Nobody knows why but they do that sometimes."

He poured the solution into a crucible. "You see that switch down there by the betatron? All right, when I move my hand, depress it. Thanks."

A matter canker takes time to establish. There were failures in the early stages of Henry's. It was more than a week after his conversation with Vela that he got the canker into its ultimate form.

He carried it out of the laboratory, Vela following, and showed it to the others, who were sitting listlessly on the grass.

"It doesn't look like much," Denis said after a pause. He was turning the big flask critically in his hands. "Except for the color, that is, how could this annoy anyone?"

"It hasn't been activated yet," Henry explained. He took the flask back from Denis and set it on the ground. "I want you both to get into your coveralls. The canker isn't very radioactive but there's bound to be some radiation. So keep well back from it."

He adjusted the timing device on the neck of the flask. While Mrs. Pettit and Denis were getting into their long white coveralls he dropped in the gray-sheathed thorium pellets which were the activating charge. Once more he adjusted the timing device. "Get back," he said. The first—second—third pellets dropped.

The flask dissolved. The gluey viscous stuff it held ran out sluggishly over the grass. Writhing, twisting, boiling, the grass was eaten away from it. The liquid disappeared. The canker was eating in.

"It's getting started nicely," Henry said.

A column of steam shot up. It enlarged, grew hollow. Now there was a hole, a growing one, in the ground. The edges curled and bubbled and smoked. The hole widened, grew deeper.

A wind blew over the surface of the grass. It freshened. In a moment the leaves of the trees were in motion. The boughs began to rock. The column of steam broke off, reappeared soaringly, broke off again. The wind was growing to a gale.

"What is this, son?" Mrs. Pettit demanded. She had to put her mouth against Henry's head to make herself heard. "Where's the wind coming from?"

"Canker's creating a vacuum," Henry yelled back. "Air rushes in to fill it faster as the canker grows. Get back! *Get back!*"

The party hurried across the slick green surface of the grass toward safety, breaking at the last into a run. The giant wind kept trying to push them back.

"Further! *Further!*" Henry yelled. *"Get back!"*

Abruptly the canker was lapping at the laboratory walls. The stones boiled evilly for a moment and no longer existed. The upper part of the structure fell in, disappeared.

Henry's face was greenish white. "It's getting out of control. *Run! Run!*" he said.

They ran. Shrieking, stumbling, trying to breathe, they ran. The canker was faster than they. With the flowing ease of a creature in a dream it gained on them. It was no more than a yard from them when they reached the site of the cooking fire. Two seconds more and it was lapping at their heels.

Vela collapsed and fell. Denis put his hands under her armpits and wildly tried to drag her along. Mrs. Pettit, her face a mask of terror inside the glazed hood of her coveralls, was screaming inaudibly. The wind was horrible.

Hathor appeared. She was standing in the air eight or ten feet above their heads. Though her eyes still had their uncanny look of remoteness and impassivity, something about her suggested exasperation consciously controlled. Standing securely on nothingness she began to make quick, plucking motions with her hands. Slipping, sliding, twisting, they moved in space and out of it.

There was a terrific lightning flash. The world dissolved in curtains of white light. Henry, staggering back from the impact of the prodigy, was amazed that his retinae had not been burned out. It did not seem possible that the eyes could be flooded with such light and still see.

There was another even vaster flash. Slowly, reluctantly, it died away. Henry looked up at Hathor with his scalded eyeballs. Her hands still moved in their twisting pattern, sliding in and out of visibility, but more deliberately than they had. Tiny veins stood out on her temples. Her lips were compressed. Plainly she was imposing some great exertion on herself. The howling wind had died away.

The earth, the horizon, the air, twanged like a plucked bowstring. In the most horrible moment of the afternoon, Henry perceived that everywhere about him were slowly opening doors. Convulsively he shut his eyes.

When he opened them again Hathor had put down her hands. The air was calm and untroubled. All around the party the grass lay as fresh, as green, as unbroken as it had been before the matter canker was set up. The only sign of its existence that the canker had left was an exceptionally heavy coating of dew. But the laboratory was gone.

Hathor fixed her impassive eyes on Henry. Her face had resumed its ordinary inexpressiveness, but he felt the fright that always came over him at mental contact with her. A huge voice began to print itself awesomely in his brain—"DON'T EVER DO THAT AGAIN."

It hadn't worked. Hathor had neither punished them nor got rid of them. And now what were they to do? The laboratory was gone. They had no way of annoying Hathor with another matter canker even if they had been minded to try it. All that was left them was to try to be unsatisfactory pets.

They discussed it night after night as they sat around the coals of their fire. They could decide on nothing. It was not until Hathor, coming to get Henry for the third installment of his training, took Denis along too, that a definite program emerged.

Denis was shaken by his experience. It amused Henry, who was becoming accustomed to the horror that Hathor's training involved, to see how shaken he was. Denis' tight little mouth was as firm as ever when he remembered to keep it firm. But in moments of inattention his jaw hung slackly and his lips had a tendency to shake.

"This can't go on," he said, pacing up and down on the grass. "Vela's not well—haven't you noticed? She needs medical attention but I wouldn't trust Hathor to prescribe for her. It's not myself I'm thinking of, it's her. We've got to get home."

"It would be nice if we could," Henry replied warily. "But—"

"But what?"

"Nothing. Do you have a plan?"

"Yes. We'll run away."

"Run away? Hathor can bring us back in ten seconds as soon as she notices we're gone."

"Yes, of course she can," Denis replied. "But if we keep on running away and she has to keep on bringing us back—you see what I mean. She only comes to visit us every four or five days, but if every time she comes we've run away, she'll soon get tired of it. Bringing us back will be so annoying she'll send us home to get rid of us."

Henry was silent.

"What's the matter?" Denis asked challengingly. "Don't you think it would work? We could save up our supplies and take food with us. Besides, there's a lot of wild fruit."

"Oh, I think it would work. That's what's bothering me."

Denis' back stiffened. For a moment he was again the martinet. "Explain yourself," he rapped out.

"I'm afraid." Henry swallowed. "Afraid to annoy her. Afraid of what she'd do."

Denis looked relieved. "Nonsense," he said heartily. "If she didn't do anything to us for setting up the matter canker she won't do anything to us no matter what we do. That's obvious. Besides, what could be worse than what she does when she's training us? That—that almost makes me sick."

Henry let his hands dangle down between his knees. His eyes had taken on an odd bright look. "That's pretty bad, isn't it?" he said. He managed a smile. "Pretty bad. But maybe something could be worse."

"Rot! I'm going to talk to Vela and her mother about it. If they agree will you come along with us? After all, you're in this too."

There was a pause. "All right," Henry replied at last. "As you say, I'm in this with you. If you go I'll go with you."

Hathor had made one of her visits only the day before. She made them at irregular intervals but it was probable that three or four days would elapse before she would visit Henry and the others again. On the third day, carrying what supplies they had been able to accumulate, the party escaped.

The escape was unspectacular. They walked for a mile or two through the rolling parkland where Hathor had established them, turned to the right and were on a road that was no more than a grassy track. Once in the distance they saw a pair of Hathor's people walking slowly along. Sometimes the big mammals walked, instead of simply materializing where they wished to be.

Denis made the party hide beside the road until the big people were safely out of sight. Later the party passed a lonely building whose walls were shimmering gray webs. Henry identified it to himself as a place where a dimension-spanning vortex, like the one which had brought them thither, was being made. By noon the party was in a rather open wood. They decided to stay there for the night.

Hathor came for them on the second day. She did not seem angry, only more than usually remote. She set them down on the sward beside the open stoa in the park where they slept, and gazed at them. Then she disappeared.

Denis was jubilant. "It's working!" he said, very pleased with himself. "The next time we run away or maybe the time after that she'll send us home to get rid of us. You'll see, old chap."

"Will she?" Henry answered with a sigh. "Well, I hope you're right."

The second attempt at escape was not very successful. Hathor came for them when they had been gone no more than a couple of hours. The third time . . .

Denis was in the lead when they reached the boundary of the park. He was talking cheerily to Vela, his head turned, as they walked along. When he faced about once more, Hathor was standing there. Her crimson-tipped crest waved gently in the breeze as she bent over and picked up Denis.

The action itself was ordinary enough but Henry felt a sickening pang of apprehension. He plucked at Vela's arm. "Run," he said hoarsely, "you and mother run and hide."

"But—what's the matter? What's she doing with her hands?" Vela's eyes were round. "Why is she holding him so tight?" Her voice went up. "Is she—he said she wouldn't hurt us. Oh! *Oh!*"

Hathor's hands were slipping smoothly in and out of the web of invisibility. Now she put one of them up to Denis' head. Eerily, unbelieveably, her fingers slid inside the skull.

Denis began to scream. It was a horrible high squeal like a frightened rabbit's. At the sound Vela pressed her fists to her ears and started to run. Mrs. Pettit hesitated, looking after her. Then, moaning and slobbering, she bobbed after the girl. Henry stayed behind, until he was sure what was going on. Then he too turned and ran.

There was little cover in the rolling park. The women were cowering behind a big granite boulder and there Henry joined them. Denis gave scream after shattering scream.

The screams stopped. Henry looked over the top of the rock.

Tears were still flowing down Denis' cheeks but the convulsed terror had gone out of his face. It had been replaced with a vegetable imbecile calm.

Hathor put him down very gently on the grass. He walked eight or ten paces uncertainly and then sat down on the sward. He pulled up a handful of grass and examined its roots.

Vela tugged desperately at the hem of Henry's sleeve. "What's she done to him?" she demanded in an agonized whisper. "Oh what is it? Henry, Henry, Henry—what's she done?"

Henry turned to face her. "We geld domestic animals to make them better pets, don't we?" he answered. His mouth twisted shockingly to one side. "Hathor's done something to his brain to make a better pet out of him. So he'll stay here always without wanting to get away, so he won't be a nuisance any more. That's what she's doing. She's making us better pets. *Better pets! Better pets!*"

He was still shrieking the words when Hathor picked him up.

WORLD OF ARLESIA

"THAT'S ODD," YOU said, looking up from the financial page. "It seems Lunar Mines is going to declare a dividend on its common stock this year after all. I heard keeping the workers in space suits all the time was running their production costs up too high, and there was supposed to be some engineering reason why they couldn't put the mines under a universal dome. But Lunar always had clever technicians. The article says they expect to cut a juicy melon at Christmas time." You folded the evening paper and looked at me. "Are we going anywhere tonight?"

"Oh, if we can find a good picture, something we haven't seen. . . . We've been to all the good ones, Bill."

"Let's see," you said, "something caught my eye in the inside pages. Here." You spread the paper open again and pointed.

There was a drawing of a woman's head, wide-eyed, flat-nosed, with subtly-smiling mouth, the filmy hair streaming out all around the head in a circle, and little fishes darting in and out through the floating meshes. "World of Arlesia," I read, "in a double bill with Diabolique. The strangest pictures ever filmed. A unique visit to another world."

"World of Arlesia," I repeated reflectively. "I think I've heard of it. They used a special filming process, and there's some reproduction of tactile sensations and smells. It's new."

"I remember the name, too," you agreed. "It's about a radio operator on a motor ship. He keeps getting messages for which he can't account. It turns out that they're coming from the people of Arlesia, the underwater world. It was filmed by some small independent company."

The theatre was in a remote part of the city, a small building, not one of the usual picture houses. Inside, the seats spread out in a semi-circle around a low stage; the walls were pale cream and the draperies dull red, of heavy velvet. The audience was of fair size.

After an interval, a woman came out and stood before the velvet curtains. She was slender, tall, with a dead-white skin and very dark red hair. She wore a quiet, well-tailored suit. She was carrying a square black box.

"Good evening," she said, bowing politely toward the audience. "Tonight I will perform for you WORLD OF ARLESIA."

She seated herself at a table to the left of the stage with the black box before her. At a slight movement of her hand, the curtain slid back from the stage and the house lights went out.

A slow play of colors began to move across the stage. After a little while the tempo accelerated; the colors grew more and more bright. They began to hurt my eyes, and I kept looking away. I noticed, Bill, that you were gazing with fixed attention at the screen, as if fascinated.

The movement on the screen reached a whirling climax and then started to slacken again. The colors dimmed and dulled; finally, with a last slow circling, they faded out. . . .

You and I were driving uphill. It was a sunny afternoon, the air pleasant and warm. We're really in the picture, I thought with dreamy satisfaction as we followed the winding road up, but it's very different from what I expected it would be.

At the top of the hill, you stopped the car and got out. I followed you. Together we walked down a brick path toward a house in the hollow.

A man came out toward us. He bowed slightly and smiled. "You're the radio operator. I suppose," I said to him. Perhaps he would tell us about his adventures, or perhaps he would take us with him on the ship.

He raised his eyebrows slightly, as if in surprise. "No," he answered, "I'm your guide." He led us down into the garden. There was a shelf built against the side of the house, and on it were three underwater masks and simple respirators.

"Do you see that shimmering ahead?" he asked, pointing through the trees. "That's where the underwater world of Arlesia begins. You are to put on your masks and respirators, and we will go hunting fish."

I hesitated. "Oh, it's perfectly safe," the guide urged. "Overhead there are tons and tons of water, of course, but the masks are of special design. See, your husband has already put his on." I looked toward you and saw you, faintly grotesque in your new accouterment, listening eagerly to what the guide said.

When I had put on my mask, he handed us each a slender spear. "We catch the fish with these," he said. "Come on." He led us forward.

The water seemed to thicken about our limbs, and we moved more slowly as we advanced. Ahead, there were opalescent swirlings in the sunny water, vagrant rainbow plays of color that might have been the motions of schools of fish. We toiled painfully after them over the level ocean floor.

You were excited. Through the thick glass of your mask I could see you smile, and once you turned to me in triumph, saying, "See the one I caught then!" and held out your bare spear for me to see.

I soon tired of the fruitless sport. I stood watching you and the guide flounder after the elusive water-whirls, feeling myself divided between dreamy acceptance of everything and a faint uneasiness which might even grow into fright.

"That's enough," the guide said at last. "Now we'll go on in." He led us through the darkening waters along a narrow path that ran between lumps of what might have been coral. A greenish building loomed up ahead.

"Excuse me," the guide said. "I want to speak to the people inside." He opened a door and called out something to the women who were standing within in the greenish dusk or moving dully at some unknown task. None of them wore respirators or masks.

Then . . . "This isn't underwater," I said, facing the guide. "There aren't tons of water overhead. If there were, you couldn't have opened the door just now; those people would have drowned. And we couldn't talk to each other underwater without a radio. I don't like it here."

"Oh, yes, yes, it is underwater." the guide replied quickly, urgently. "It's all underwater, everything. What gives you such a strange idea? This is Arlesia, the underwater world." He pointed upward, to where the light was coming down thickened, as through layers of greenish gauze. "See how the light is, filtered through those fathoms and fathoms of water above us? Now do you believe this is what I say it is?"

I looked down at my hands, my feet. I wasn't even wet. "No," I replied.

"I'll have one of the women finish showing you about," the guide said with agitated haste. "As soon as you've seen more, you'll be convinced." He motioned to one of the women in the room and she came drifting up to us, her face a dim, brownish oval. "Take her on in," he bade her. "See that she sees enough. Be sure."

The woman put her hand on my wrist and began to draw me into a corridor. "Where's my husband?" I asked, looking back.

"He's being taken on in," she replied in a monotone. "He's all right. Don't worry. He's perfectly all right."

We moved down a long dim passage toward a heavy door. "Come in here," she said. "After you've been in here, you'll understand things better. It won't be any trouble for you to believe." She pushed the door open with her shoulder and tried to draw me inside.

I pulled back. I had caught a glimpse of complicated machines, of a huge screen on which coruscated just such dazzling colors as those I had already seen in the theatre. An inhuman gobbling and whirring came from the room.

"I won't," I said. "You're trying to do something to me, something to my mind. I won't go in there."

"Ah, well," she said. She dropped my wrist and was silent. She looked at me with a vague half-smile. "You get tired of living underwater all the time," she said in a tone of tremulous confiding.

She clasped her long fingers around my wrist once more. I followed her reluctantly. Was *this* the picture, World of Arlesia? Wasn't the pretence, rather, that I was in some fantastic place designed to hide from me the fact that this was *real,* that something real and *bad* was going on?

"You ought to've gone in that room," my guide said, turning to me in faint reproach. "You'd've understood everything better then. But see." She held open another door for me to look within. Under a flickering blueish-green light, with the sharp smell of ozone in the air, I saw naked women lying on couches, row after row of them, tier after tier. There seemed to be some sort of electrical terminals at their heads and at their feet. In the difficult light I fixed my eyes on the face of one nearest me; her face was tense and contorted, deathly white, and blood trickled slowly from her lips.

"What are you doing to them?" I cried. "She's being hurt! What are you doing?"

"Why, they're having the most beautiful dreams," the woman said, wearing a faint smile. She lowered her voice. "I heard them talking about it once. They said something about transmitting them, or something like that."

Still leading me by the wrist, she took me through the long rooms into another of only slightly smaller size. Stacked up in layers against its sides were what I at first took to be brocaded rolls of silk. Then I saw that they were the swaddled bodies of women, shrunken and dry.

"What has happened to them?" I demanded, shrinking back and pointing at the piles. "Are they dead? They look dried up, as if all the blood has been sucked out of them."

"Oh, no, of course not. They're learning to be mermaids, dear."

"To be mermaids? That's ridiculous." I felt faint.

The woman came close to me, her eyeballs swiveling from side to side as she looked agitatedly around the room. She put her face close to my ear, "Once I heard a leader say," she breathed, her voice a mere shred of sound, "that they had been transmitted to the moon. To work in the mines. They don't need air or food. They're part on the moon and part here."

"On the moon? What—"

"Hush, hush! They're learning to be mermaids, dear. That's the way it really is."

She led me on through the room and out into another corridor. We stopped at a little door near an ascending stair.

"Go in there and take off your things, dear," she bade me. "All of them. Then we'll go back." She gave me a little push and a dim smile.

I clutched the door jamb. "I won't," I said. "I won't go in there. I want my husband back. I want out of here." I began to cry.

"But you've got to!" She pulled at my wrist, using an unsuspected strength. She was speaking from between clenched teeth. "You've just got to! You can't act like this!"

I tried to pull away. Then I saw a woman hurrying down the stair toward us. She looked brisk and wide-awake; she almost seemed normal. It seemed to me she was some sort of a matron or wardress. Diamonds glittered at her ears, her neck, her plump wrists.

"What's all this, Xenia?" she snapped. "What are you doing? Using *force*? I won't have that, it's too dangerous."

"She won't take her things off," the other woman whined. "She doesn't want to—to start dreaming."

"Won't take her things off?" She was close to me, frowning. "Then how did she get in as far as this?"

I was sick with fright. But I tried not to show it, to stop crying.

"I want out of here," I said. "I want my husband back. Now!"

"But, child, that's impossible." Her voice was reasonable, kind, even, but her eyes glittered with a colder fire than did her diamonds. "You must see that. You can't be processed if you're unwilling. And if you stay here, you might raise the sleepers. And that would start something it would be hard to stop."

"You could exhaust her," Xenia said eagerly. "She wouldn't have to be willing . . . for that."

I felt the stout woman's plump hand under my chin, saw her cold eyes boring into mine.

"Perhaps. Hmmn." She shook her head. "No. Not this type. She would be of no use to us whatever. And what would we do with the body?"

I tried to keep the eagerness and the terror out of my voice. "You could let me go. It's not impossible. Don't you see, no one would believe that this was anything except the movie, World of Arlesia? All this is in the picture, isn't it? I saw what I was meant to see—the radio operator's adventures—the fish-hunting."

It was no use. The stout woman shook her head.

"You're clever, girl," she said. "You would be, of course. And you've seen too much. Very much too much. We can't have you free, to give away trade secrets."

"Then you'll have to kill me," I cried. "I—I won't give in—I won't *let* you do—whatever you want to do to me!"

"You'll suffer for this, Xenia!" The stout woman's arm shot out, pulling Xenia violently toward her. She shook her so hard I thought Xenia's spine would crack. "You'll have no more of—of what you *need*! I'll take it away from you. Forever! Forever, do you hear?"

The listless Xenia was suddenly filled with energy. She pulled herself free and her face contorted with desperate anger.

"Then I'll tell them about her. I'll tell the one who always hurts. You'll get yours, then. The penalty for mis-management."

The stout woman bit her lip savagely. "All right, then! Let her go. Take her out, all the way! I will settle with you, later."

My knees began to shake, then, and I wanted to run. Xenia's dusky hands were pushing me out, away from there, but I wouldn't go.

"I won't go without my husband. I want him back!"

"Hush!" the stout woman almost screamed. Her face was murderous. "You'll get him. Take him out, too, Xenia. Hurry, now, before—before they find out!"

We were sitting in the theater again. Everyone else had gone; the building was chilly, and only a few dim lights burned. You yawned and stretched.

"I certainly got cramped sitting still so long," you said. "But the picture was interesting, didn't you think?"

"Yes," I replied.

"It was all so real. I like that part about catching the fish— remember all those big fish I caught, twenty or so, all colors, and some even with stripes?"

"Yes, that was fun."

"And all those mermaids, swimming around? When the guide went into the cave to talk to them? That was really beautiful."

"Yes, I liked that."

"It was quite a picture," you said. "But I thought the ending was too abrupt. They were just about to turn me into a merman, with gills and everything, so I could enjoy being in Arlesia without having to wear a mask and respirator, and then it just stopped. Didn't you think the ending was a little too abrupt, Marie? It would have been more artistic to have us become underwater people like the others in Arlesia."

"Oh, I don't know," I replied. My voice was a trifle unsteady, but I don't think you noticed it. "I'm just as glad it ended when it did, I think."

THE LITTLE RED OWL

"By now the fire was getting very close to Billy and Gwendolyn," Charles said unctuously. "They could feel the heat against their faces, and it frightened them. All around them the leaves and branches were bursting into flame. They pulled as hard as they could against the ropes the Vulture Man had tied them with, but they could not get loose. Billy began to scream."

He paused in his narrative and looked archly at the children. They were listening intently. He observed with pleasure that they were both pale with excitement and what was pretty certainly distress. "What do you think happened to Billy and Gwendolyn?" he urged them. "Go on, tell me what you think happened to them."

"I know!" Peter said, almost shouting, "I know! The Little Red Owl came and got them out!"

"I'm afraid not," Charles answered smoothly. "Don't you remember, I told you at the beginning of the story tonight that the Little Red Owl has been hurt? He's not strong the way he used to be. The Vulture Man caught him and broke the bones in both his wings. Now he can't fly. All he can do is lie on the ground. And the broken wings hurt him very much."

Charles transferred his attention to Carlotta, who was chewing anxiously on the end of one of her short blonde braids. "What do you think happened, Lottie?" he asked.

She pulled the wisp of hair out of her mouth. "He's not really hurt, is he, Uncle Charles?" she asked anxiously. "Not the Little Red Owl? He's all right. He'll save them. You're just making it up."

Charles sighed. "Both the Little Red Owl's wings are broken," he said patiently. "He can't help Billy and Gwendolyn. He needs help himself. Carlotta. Do you know what is going to happen to Billy and Gwendolyn?"

She put her arm around Peter and hugged him up to her. "What, Uncle Charles?" she asked, as if the contact with her brother strengthened her.

"Why, they're going to be badly burned. Perhaps they will even die before the fire goes out. Do you remember how much your arm hurt when you burned it last week, Lottie?" He pointed to the bandaid on Carlotta's forearm. "Well, then."

Lottie's face puckered up. Her small chest heaved. For a moment Charles thought she was going to scream or slap at him. Then she began pulling her brother toward the door. "Come on, Peter," she said, almost in a whisper. "It's time for bed."

From the hallway she spoke to her uncle in a clear if somewhat wobbling voice. "I don't care what you say. I don't believe it. The Little Red Owl . . . the Little Red Owl isn't hurt. He's all right!"

Charles heard her and her brother stumbling down the hall toward their bedroom. For a moment his eyebrows went up. Then he relaxed. He chuckled. This defiance, of course, meant that Lottie was frightened. Not ill-pleased with himself, he rose from his chair.

Mrs. Morris, his housekeeper, was in the back sitting room. Under the placid light of a floor lamp she was knitting steadily away on a blue pullover for Peter. After a moment she put her work down and looked at him.

"Are the children all right, sir?" she asked in her pleasant voice, "I thought their voices sounded a little worked-up."

"I was telling them rather an exciting story," Charles said easily. "You know how children are."

"Yes, sir." Mrs. Morris hesitated. "Why do you tell them stories like that, sir? Just before they go to bed?"

Why, indeed? Charles thought. He felt his throat contract in an inaudible chuckle. For he loved them, he loved children, he loved

Billy and Gwendolyn—no, their names were Carlotta and Peter—tenderly. "They enjoy the excitement," he said lightly. "Didn't you like ghost stories yourself when you were young?"

"Oh, ghost stories." Mrs. Morris' face relaxed. She stuck the needle in her knitting, put it in the knitting bag. "I'll go tuck them in, sir," she said, "I wouldn't want them to have bad dreams."

She went out. Charles, left alone in the room, stood on the hearth rug jingling the change in his pockets restlessly. Should he have a drink? No, he wasn't thirsty. He picked up a newspaper and put it down again. At last he pulled an arm chair up to the fire. He sat down, picked up the poker, began to tap with it against the burning logs. A cloud of sparks darted up.

Charles watched, smiling. Whenever the swarm of sparks started to die away, he tapped on the logs again. At last he laid the poker aside and sank back in his chair. He began to plan the story he would tell the children on the next day.

The morning was rainy, in the afternoon there were scattered showers. It was not until late afternoon that Mrs. Morris thought it advisable to let the children out of the house. Charles watched from his study window.

Shouting and laughing, the children ran straight for the wall. Since the wall was less than five feet high it wasn't—Charles thought—exactly dangerous, but it had for the children the special attraction of the disapproved. Lottie clambered up first and then, from her eminence, gave Peter a helping hand. Soon, arms outstretched, they were balancing dramatically as they tightrope walked.

It began to grow dark. Charles came up to them, walking quietly in the dusk. "Lottie," he said, "it's time for you two to go in. I have a new story to tell you tonight."

From under her upraised arm Lottie peered at him. "I don't want to go in," she said sullenly. "Peter and I, we don't like your old stories. We don't want to listen to them."

"Carlotta, do you know what happens to little girls who are rude?"

"N-no," she answered uneasily. He could see that she was getting scared.

"They fall down and break their bones," he said impressively. "It hurts them very much. Carlotta, you're going to fall and break your arms and legs, like the Little Red Owl. That's because you were rude to me."

Lottie's mouth opened. She stared at him. Then she turned to run. Her foot caught. Over she went.

She began to scream hysterically. What a fuss about nothing, Charles thought, going up to her. Because of course she hadn't broken anything; bones at her age were soft, not brittle. Even though she should have. He tried to pick her up, and she crawled away from him, shrieking. And then of course Mrs. Morris had to come out.

Carlotta's knees were bathed and bandaged, she and Peter were given supper on a tray in their bedroom. Mrs. Morris spent a long time with them before she closed the door behind her and came out.

There would, Charles expected, be some kind of interview. He was standing on the hearth rug waiting when she came in.

"I want to speak to you about the children, sir," she said, plunging.

The courage of the timid! Charles thought. "Yes?" he said. He was careful to get the inflection of the word exactly right.

She moistened her lips. "Lottie says—Lottie tells me that you threatened her, sir. She says you told her she would fall and break her bones. As a punishment."

"She was exceedingly rude to me," Charles responded indifferently. Not that it would do him any good to be indifferent—it was an article of faith with Mrs. Morris that children were always right.

"Maybe so, sir. But you mustn't talk to her like that. She might really have hurt herself." She hesitated. "I'll have to tell her mother, sir, when Mrs. Gibbs gets back."

"Tell away," Charles answered, though he could feel himself trembling. It was the unfairness that bothered him. "Carlotta was unbearably rude."

Mrs. Morris bowed her head. It might have been in agreement. After an instant's silence, she continued. "And, sir, you must not tell them any more of those stories. I won't have that."

"Won't?" Charles mocked her.

"Yes, sir. Won't." She looked at him. Her face softened. "I think you ought to see a doctor, sir," she said. "You're not well."

"I never felt better in my life!" It was true. The energy, the force that filled him—it was like a fountain of life bubbling up. He was in love with them. Until now he had not really lived.

"I don't mean that kind of a doctor, sir. I mean—somebody who knows about the nerves. I beg your pardon, Mr. Gibbs. But I can see that as far as your nerves go, you're not well."

There were heavy candlesticks over the mantel. Charles clenched his hands in his pockets. No, he wouldn't. "Perhaps you're right, Mrs. Morris," he said disarmingly. "I haven't been quite myself lately. When Mrs. Gibbs comes back, I'll certainly go see someone."

"Thank you, sir. I'm sure it would do you good."

Her righteous back receded in the hall. But now what was he to do? If he told Mrs. Morris to go, pack her things, get out, *get out,* her first action would be to communicate with Sally Gibbs. And that would mean having his sister-in-law to deal with. Charles grimaced.

After a moment he sat down in the arm chair and began prodding absorbedly at the fire.

The days passed slowly, emptily. He kept away from the children and they kept out of his way. Mrs. Morris was always near them, watchful, well-mannered, alert. He had not known time could pass so slowly. He had nothing to live for now.

At the end of the week he went to the city to see a dealer in rare books. "Oh, yes, Mr. Gibbs," the man said pleasantly. "I've a new book, only came in yesterday, in which I think you might be interested. "Here," he handed a copy of *The Secret Museum of Naples* to him.

Charles pushed it away distastefully. "No, not that," he said, trying to keep the scorn out of his voice. "I'll tell you the sort of thing I want." He went into details.

The bookseller listened intently, smiling at first, and then beginning to frown. "Let me see," he said when Charles paused. "Would this be it?" He got a large floppy folio from under the counter and opened it a page.

Charles couldn't help smiling at the picture, but he had to refuse the book. Once more he explained his wants.

"I'm afraid I can't help you," the dealer said at last. "You can see yourself that such a book would be rather, h'um, rather special. I doubt that it exists. A child's coloring book, you say, with a particular picture. Let me think."

He wrinkled up his forehead. Then he scribbled an address on a sheet from a note pad and handed it to Charles. "That's the artist who did the picture you were just admiring," he said. "You might find it worth while to talk to him."

The artist's studio was on the third floor, a big, empty room whose walls were decorated with innocuous flower pastels. The artist himself was a small man with a tight face and watchful eyes. After Charles had talked to him for a while, however, he became more friendly. He got out a portfolio of his drawings; they were very amusing, very amusing indeed. Not at all like the pastels on the wall, Charles congratulated him on his talent. And the artist showed a gratifying readiness at understanding what it was Charles wanted him to do.

He drew a sketch; it was even better than the ideas Charles had had. He knew a printer who could, he thought, reproduce the picture as Charles wanted it. The sum the artist wanted for making the drawing and overseeing its insertion in the books—Charles thought it would be better to have two of them prepared—was certainly large. It was so large that Charles hesitated briefly. But after all, why not? What is money given us for, if not to enjoy ourselves?

On the eleventh day the artist telephoned from the city to say that the books were ready. Would Mr. Gibbs come after them? Certainly, Charles said, certainly. His fingers trembled with excitement as he dressed.

"It's page six," the artist said, giving him the picture books. "Of course, until it has been gone over, it doesn't look like much."

Charles examined the inserted page and nodded. Page six could not be distinguished, superficially, from any of the other pages. It, like they, bore on its surface numerous tiny colored dots, widely spaced, and an occasional solid line.

"I had the printer run off some extra copies of the page," the artist said, picking up a brush. "I'll show you how it comes out. Watch." He dipped the brush in water and began to paint the water carefully over a loose sheet which bore the numeral 6. "There! What do you think of it?"

Charles could only nod with satisfaction. A beautiful job! Of course, the children would probably smear it. It was unlikely that they would paint as carefully as the artist had done. But enough would come through—there was plenty on the page—to have an effect. Oh, yes.

He paid the painter, and left. He carried the books, an innocuous brown paper parcel, under his arm. All the way home, in the taxi, in the station, on the train, he kept caressing it. The feel of the paper against his fingertips delighted him.

It was such a pleasant afternoon that he decided to walk from the station to his house. It would give him more time to plan and anticipate. But when he was about a block away from home he remembered, with a stab of dismay, something he'd forgotten to plan for: Mrs. Morris. Oh, dear.

How could he get her out of the house? A faked telephone message? No, his voice couldn't possibly pass for that of Mrs. Morris' daughter Jean. A telegram? But telegrams always have the name of the receiving office at the top, and Jean lived in Connecticut. If Mrs. Morris noticed *that* little discrepancy, the fat would be in the fire.

Was his whole Argosy of enjoyment going to be wrecked on the rock of Mrs. Morris? After all the trouble he had gone to? It was abominable. His lips shook. But, after all, perhaps he was distressing himself for nothing. It would be difficult to get Mrs. Morris out of the house; but was getting her out of the house absolutely necessary? Wouldn't there, indeed, be an especially subtle pleasure in going ahead with what he was going to do while she was present? He'd have to be careful, but he could manage it. Satisfied, Charles began to hum lightly as he walked along.

When he got home he gave Mrs. Morris the parcel. "I bought these for the children in the city," he said. "Happened to see them in the window of a novelty shop. Do you think Lottie and her brother will care for them?"

Mrs. Morris undid the string. The dubiety left her face as she looked at the lettering on the covers of the big gay paper books. "The Paint-With-Water Color Book," she read aloud. "All you need is water and a brush."

"You understand how it works?" Charles said carefully. "You just take a paintbrush and water, and paint over the pages inside. And the water makes the colors and the pictures come out."

Mrs. Morris nodded. "Yes, I know. Jeanie used to have a coloring book like that."

She began to flip over the pages. Page one. Page three. Page five. Page seven. She hadn't noticed anything. Charles felt weak with pleasure. He licked his lips.

"Yes, they'll like them," Mrs. Morris said. "Thank you, Mr. Gibbs, for thinking of the children. I'm glad you're feeling better. They've been wanting something to do. I'll go give the paint books to them now." She went out.

Charles sighed at the exquisiteness of the moment. She was cooperating delightfully. And he'd been right, it was much better fun to do it this way.

He took off his shoes. In stockinged feet, he slid into the hall. He listened. He heard a babble of excited voices, then the rush of water in the bathroom. Lottie was saying something to Peter, something about spilling. (So typical of Lottie, the pretense of neatness. He wasn't fooled by it.) The children, it was clear, were getting water and starting at once on their painting books. How long would it take them to get to page six?

After supper he listened again. Mrs. Morris was ironing in the kitchen. The house was quiet except for the occasional murmur of the children's voices. Charles was keyed-up and tense, but he found he didn't mind waiting at all. There was something quite delightful in the thought of the children painting steadily ahead, while their industry brought them nearer and nearer to page six.

His hearing seemed exceptionally acute. He could hear the pages rustle as the children turned them, the weak scratch of their brushes on the paper, even the gurgle of the water as the brushes were dipped.

The moment came as he had imagined it, at the end of a long silence. Lottie gave a faint cry. A chair was pushed back. Still remembering caution, Charles ran down the hall on tiptoe to their room.

The paint book was open on the table. Both Lottie and Peter were looking at it. It must be Lottie's book, for the painting had been done with considerable care.

The picture was even better than Charles had remembered. The Little Red Owl hung upside down, crucified through his shattered wings. The flames, the blood, the beautiful blood dripping from his eyes. And, in the background, Billy and Gwendolyn.

Charles grasped Lottie by the shoulder. Now that the time had come, he forgot what he had meant to say. He shook her. He said, "That's what happened to the Little Red Owl."

Carlotta pulled out of his grip. She faced him. She was pale, but her eyes shone. "The picture's a big lie," she said.

Charles drew in his breath. Defiance? It was impossible; he'd had the picture made so she'd be convinced.

"I'll tell you how it really was," Carlotta said. Her voice rose.

"The Little Red Owl's not hurt! When the bad Vulture Man tried to catch him, the Little Red Owl flew in his face. The Vulture Man fell down, and the fire roared up over him. Then the Little Red Owl went and saved Billy and Gwendolyn. They got away. They're safe." She hesitated. Her breath was coming in gasps. Then she tore the picture out of the book. It left a jagged edge. Using both hands, she crumpled it up.

Oh, she thought she was a heroine! Charles caught her once more and began to shake her. She felt small and soft under his hands. Would her bones be brittle, like plant stems, or would they bend before they could break?

"You little . . . little . . . to tear a thing like that!" He hit her savagely, forgetting caution, and then again. Peter began to scream; Charles couldn't attend to both of them at once. It was almost a relief when Mrs. Morris came running in.

He was helped by dignity, pride, self-respect. He managed to listen to her tirade with his head proudly erect, and when she halted for breath he said coldly, "Are you quite through?"

But there is a price set on such severe self-control, and later he had to pay it. After Mrs. Morris had herded the children upstairs to her room for safekeeping, he sat huddled over the fire in the sitting room, shivering without being able to stop himself. His hands were shaking too much for him to be able to pick up the poker.

Why hadn't he silenced her? Charles asked himself. He could have hit her repeatedly on the mouth. He was stronger than she was. But the moment had passed. He couldn't possibly nerve himself to it now. Too late. Now Mrs. Morris was in the kitchen telephoning, calling number after number as she tried to locate Sally Gibbs.

What would happen? Well, he rather thought Sally would tell Mrs. Gibbs to take the children to some hotel and stay with them tonight. But that wasn't quite what he meant. What would happen to him?

His attention wandered. He tried to concentrate on what Mrs. Morris was saying, but gave it up after a second. His fate would be decided after all, he rather thought, not by what Mrs. Morris was saying, but by the sentences of a quite different voice, the voice he had begun to hear within his head.

He listened. The outer world sank away through gauzy layers into a profound silence. The . . . the children. Yes. He started to get up. Then he sat down in his chair again. He took a newspaper from the table beside him. He folded it carefully into a long, many layered lath-shape. He thrust the end of the newspaper into the flames in the grate.

"Were you scared, Lottie?" Peter asked. After their experience their mother had taken them to a psychologist who specialized in children. He had advised that they be allowed to talk if they wished, but not pressed to it. This was the first time that either one of them had referred to what had happened, even to the other one.

They had been playing earlier in the day with plasticine. Lottie pressed a blob of it out from under her fingernail before answering.

"Yes," she said honestly, "when he broke the door down. Why, Peter? Weren't you?"

"Not then," her brother answered with a hint of superiority, "I thought Mrs. Morris would come for us."

"But when you saw how the hall was all on fire, Peter? He'd set it on fire behind him, so nobody could get in to us."

"Yes, I was scared then, Lottie. But you know what scared me most? It was when I saw how his face was all wet and shiny and the light from the fire shined on his face."

"*Shone*," his sister corrected automatically. "What I minded most was when he came in the room. All the smoke and fire."

"When did you stop being scared, Lottie?"

"When I heard him whistle."

"Who whistle?" Peter asked uncertainly. "Uncle Charles?"

"Oh, Peter, don't be silly. You're older than that. You know. *Hint*."

"Oh. His whistle's pretty, isn't it?"

"Um-hum. Low and sweet and soft. Not like an owl, really. More like a dove."

"Lottie—did it really happen?"

Carlotta stared at him. "Did *what* really happen?" she demanded. "You mean, did the Little Red Owl really lead us through the smoke over to the window? And show us how to climb down the drainpipe to the rose bed? Of course he did."

"No, not that. Just because you're bigger, Lottie, you don't need to think you're the only one that knows things. I mean, did he really fly in Uncle Charles's face?"

Carlotta did not answer immediately. She went over to the window and looked out. The children's nursery was on the second floor. She could see a street lamp and a portion of the quiet street. "I didn't see him do it," she said, without turning. "But I heard the noise. And I saw Uncle Charles fall."

Mrs. Gibbs came in. "Bedtime, darlings," she said brightly. "Come along."

They were taken to the bathroom, washed, tooth-brushed, toileted. Mrs. Gibbs saw them into bed with hugs and kisses. She turned out the light. There was a silence. Then Lottie said, "If you want to, Peter, you can sleep in my bed tonight."

"All right." He crossed the room to her, skirting the play table and a couple of chairs. They snuggled together in the bed.

"Do you think we'll ever see him again?" Peter asked when they were settled. "The Little Red Owl?"

"Maybe," Lottie said thoughtfully, "maybe we would if we were scared or in trouble. Maybe he'd come for us then and help. I'll tell you, Peter. Let's try real hard to dream about him tonight. Maybe if we try real hard we can see him." Her voice was rich with longing. "Our own dear Little Red Owl."

There was a silence. Then Lottie said, "Have you still got the feather he gave you, Peter? Are you taking good care of it?"

In the darkness Peter nodded. "Don't you worry, Lottie," he said sleepily. "I've got it in a good safe place. Yes."

THE HOLE IN THE MOON

THE MOON, NOT quite full, was coming up over the Berkeley hills in yellow splendor. There was a big black hole, a flaw, against the bright part, where the first lunar explosion had driven a pit miles deep into the sterile rock. Hovey sat on the doorstep of his shack in the junk yard and watched the moon rising. He was smoking—he had found a dozen cartons of cigarettes in a drugstore on Wednesday—and enjoying it. He was feeling good.

He was lonesome, of course, but that he was used to. He had grown so familiar with the hollow feeling in his chest that he no longer bothered to name it. Besides, what difference did it make? There was nothing for him to do except wait.

And keep on waiting. After the incandescent horror of the first few months of war there had come more subtle thrusts, and then a long, mutual, exhausted silence. Hovey had made his way down the coast from Canada, where he had been stationed, to the junk yard. It had seemed like a place to go to. He had worked there once, in the days when the Eastshore highway had been crowded with traffic, and he had always liked it. On the junk yard side of the fence the huge cubes of compressed, rust-red metal and the corded bundles of newsprint and magazines; on the other side, the highway, with the cars shooting smoothly past all day and the big diesel trucks slipping along at night. Why shouldn't he like the junk yard? It had been something to come back to, a home, homelike. Now the highway was cracked and grass was coming up in the cracks.

Hovey shifted his position and lit another cigarette. He blew smoke out through his nose. Tomorrow, if he could spare the time from

91

food-hunting, he'd carry a couple of bundles of magazines across the highway and throw them into the water of the bay. Then he'd bring in those fenders from the two cars further down the road. He liked to do things like that. It kept the junk yard from seeming too stagnant. Of course, there was really nothing to do except hunt food and wait.

The night was windless and silent. Somewhere in the yard he heard a scratching of claws that might have been made by a rat. It probably wasn't. Rats rarely came to the junk yard, where there was little to attract them. And besides, there weren't many rats now. They had died from the plagues of which they had been carriers.

The plagues. Were there any women anywhere who weren't infected? Hovey thought not; they had all caught it, every woman; he didn't want to think of it. He sighed and rubbed one hand over his eyes. But that had been the enemy's masterstroke, surely, as good as anything Hovey's own people had ever delivered. To scatter an infection that fastened only on the female half of humanity, an infection that drove them, young or old, modest or wanton, irresistibly toward the male, urged by the inward fire of the disease. . . . Nothing else could so have poisoned human life, could so have maimed the human race.

In women the plague smouldered quietly. It betrayed itself only in their pitted skins, their roughened voices, their cracked lips. But the men who received the virus from them, transmuted by its incubation in their bodies, died quite quickly and, Hovey thought, quite unpleasantly. There was a gangrenous rotting and a smell. No doubt of it, that plague had been the enemy's masterpiece.

Hovey put his cigarette out against the wood of the doorstep. It was time for him to go to bed.

A voice somewhere in front of him said softly, "Dear, are you there, dear?"

Hovey jumped to his feet. His heart was pounding. He felt a horrible fear and a horrible longing. A woman. He picked up a piece of rusted angle iron from the ground and hefted it. He'd kill her if she came near him. He must drive her away. She . . . It had been so many years.

The woman was suddenly visible, stepping, it seemed, into the moonlight from shadow. She had coppery hair, and her skin was white and shining. He had not known she was so near him.

Hovey was trembling. He bit his lips and swallowed. He said, "Go away, you devil. Do you hear me? I'll kill you. Go away." He made a motion with the piece of iron at her.

She lowered her head, smoothing the skirt of her white print dress. She was wearing high-heeled slippers. She said, in a voice as smooth as cream, "Dear, isn't it really you?"

Hovey panted, "Go away!"

She said, "Oh, no." She moved toward him lightly, floating. He looked into her eyes. He thought—but could you tell colors in the moonlight?—he thought they were blue.

"Oh, no," she repeated softly. "Don't drive me away. I couldn't come back. And you love me, don't you? You want me to stay." Her voice was soft and sweet, almost cooing. He had heard voices like hers, women's voices, years ago on the radio.

Hovey was puzzled. Trembling, he let the iron bar drop on the ground. He stared at her. She smiled at him. Her skin looked smooth and cool and inviting.

"Then you're re— not—"

"Not what, dear? I'm whatever you made me."

He gaped at her a moment more, longing, believing, disbelieving. Then he took her in his arms.

Her skin was cool and glazed as paper. He couldn't hear her breathing; he liked that. The infected women always panted. Under the light print dress her body was young and thin.

When he let her go, he was dizzy. He wanted to hold on to something, to sink down on the doorstep. It had been so many years.

He took her smooth hand and pulled her toward the cabin. In a moment he would cry, make a fool of himself. "Come in," he said, "please come in with me."

She hung back, smiling a little. "You do want me? Really? You love me, dear?"

"Oh, yes." For an instant the storm of desire abated. He breathed deeply. "Who are you? Where did you come from?" he asked.

She shook her head. "You wouldn't understand."

At once he was suspicious and afraid. "What do you mean by that?" he demanded harshly.

"Well," she answered reasonably, "I came from the yard, the junk yard." She was twisting a copper bangle around one wrist. "Partly the place made me, the way hills and big trees make people. And partly you made me, because you were lonesome. You didn't make me very much, though. That's why I'm not strong. I'm not like my sisters. I told you you wouldn't understand."

She was a little crazy, he thought in relief, just a little crazy. She had a right to be, didn't she? Anybody—everybody—did.

He put his arm around her. At the touch of her body under the thin fabric he felt the fire leap in him again. "Come in the cabin, dear," he said, "please."

She leaned back against his arm and smiled at him. She put her white hands against his chest amorously. "Do you think I am beautiful?" she asked.

"Very. Yes." Again the sweet fire.

"Oh, you should see my sisters!" she replied laughing. "If you saw them, you would not care for me."

"I only want you. *Please* come in the cabin with me." He pulled at her arm.

"They are really beautiful," she said, as if dreaming. "They are strong, because they come from strong places, and because so many men have loved them. They live in the ruined cities. Their hair is as red as fire, and their skin is rough and pitted like masonry. Or they are black all over, dressed in charcoal, and their hair is coils of oily smoke. They are more beautiful than I. I am jealous. But we are of the same stock."

His arm was still around her, but he no longer felt the contact. His thoughts were coming in pulsations, wild and confused. She was crazy. Her sisters, who had pitted flesh and lived in cities. Many men had loved them. The plague. All women had it. She was crazy, she didn't know what she was saying. What was she trying to say? Who were the sisters she was talking about?

His arm dropped away from her waist. Abruptly he was wild with frustration, with desire and anger and hate. "So it was only a trap?" he said in a breaking voice. "You put cosmetic on your skin, you thought you'd fool me? Make me want you so much I couldn't let you go?"

She did not seem to have heard him. She slipped one hand inside his shirt and caressed the muscles of his chest. "Let's go to the cabin now, dear. I want to. You must love me and make me strong."

He wanted to cry, to hit himself, to throw himself down on the ground. He picked up the angle iron. He said, "Go away. Or I'll kill you. I can do it. Right here, like this."

"No! You mustn't make me go away. You mustn't. I couldn't come back."

He struck at her. She slipped away, into the shadows, and he ran after her. She was hiding; he'd find her, he'd kill her. He wanted to kill her because he wanted her so much.

Her dress fluttered at him from a corded bundle. He ran toward it, weeping, and found a scrap of blotched magazine cover moving on top of the bale. It had looked like the pattern of her dress.

He stood, shaking and blubbering, trying to think. She must be hiding. She was cruel. He'd get her yet.

Her white hand waved at him from behind a heap of metal. But when he reached it, it was white paper, glinting in the light of the moon. He touched it, unable to believe. It felt cool and glazed.

Her mop of copper-colored hair winked and beckoned. It was here, it was there, no, over there. He ran after it, sobbing and rubbing his eyes. The moon tricked him; when he put out his hand to touch her hair, it was always one of the cubes of rust-red metal that he touched.

He stopped at last, in the middle of the junk yard, sinking down on his knees in fatigue.

He was so filled with bitterness he did not see how he could possibly continue to breathe.

Next day he hunted through the drugstores (the liquor stores had been looted long ago) until he found a carboy of grain alcohol. He brought it back to the shack and drank it, mixed with vanilla extract and water, all that day. He lay on his back on his cot, sipping the mixture and smoking. He did not understand anything. Who she had been, where she had come from, who her sisters were, even whether she had been real—the more he tried to understand these things, the more he was conscious of his corroding, unbearable loneliness.

On the third night the moon was full. It rose higher and higher, a big yellow globe with a black hole in the lower part, like a bite taken out of an apple. Hovey sat on his doorstep in the moonlight, drinking the last of his alcohol and humming an old tune to himself. *Juanita*, its name was. He heard footsteps coming down the highway toward him.

He got up and went to the fence around the junk yard. It was a woman, and when she caught sight of him, she began to talk and gesture. Her voice rasped like unoiled metal, and even from that distance he could see the pitting of her skin.

He opened the gate with a flourish. "Come in," he said to her as she joggled and posed in the moonlight. "Do come in. You're real, anyhow. I won't hurt you. You can stay."

THE CAUSES

"GOD ROT THEIR stinking souls," the man on the bar stool next to George said passionately. "God bury them in the lowest circle of the pit, under the flaying ashes. May their eyeballs drip blood and their bones bend under them. May they thirst and be given molten glass for liquid. May they eat their own flesh and sicken with it. May they—" He seemed to choke over his rage. After a moment he lifted his glass of stout and buried his nose in it.

"You Irish?" George asked with interest.

"Irish? No." The man with the stout seemed surprised. "I'm from New Zealand. Mother was Albanian. I'm a mountain climber. Why?"

"Oh, I just wondered. What are you sore about?"

The man with the moustache patted the newspaper in his pocket. "I've been reading about the H-bomb," he said. "It makes me sick. I'm cursing the scientists. Do they want to kill us all? On both sides, I'm cursing them."

"Yes, but you have to be reasonable," the man on the second bar stool beyond George argued, leaning toward the other two. "None of us like that bomb, but we have to have it. The world's a bad place these days, and those Russians—they're bad cookies. Dangerous." Uneasily he shifted the trumpet case he was holding on his lap.

"Oh, sure, they're dangerous." The man with the stout hesitated, sucking on his moustache. "But basically, the Russians have nothing to do with it," he said. He cleared his throat. "I know what you're going to say, but it's not true. Our real trouble isn't the Russians . . . We're in the mess we're in because we've lost our gods."

"Hunh?" said the man on the second bar stool. "Oh, I get it. You mean we've become anti-religious, materialistic, worldly. Ought to go back to the old-time religion. Is that what you mean?"

"I did not," the man with the stout said irritably. "I meant what I said. The gods—our real gods—are gone. That's why everything is so fouled up these days. There's nobody to take care of us. No gods."

"No gods?" asked the man on the second bar stool.

"No gods."

The interchange began to irk George. He finished his drink—bourbon and soda—and motioned to the bartender for another. When it came, he said to the man with the moustache, "Well, if we haven't got any gods, what's happened to them? Gone away?"

"They're in New Zealand," the man with the moustache said.

He must have sensed the withdrawal of his auditors, for he added hastily, "It's all true dinkum. I'm not making it up. They're living on Ruapehu in Wellington—it's about 9,000 feet—now instead of Olympus in Thrace."

George took a leisurely pull at his drink. He was feeling finely credulous. "Well, go on. How did they get there?" he asked.

"It started when Aphrodite lost her girdle—"

"Venus!" said the man on the second bar stool. He rolled his eyes. "This ought to be hot. How'd she lose it?"

"Her motives were above reproach," the man with the stout said stiffly. "This isn't a smutty story. Aphrodite lent the girdle to a married woman who was getting along badly with her husband for the most usual reason, and the girl was so pleased with the new state of things that she forgot to return it. The couple decided to take a long cruise as a sort of delayed honeymoon, and the woman packed the girdle in her trunk by mistake. When Aphrodite missed it—Olympian society goes all to pieces without the girdle; even the eagles on Father Zeus's throne start fighting and tearing feathers—it was too late. The ship had gone so far she couldn't pick up any emanation from it."

"When did all this happen?" George asked.

"In 1913. You want to remember the date."

"Well, as I was saying, she couldn't pick up any emanation from the girdle. So finally they sent Hermes out to look for it—he's the divine messenger, you know. And he didn't come back."

"Why not?" the man on the second bar stool asked.

"Because, when Hermes located the ship, it had put in at New Zealand. Now, New Zealand's a beautiful country. Like Greece, I guess—I've never been there—but better wooded and more water. Hermes picked up the girdle. But he liked the place so much he decided to stay.

"They got worried then, and they sent others of the Olympians out. Iris was first, and then the Muses and the Moirae. None of them came back to Olympus. Those left got more and more alarmed, and one big shot after another went out hunting the girdle. Finally by 1914 there wasn't anybody left on Olympus except Ares. He said he didn't much care for the girdle. Things looked interesting where he was. He guessed he'd stay.

"So that's the situation at present. All the gods except Ares, and once in a while Athena, are on Ruapehu. They've been there since 1914. The Maori are a handsome people anyhow, and you ought to see some of the children growing up in the villages around there. Young godlings, that's what they are.

"Athena doesn't like it there as well as the others. She's a maiden goddess, and I suppose there isn't so much to attract her. She keeps going back to Europe and trying to help us. But somehow, everything she does, no matter how well she means it, always turns out to help that hulking big half-brother of hers."

"Interesting symbolism," George said approvingly. "All the gods we've got left are Ares, the brutal war god, and Athena, the divine patroness of science. Athena wants to help us, but whatever she does helps the war god. Neat. Very neat."

The man with the moustache ordered another bottle of stout. When it came, he stared at George stonily. "It is not symbolism," he said, measuring his words. "It's the honest truth. I told you I was a mountain climber, didn't I? I climbed Ruapehu last summer. I *saw* them there."

"What did they look like?" George asked lazily.

"Well, I really only saw Hermes. He's the messenger, you know, and it's easier for people to look at him without being blinded. He's a young man, very handsome, very jolly-looking. He looks like he'd play all kinds of tricks on you, but you wouldn't mind it. They'd be good tricks. He—you could see him shining, even in the sun."

"What about the others?"

The man with the stout shook his head. "I don't want to talk about it. You wouldn't understand me. They're too bright. They have to put on other shapes when they go among men.

"But I think they miss us. I think they're lonesome, really. The Maori are a fine people, very intelligent, but they're not quite what the gods are used to. You know what I think?" The man with the moustache lowered his voice solemnly. "I think we ought to send an embassy to them. Send people with petitions and offerings. If we asked them right, asked them often enough, they'd be sorry for us. They'd come back."

There was a stirring four or five stools down, toward the middle of the bar. A sailor stood up and came toward the man with the moustache. "So you don't like the government?" he said menacingly. There was a beer bottle in his hand.

"Government?" the man with the moustache answered. George noticed that he was slightly pop-eyed. "What's that got to do with it? I'm trying to help."

"Haaaaaa! I heard you talking against it," said the sailor. He swayed on his feet for a moment. Then he aimed a heavy blow with the beer bottle at the center of the moustache.

The man with the moustache ducked. He got off the bar stool, still doubled up. He drew back. He rammed the sailor hard in the pit of the stomach with his head.

As the sailor collapsed, the man from New Zealand stepped neatly over him. He walked to the front of the bar and handed a bill to the bartender who was standing, amazed, near the cash register. He closed the door of the bar behind him.

After a moment he opened it again and stuck his head back in. "God damn everybody!" he yelled.

After the sailor had been revived by his friends and pushed back on a bar stool, the man with the trumpet case, who had been on the far side of the stout drinker, moved nearer to George.

"Interesting story he told, wasn't it?" he said cheerily. "Of course, there wasn't anything to it."

"Oh, I don't know," George answered perversely. "There might have been."

"Oh, no," the man with the trumpet case said positively. He shook his head so vigorously that the folds of his pious, starchy, dewlapped face trembled. "Nothing like that."

"How can you be sure?"

"Because . . ." He hesitated. "Because I know what the real reasons for our difficulties are."

"Well, what's your explanation?"

"I—I don't know whether I ought to say this," the starchy man said coyly. He put his head on one side and looked at George bright-eyed. Then, as if fearing George's patience might be on the edge of exhaustion, he said, quite quickly, "It's the last trump."

"Who's the last trump?" the man on the bar stool around the corner from George asked, leaning forward to listen. George knew him by sight; his name was Atkinson.

"Nobody," the starchy man answered. "I meant that the last trump ought to have been blown ages ago. The world is long overdue for judgment."

"H. G. Wells story," George murmured.

"I beg your pardon?" said the starchy man.

"Nothing." George motioned to the bartender and ordered a round of drinks. Atkinson took gin and ginger ale, and the starchy man kirschwasser.

"Why hasn't the trump been blown?" Atkinson asked, with the air of one tolerating noisy children.

"Because it's lost," the starchy man replied promptly. "When the time came to blow it, it wasn't in Heaven. This wicked, wicked world! Ages ago it should have been summoned to meet its master." He drooped his eyelids.

George felt his tongue aching with the repression of his wish to say, "Plagiarist!" Atkinson said, "Oh, fooey. How do you know the trump's been lost?"

"Because I have it here," the starchy gentleman answered. "Right here." He patted his trumpet case.

George and Atkinson exchanged a look. George said, "Let's see it."

"I don't think I'd better . . ."

"Oh, go on!"

"Well . . . No, I'd better not."

Atkinson leaned his elbows on the bar and rested his chin on his interlaced fingers. "I expect there's nothing in the trumpet case actually," he said indifferently. "I expect it's only a gambit of his."

The soft, wrinkled skin of the man who was drinking kirschwasser flushed red around the eyes. He put the trumpet case down on the bar in front of George with a thump, and snapped open the lid. Atkinson and George bent over it eagerly.

The trumpet case was lined with glossy white silk, like a coffin. Against the white fabric, gleaming with an incredible velvety luster, lay a trumpet of deepest midnight blue. It might have been black, but it wasn't; it was the color of deep space where it lies softly, like a caress, for trillions of miles around some regal, blazing star. The bell of the trumpet was fluted and curved like the flower of a morning glory.

Atkinson whistled. After a moment he paid the trumpet the ultimate tribute. "Gosh," he said.

The man with the trumpet said nothing, but his little mouth pursed in a small, tight, nasty smile.

"Where'd you get it?" George queried.

"I'm not saying."

"How do you know it's the last trump?" Atkinson asked.

The starchy man shrugged his shoulders. "What else could it be?" he asked.

The door at the front of the bar opened and three men came in. George watched them absently as they walked the length of the bar counter and went into the rear. "But . . . you mean if this thing were blown, the world would come to an end? There'd be the last judgment?"

"I imagine."

"I don't believe it," Atkinson said after a minute. "I just don't believe it. It's an extraordinary looking trumpet, I admit, but it can't be . . . that."

"Ohhhhh?"

"Yes. If it's what you say, why don't you blow it?"

The starchy man seemed disconcerted. He licked his lips. Then he said, in rather a hostile tone, "You mean you want me to blow? You mean you're ready to meet your maker—you and all the rest of the world—right now? Right this minute? With all your sins, with all your errors of commission and omission, unforgiven and unshriven on your head?"

"Sure. That's right. Why not? The longer the world goes on existing, the worse it'll get. As to sins and all that, I'll take my chances. They couldn't be much worse than what—" Atkinson made a small gesture that seemed to enclose in itself the whole miserable, explosive terrestrial globe—"than what we have now."

Under his breath. George quoted. " 'We doctors know a hopeless case—' "

The starchy man turned to him. "Do you agree with him, young man?" he demanded.

"Yep."

The man with the trumpet turned bright red. He reached into the case and picked up the trumpet. As he lifted it through the air, George noticed what a peculiarly eye-catching quality the celestial object had. Its color and gloss had the effect on the eye that a blare of horns has on the ear. Heads began to turn toward it. In no time at all, everyone in the bar was watching the starchy man.

He seemed to pause a little, as if to make sure that he had the attention of his audience. Then he drew a deep, deep breath. He set the trumpet to his lips.

From the rear of the bar there burst out a jangling, skirling, shrieking, droning uproar. It was an amazing noise; a noise, George thought, to freeze the blood and make the hair stand upright. There must have been ultrasonics in it. It sounded like a thousand pigs being slaughtered with electric carving knives.

Everyone in the bar had jumped at the sudden clamor, but the effect on the starchy man was remarkable. He jumped convulsively, as if he had sat on a damp tarantula. His eyes moved wildly; George thought he had turned pale.

He shouted, "They're after me!" He shouted it so loudly that it was perfectly audible even above the demoniac noise of the bagpipes. Then he grabbed up the trumpet case, slammed the trumpet in it, and ran out of the bar on his neat little patent leather feet.

The two bagpipers came out from the rear of the bar, still playing, and began to march toward the front. Apparently they had noticed nothing at all of the episode of the dark blue trumpet. The third man followed in the rear, beating on a small drum. From time to time he would put the drum sticks to his upper lip and seem to smell at them.

"Remarkable, isn't it?" Atkinson said to George over the racket. "Only bar I ever was in where they kept bagpipes in the rear to amuse the customers. The owner's Scottish, you know."

The instrumentalists reached the front of the bar. They stood there a moment skirling. Then they executed an about-face and marched slowly to the rear. They stood there while they finished their number. It was long, with lots of tootling. At last they laid their instruments aside, advanced to the bar, and sat down on three bar stools near the center. They ordered Irish whiskey.

"Wonder where he got that trumpet," Atkinson said thoughtfully, reverting to the man with the trumpet case. "Stole it somewhere, I shouldn't be surprised."

"Too bad he didn't get to blow it," George answered. He ordered Atkinson and himself another drink.

"Oh, that!" Atkinson laughed shortly. "Nothing would have happened. It was just a fancy horn. You surely don't believe that wild yarn he told us? Why, I know what the real reason for all our troubles is!"

George sighed. He drew a design on the bar counter with his finger. "Another one," he said.

"Eh? What? Oh, you were talking to yourself. As I was saying, I know the real reason. Are you familiar with Tantrist magic and its principles?"

"Unhunh. No."

Atkinson frowned. "You almost sound as if you didn't want to hear about this," he observed. "But I was talking about Tantrist magic. One of its cardinal tenets, you know, is the magic power of certain syllables. For instance, if you persistently repeat Avalokiteshvara's name, you'll be assured of a happy rebirth in Heaven. Other sounds have a malign and destructive power. And so on."

George looked about him. It was growing late; the bar was emptying. Except for himself and Atkinson, the pipers and the drummer, and a man around the corner of the bar from George, who had been sitting there silently against the wall all evening, the stools were empty. He looked at Atkinson again.

"About 1920," Atkinson was saying, "a lama in a remote little valley in Tibet—" George noticed that he pronounced the word in the austere fashion that makes it rhyme with gibbet—"got a terrific yen for one of the native girls. She was a very attractive girl by native standards, round and brown and plump and tight, like a little bird. The lama couldn't keep his eyes off her, and he didn't want to keep his hands off either. Unfortunately, he belonged to a lamistic order that was very strict about its rule of chastity. And besides that, he was really a religious man.

"He knew there was one circumstance, and one only, under which he could enjoy the girl without committing any sin. He decided to wait for it.

"A few months later, when the girl was out pasturing the buffalo, or feeding the silk worms, or something, she saw the lama coming running down the side of the hill toward her. He was in a terrific froth. When he got up to her, he made a certain request. 'No,' the girl answered, 'my mother told me I mustn't.' You see, she was a well-brought-up girl."

George was looking at Atkinson and frowning hard. "Go on," he said.

"I *am* going on," Atkinson answered. "The lama told her to go home and ask her mother if it wasn't all right to do what the holy man told her. He said to hurry. So she did.

"When she came back the lama was sitting on the field in a disconsolate position. She told him it was all right, her mother had said to mind him. He shook his head. He said, 'The Dalai Lama has just died. I thought you and I could cooperate to reincarnate him. Under the circumstances, it wouldn't have been a sin. But now it's too late. Heaven has willed otherwise. The job has already been attended to.' And he pointed over to a corner of the field where two donkeys were copulating.

"The girl began to laugh. As I said, she was a well-brought-up girl, but she couldn't help it. She laughed and laughed. She almost split her sides laughing. And the poor lama had to sit there listening while she laughed.

"You can't excuse him, but you can understand it. He'd wanted her so much, he'd thought he was going to get her, and then those donkeys— Well, he began to curse. He began to curse those terrible, malign Tantrist curses. He's been cursing ever since.

"Ever since 1920, he's been cursing. Once in a while he pauses for breath, and we think things are going to get better, but he always starts in again. He says those dreadful Tantrist syllables over and over, and they go bonging around the world like the notes of enormous brass bells ringing disaster. War and famine and destruction and revolution and death—all in the Tantrist syllables. He knows, of course, that he'll be punished by years and years of rebirths, the worst possible kind of karma, but he can't help it. He just goes on saying those terrible syllables."

George looked at him coldly. "*Two Kinds of Time*," he said.

"Hunh?"

"I said, you read that story in a book about China called *Two Kinds of Time*. I read it myself. The donkeys, the lama, the girl— they're all in there. The only original part was what you said about Tantrist curses, and you probably stole that from someplace else." George halted. After a moment he said passionately, "What's the *matter* with everybody tonight?"

"Oh, foozle," Atkinson replied lightly. *"Om mani padme bum."* He picked up his hat and left the bar.

After a minute or so, the two pipers followed him. That left George, the silent man in the corner, and the instrumentalist who had played on the drum. George decided to have one more drink. Then he'd go home.

The silent man who was leaning against the wall began to speak. "They were all wrong," he said.

George regarded him with nausea. He thought of leaving, but the bartender was already bringing his drink. He tried to call up enough force to say, "Shut up," but his heart failed him. He drooped his head passively.

"Did you ever notice the stars scattered over the sky?" the man in the corner asked. He had a deep, rumbling voice.

"Milky Way?" George mumbled. Better hurry and get this over with.

"The Milky Way is one example," the stranger conceded. "Only one. There are millions of worlds within the millions of galaxies."

"Yeah."

"All those millions of burning worlds." He was silent for so long that George's hopes rose. Then he said, "They look pretty hot, don't they? But they're good to eat."

"Hunh?"

"The stars, like clams . . ."

"Beg your pardon," George enunciated. He finished his drink. "Misjudged you. You're original."

The man in the corner did not seem to have listened. "The worlds are like clams," he said rapidly, "and the skies at night present us with the glorious spectacle of a celestial clambake. They put them on the fire, and when they've been on the fire long enough, they open. They're getting this world of yours ready. When it's been on the fire a little longer, it'll open. Explode."

George realized that that last drink had been one too many. He didn't believe what the man in the corner was saying. He wouldn't. But he couldn't help finding a dreadful sort of logic in it. "How'ju know this?" he asked feebly at last.

The man in the corner seemed to rise and billow. Before George's horrified and popping eyes, he grew larger and larger, like a balloon inflating. George drew back on the bar stool; he was afraid his face would be buried in the vast unnatural bulk.

"Because," said the inflating man in a high, twanging voice, "because I'm one of the clam-eaters!"

This horrid statement proved too much for George's wavering sobriety. He blinked. Then he slid backward off the bar stool and collapsed softly on the floor. His eyes closed.

The billowing form of the clam-eater tightened and condensed into that of a singularly handsome young man. He was dressed in winged sandals and a winged hat; from his naked body there came a soft golden light.

For a moment he stood over George, chuckling at the success of his joke. His handsome, jolly face was convulsed with mirth. Then, giving George a light, revivifying tap on the shoulder with the herald's wand he carried, the divine messenger left the bar.

THE ISLAND OF THE HANDS

EVER SINCE HE had begun to have the dreams about Joan, there had been a compass in his head. He felt that he could go as directly to the spot from which she was calling him as a homing pigeon returns to its cote. He woke from those dreams—dreams in which she stood before him pale and disheveled, weeping bitterly, imploring him, "Come, oh, come!"—as surely oriented as an arrow in flight. Joan was the magnet, and he the steel. But Joan was dead.

They had hunted for her for nearly a week after her plane had crashed. Over and over the water, day after day, sectioning and resectioning the area where she must have gone down. There had never been any trace. How could there be? Earth was a water world for thousands of miles around the area. The best that could have happened was that she might have floated for a few hours, for a few days, before she drowned.

Dirk had been talking to her by rad when her plane had crashed. The flight had been going splendidly, rather monotonous really. She hoped to see him in a few hours. And then her voice had soared up suddenly in a shocking scream. "The plane! What—oh, my God!" Seconds later he had heard the final roaring crash.

Something had happened to Joan's plane in perfect weather, with visibility unlimited, with the engines purring silkenly. What? What had caused the crash?

Not long after the search for his wife was officially abandoned, Dirk began to have the dreams. Night after night with the compass in his brain pointing, nearly three months of nights, until he began to wonder whether grief for Joan—too soon lost, too well loved—

was breaching the wall of sanity in him. And then his decision, no sooner reached than rejoiced in, the decision to abandon rationality and go to look for a woman who was certainly dead.

Dirk Huygens went to Larthi, the little settlement from which the official rescue planes had set out. He could pilot a plane himself, but in Larthi he hired a quadriga with two navigators to spell each other. He did not want the duties of piloting to distract him from the pointing of the needle in his head.

Sokeman was the name of the chief navigator, a lean nervous man who smoked and coughed continually. Ross, the second pilot, was of very different physical type—bull-necked and broad-shouldered, with a ready grin. They had good references.

"What were those coordinates again?" Sokeman asked suddenly. The three men were having a drink together in a waterfront bar in Larthi to bind the bargain they had made.

"63° 11' west, 103° 01' north," Huygens said. "Or thereabouts. As I told you, I can't be quite sure. I want the whole area searched."

"Um." Sokeman ordered another round of drinks.

"Why?" Huygens asked. He swallowed. "Is it—did you ever hear of land there?" Hope had begun a thin hammering in him.

"Land? Oh, no. Nothing out there but water. But it seems to me I've heard those coordinates before. Do you remember, Ross? Wasn't there a man a year or so ago asking about them?"

"I think so," Ross answered. "And a dame six months or so before that. A good looker." He grinned.

"What happened to them?" Huygens asked absently. The two pilots had told him it was too late to begin the search tonight.

Sokeman shrugged. "Don't know," he answered. "Maybe they hired boats. They didn't hire our rig."

The next day at dawn the search began. Hour after hour the quadriga beat back and forth across the water. Huygens, his hand pressed to his head, muttered directions. To the west. Now, back. West again. South-south west. Steady as she goes. North. North through east. Back. . . ." And hour after hour the quadriga obeyed him, hunting patiently, tirelessly, fruitlessly.

The day passed in a dazzle of empty waters. Then it was dark and time to go back to Larthi. So it was that day and the next day and the next and the next. Huygens saw that even the pilots, though they were being paid for the time spent in hunting, were growing impatient at the futility of their task.

On the fifth day he turned abruptly to Sokeman, who was piloting. "Go back," he ordered harshly. "Back to Larthi. It's no use."

Sokeman bit his lip. His eyes narrowed. Huygens thought he must be considering whether he and the rig could claim to have earned a full day's pay. "It's almost sunset," he said. "Only an hour or two more. Let's finish out the day, eh. Mr. Huygens? Then we'll go back."

"All right," Huygens said unemotionally. He sank back in his seat, his hands pressed over his eyes. Hope had made him sick. A thousand times in the last few days, it seemed to him, the voice in his brain had said "Here!" imperatively. And there had never been anything but the flat surface of the empty sea.

The quadriga wheeled and banked. Sokeman sent it back and forth in long sweeps above the water. Huygens endured the ship's motion impatiently. Now that he had come to a decision, he wanted to get it over with. He wanted to be back in the rooming house in Larthi, done with hope, getting ready to go back to Zavir. There was work waiting for him in the city. It would help him to forget.

The ship shook abruptly from stem to stern. Huygens had a sudden amazed conviction that it had rammed an invisible wall. Sokeman screamed shrilly, like a woman. It was as though a crushing weight pushed the quadriga down irresistibly toward the surface of the sea. Huygens heard a wild roaring in his ears. And then it was all black.

Huygens came back to consciousness to find he was vomiting. He levered himself up with one arm and looked around the quadriga's cabin. Sokeman was lying back in the pilot's seat, a huge lump swelling on his temple where it had struck against the side of the ship. Ross was stretched out in the aisle, but as Huygens watched he stirred and raised his head. The quadriga's stout frame was buckled and pleated and crumpled in a hundred places. The ship must be completely wrecked.

Ross groaned. He sat up, holding on to the back of the pilot's seat. "Where are we?" he asked. "What happened to the ship?"

"I don't know," Huygens answered. Shakily he made his way to one of the ports and looked out. "We're on a little beach," he reported. "It's rocky and steep. I can't see much. There're trees and brush on three sides of us."

"It's land, anyway," Ross answered. He looked at Sokeman and whistled. Carefully he felt over the unconscious man's skull. "I don't think he's hurt bad," he said after a minute. "Anyhow, there's nothing we can do for him. Let's go outside and see what we can find."

The quadriga seemed to have crashed in a little cove. A dark mass of heavily-foliaged trees and brush came down almost to the edge of the water. "I don't think we can get through that," Huygens said, studying it. "Let's walk along the beach and see if we can find a trail."

They had gone crunching over the pebbles for perhaps a quarter of a mile when Ross said, "This is a funny place. Notice how misty the air is, and cold and still? It was a fine bright day, a little windy, when the ship crashed. And notice those trees. I never saw trees like that before, such a dark green, with little needles making up big flat leaves."

Huygens nodded. "I thought at first they were pseudo-conifers," he said, "but—what's that at the edge of the water up ahead?"

The two men exchanged glances. "A motor boat," Ross said slowly. "There must be people here. A motor boat."

A little farther along they saw a cabin cruiser, drawn up carelessly on the shingle, and then another smaller boat. They might have been there a long time. A little beyond the last craft there was an opening in the heavy blackish brush. Overgrown as it was, it seemed to be a trail which led inward.

"Those motorboats are as queer as everything about this place," Ross said as the two men started back to the quadriga after Sokeman. "What are they doing here, so far from the nearest port? It reminds me of something. . . ." He fell into a frowning abstraction.

Sokeman was standing outside the quadriga when they got back, though he looked white and sick. Huygens went into the ship for the aid kit, blankets and other supplies. Then they started along the beach again, supporting Sokeman between them.

The trail was badly overgrown, and they had to stop frequently for Sokeman to rest. It was nearly dark when Ross said, "There's something off to the right, where the trees are sort of mashed down. Do you see it? Looks like it might be a wrecked plane."

They got up to it, and Ross was right. It was a wrecked plane, thoroughly wrecked, Huygens read the name on the fuselage— "Coma Berenices"—twice before he admitted to himself whose plane it was. "Coma Berenices" had been the name of Joan's plane.

He said something to the others. He dropped Sokeman's arm and ran crazily around the plane, looking for Joan. He found her under a bush to one side. She had been lying there for about three months, but there were things that made the identification unmistakable—a bracelet he had given her, her long bright hair, her wedding ring.

"Was that what you were . . . looking for?" Ross asked when he had gone back to where they were waiting for him.

"Yes," Huygens answered carefully. "It wasn't—quite what I wanted to find."

He took one of the blankets and spread it carefully over Joan. Ross said, "We'll come back tomorrow and—fix things up." Huygens made no answer.

They went a good deal farther on before they made camp. Huygens, when he did sleep, slept soddenly. He did not dream. There was no reason for him to. Joan was dead.

Huygens woke early the next morning, before there was much light in the sky. Little streamers of mist floated in the still, heavy air. Sokeman and Ross were still asleep.

He was thirsty. They had found a tiny spring last night, welling up softly under a clump of blackish brush. He went over to the spring, scooped up the cold water in his hand, and began to drink. He was just rising to his feet when he saw Joan coming toward him through the trees.

He ran toward her, his heart hammering insanely. When he was about ten feet from her he stopped suddenly, as if the impulse which had borne him on was exhausted. Foreknowledge was already in him. He could see, now, that the woman was not Joan; in a sense he had known that she was not Joan when he began to run. But this moment of realization was more cruel than any yet had been.

She was not Joan. She differed from her in a hundred, a thousand, tiny ways. Her face was a more perfect oval than Joan's, her hair brighter, her eyes hazel instead of gray. She was taller than Joan and under her thin golden tunic her body was rounder and more lithe. She walked with a more deliberate grace than Joan had. But for all the differences the resemblance was uncanny, astonishing, incredible. Huygens stared at her, and belief and disbelief alternated in him like systole and diastole in the beating of the heart.

The woman smiled at him and held out her hands in welcome. "Hello, Dirk," she said.

"Are—you're not Joan."

"No."

After a minute Huygens said, "How did you know my name?"

She smiled at him again, but did not answer. A tatter of mist floated between them. Huygens would not have been surprised if she had dissolved in it. But when the mist cleared she was still there.

The sound of their voices had wakened the other two men. Ross came up, looking about alertly. When he saw the woman, he whistled softly. "Introduce me to your friend," he said in Huygens' ear.

"What's your name?" Huygens said to Joan-not-Joan.

He would have sworn the question was new to her. She looked troubled and disturbed. "Miranda," she answered, as if after thought.

Sokeman had been looking at the girl in silence, frowning. Now he said, "Our plane was wrecked. What's the name of this place?"

"This is the place of shaping. Its name is the Island of the Hands."

Sokeman's face remained blank, but Ross let out his low whistle again. He said stumblingly, "I think, I seem to remember, I believe I've heard . . ."

"Maybe," Miranda answered distantly. "The island is known to some people on Earth."

Ross's self-assurance was coming back. "Look here, Miranda," he said, "aren't there other people on the island? You know, people. A settlement, a town."

"Yes, there are people," Miranda replied. She had a low, musical voice, sweeter than Joan's had been. She moved closer to Dirk, smiling, and fingered the stuff of his sleeve. He saw that she was very beautiful. Without looking at Ross she said, "Shall I take you to them?"

Sokeman and Ross exchanged glances. "Yes," Ross said.

Miranda waited while the three men broke camp. Her eyes followed Dirk Huygens as he worked, and always she smiled. When they were ready she led them along the trail.

They walked for a long time, always slightly up, through the heavy, quiet air. Miranda said at last, "We turn to the right here. Do you see?" She indicated a barely perceptible track. "This is the way to the people, to those who have their desire. The other way leads to the Hands."

There were too many questions in Huygens' mind for him to ask any of them. He walked beside Miranda silently. Behind him the two men were talking in low tones. He heard Ross say something like, "When I was a child . . . this place . . ." and then Sokeman's murmured, inaudible reply.

They came to the top of a slight rise. Below them, in a shallow valley, was a group of squat structures in a semi-circle. They were small, almost huts, and there was about them an indefinable air of desolation and abandonment. "This is where the people live," Miranda said, turning to speak over her shoulder. "Shall we go down to them?"

Sokeman and Ross said "Yes" almost together. Ross was frowning and his lips were tight.

They had gone a few steps when a man came stumbling up the slope toward them. He collapsed almost at their feet. He was gaunt to the point of emaciation, with staring, bloodshot eyes, and his scanty clothing hung in tatters around him. Miranda walked around him with calm indifference. Huygens saw that the man was dead drunk. As they passed him, he tipped a phlomis bottle up with a shaking hand to get the last few drops from it. The bottle gave an unlikely gurgle as he lowered it.

There was a flash of movement ahead in the clear space where the houses were. Miranda led the three men toward it. When they had got close enough Huygens saw that it was a woman—surely an elderly woman, dressed in faded violet taffeta—who was moving in the measures of an intricate dance with a huge young man. The man moved with the precision of clockwork, as smoothly as if inaudible music were regulating him, but the woman stumbled from time to time. About and about they went in their fantastic dance against the background of the blackish trees, while streamers and tags of mist drifted slowly toward them.

As they moved closer to Huygens in their rhythmic circling, he saw that the woman was, as he had thought, wrinkled and old. Her partner, however, had the bland, impossible perfection of a dummy in a display of fashionable clothing. His empty face was bent down to the gray-haired woman in what was almost a caricature of admiring attentiveness.

Three other men, as alike him as peas, were waiting at the edge of the clear space. One of them stepped up to the dancing couple and tapped the huge man on the shoulder. And docilely the dancing giant resigned the gray-haired woman to the second man. He moved off with her in the perfect and uncanny clockwork step.

"She dances," Miranda said as if in explanation. "Always she dances. It is her desire."

The elderly dancer stopped abruptly. "I'm tired," she whimpered. Instantly the man who had been dancing with her knelt before her and kissed her hand. It was a parody of adoration. Then he picked her up in his enormous arms and, holding her as if she were something infinitely precious and frail, carried her off to one of the huts. The other three men followed behind.

The grotesque spectacle had kept Huygens silent. Now he turned to Miranda. "What is it?" he demanded. "I don't understand. Are they all like this?"

"All? Oh, no." Miranda shook her bright head. "Their desires are different, you see." She hesitated. "They stay in the huts most of the time," she said. "If you want to see them, you must look in the windows. They will not care. They will not notice you."

Ross had already gone to the window of the nearest hut and was looking in. After an instant Huygens followed him.

The light was bad. At first all Huygens could see was a heap of something on the floor and, seemingly buried in it, the head and shoulders of a man. Then he perceived that the heap was a glinting mass of faceted jewels, sending out sparks of purple, red, green, topaz, and gold. A naked man, wizened and under-sized, was standing waist-deep in the pile. He was plunging his hands in it over and over, bringing up handfuls of corruscating jewels and letting them drop over his head and breast.

In the next hut a woman sat on a low bed. In her arms she held a young child. She talked to it, played with it, rocked it in her arms. And all the time the child was perfectly passive and mute. Once only it moved its hands a little. There was something horrible in its inactivity.

"Have you seen enough?" Miranda asked as he turned from the window. "Are you ready to go to the place of shaping, to visit the Hands?"

Ross drew in his breath. Almost diffidently he asked, "Is it allowed? May anyone . . . shape with the hands?"

"Oh, yes," Miranda answered with a grave smile. "This is the Island of the Hands."

She turned and began leading them around the semicircle of buildings. Huygens followed her automatically. His mind was in confusion. As they began to walk uphill again he said, "What is this place, Miranda? Ross and Sokeman seem to understand, but I don't."

"What do you want to know?" Miranda asked in her sweet voice.

"What the island is, what those people are doing here, what the Hands are—everything. How was it we didn't see the island? What made our plane crash?"

"I will tell you what I know," Miranda said. She put out her hand and touched his arm lightly, smiling. With a shock of surprise he saw that on her finger there was a gem-set wedding ring.

"The Island of the Hands was made by a great, by a supreme, man of science long ago. He had lost his wife, and he felt he could not live without her. He made the place of shaping so he could bring her back. You will understand that part better when you see the Hands.

"After he died, the island remained. People began to come to it, one or two a year, people who had desires they could not bear to leave ungratified. They come to the island, and with the Hands they make their desires. And they live in the huts—I don't know who built them—until they die.

"The island cannot be seen from above. Only a little of its coast is visible from the water's edge. There is a—a space around the Hands that bends the rays of light. And force goes up from the place of shaping. Your plane crashed against that force."

Some of Huygens' confusion was gone, but a mystery remained. "Who are you?" he said to the woman who looked so uncannily like Joan, "What are you doing here?"

"I am Miranda," she answered readily. "This is where I live."

"But—" Huygens bit his lip. He fell silent, his head lowered, as he tried to think.

Ross and Sokeman were talking behind him. He heard Sokeman say something about the rucksack of food Ross had left behind at the camping place, and then remark, "I'm not hungry. That's strange. We haven't had anything to eat today."

"I don't think we need to eat here," Ross answered. In a more intimate tone he said, "What are you going to make for yourself, Chet?" There was a pause. Then, for answer, came only Sokeman's nervous laugh.

The place of shaping surprised Dirk. He hardly knew what he had been expecting—an amphitheatre, a building like a temple, a huge cave. But Miranda merely led them to a level spot, clear of trees, where the white mists that floated over all the island were almost chokingly thick. Then, as he peered and strained his eyes, he saw, very dimly through the mist, the outline of a huge, a gigantic, a cyclopean pair of hands. The fingers of one hand rested lightly on the back of the other, and though the hands were as quiet as if they had been hewn out of stone, it was as if they but rested from the labor of creation, and would again create.

"Go no nearer," Miranda said warningly. "Do you see the line?" She indicated a luminous mark, as slender as thread, that ran off on both sides into the thick white mist. "You must not step over that. It is very dangerous.

"Now, this is the way that the shaping is done. The one who would create his desire for himself kneels in front of the line and stretches his hands over the line into the fog. And what he wants he thinks of with all his heart and his soul and his hope. And the Hands shape his desire for him.

"Dirk, I am not that Joan whom you lost. Will you be the first to use the Hands? Will you have the Hands shape her again for you?"

Huygens' heart gave a bound. He realized now that he had repressed awareness of the possibility of which Miranda spoke into the depths of his brain. It was impossible, it was wonderful, it was horrible. He thought of the child, inert as a dummy, that he had seen on the woman's lap in the hut. He thought of the blank, fatuous faces of the men who had danced with the woman in the violet dress. "Would she—would she be really Joan?" he asked. "Would what I made be Joan the way she really was?"

Miranda raised her shoulders in a tiny shrug. "There are two things, I think, that determine what the hands shape. One is the force of the longing, the force of the desire. The other is the clearness of the image in the mind. But if the shaper does not like what the Hands have shaped for him, he can let the creation slip back into the mist.

"One thing more I must tell you. You may use the Hands for shaping but once. You may stay here as long as you like, having the Hands shape and reshape your desire for you, until it is as close as may be to what is in your heart. But once you have taken your hands from the fog, you can never put them in again. No one is strong enough. You would be lost."

"A radiation," the part of Huygens' brain which could still function was saying. "Perhaps a radiation to which a second exposure brings death . . . Joan, Joan, Joan! What shall I do?"

Miranda was studying him with her hazel eyes. "Let one of the others be first, then," she said. "Watch one of them use the Hands, Dirk."

Sokeman stepped forward. His grayish face was faintly flushed. He knelt down on the ground. Slowly he stretched out his hands over the line into the fog. They disappeared. And the gigantic Hands in the fog before him—were they a long way off, or were they close?—began to stir.

Sokeman's eyes were closed. He seemed to be barely breathing. The Hands hesitated, trembled. Then, working in the mist like a sculptor shaping plastic clay, they began to create.

An opalescent flask of xoanon floated phantasmagorically in the mist. It faded, was followed by a succession of bottles and flasks. Dirk recognized among them one or two liquors which had the reputation of being nerve poisons, A stack of currency flicked into being and out of it again. There followed more bottles and flasks.

"None of those is what he really wants." Miranda said softy in Dirk's ear. "Wait. He will get over being shy in a little while."

The Hands paused. Then they began to work again, but not as before. This time there was a purpose and intentness which had been lacking. The Hands worked in the fog, slowly and thoughtfully, for a long time. Sokeman's face had a dark, congested look. But at last he drew his hands out of the fog. There was a golden phial in one of them.

"What is it?" Dirk said to Miranda.

"A drug, I think. Yes." Sokeman had gone a few steps with the phial in his hand. Now he halted, half-turned away from them, and tipped something from the phial on the back of his wrist. He raised the wrist to his lips and touched it with the tip of his tongue.

"Will you be next, Dirk?" Miranda said.

"I—" He saw that her whole body was trembling. Her hands were clenched until the knuckles were white. "Why do you want me to try?" he asked.

She looked so exactly like Joan as she answered, "Because, because I have to know," that a wave of longing swept over him. Without a word he knelt down by the shining line and thrust his hands into the mist.

It was as if he had plunged them into a swift cold stream. The force seemed to tug and wrench at his body. And along with the sensation of coldness and swift motion there was a peculiar languor and fatigue, as if his will were being sucked away from him.

Huygens bit his lip. The Hands were stirring. With all his force he brought Joan before his mind, Joan as she had been one day late in spring when they had gone cruising among the islands. She had stood by the prow of the cruiser, leaning forward into the wind and laughing, and her youth had been like the flash of the sun on the ripple of the water. He could not live without her. He would bring her back.

The Hands paused in their labor. Joan moved toward him through the mist, smiling, her head held high; and if there was a blankness in her eyes, he could ignore it, he needed her so. But when she was almost up to him she wavered like a reflection in disturbed water. For all his desperate trying she grew dimmer and at last dissolved. There was nothing there in the mist.

Another phantasm of Joan came toward him. She faded, was replaced by another image and another one. Always they had that curious blankness in the eyes. Dirk felt that his life was going out into the images his desperation created. And yet they would not live.

His mind caught at other aspects of Joan. A wave of perfume— the perfume she had used—came toward him from the mist. It was fresh and mysterious and exciting all at once; it made his heart pound with longing for her. For a moment, before the perfume floated away, Huygens felt the warmth and enveloping tenderness of Joan so clearly that he was certain she must be standing beside him. Then the perfume faded and a second later the sense of Joan's physical presence went too. Huygens, his hands tingling with that cold languor, strove desperately to bring her image before his mind once more. But something always eluded him in her—the look in the eyes, the lift of the chin, the shape of the face.

He kept on trying long after he knew its hopelessness. Time after time he created, while Miranda waited patiently. The Joans he made had grown as frail as candlesmoke, before he gave up at last. He turned to Miranda and said, "I loved her, though."

"Yes." Miranda's face was expressionless, but she seemed taller than she had been, and her eyes glowed. After a moment she said, "I think that is why you could not make her, Dirk. When a man loves a woman, he cannot detach her enough from him to see her clearly. His love for her makes a mist. Joan was not a woman for you, but a climate within which you could feel and think. *He*—" she motioned to Ross, who had knelt down by the line as soon as Huygens had risen—"will have no such difficulty in shaping a woman for himself."

It was true; the Hands were shaping a voluptuous, full-bodied woman for the other pilot. He was grinning and his eyes were hard. Huygens watched unseeingly for a moment. Then he turned away.

"Where are you going?" Miranda asked quickly.

"Back to the wreck of Joan's plane. To bury her."

He had buried her, and night had come on. Now he sat sleepless under one of the black trees and listened to the hiss . . . hiss . . . hiss . . . of the waves as they rolled on the beach. His mind was full of loss and pain.

A shadow moved. Miranda came toward him. She sat down beside him. For a time there was silence; then Miranda said in her sweet voice, "Do not grieve so, Dirk."

He turned on her savagely. "Don't grieve! When I've lost her! When—" He could not go on.

"Poor Dirk."

"Who are you, Miranda? I know you're not Joan. But you're so like her . . . I keep thinking that you'll say to me, 'Yes, I'm Joan. It was only a joke, I was only teasing you. I won't tease you any more. I'm Joan, your wife.'"

Miranda laid her hand over his and he felt such a warmth of tenderness flow out from her that it dizzied him. He caught at her, not in desire, but in loneliness and despair. "Whoever you are—oh, be Joan! Be Joan!" he said.

She put her arms around him tenderly. "Dirk, sweetheart. Darling. Oh, yes. I'm whoever you want me to be."

When the gray day had come and it was light, he said to her, "Why do you look at me so much, Miranda? Whenever I look at you, you are watching me."

She scooped up sand and let it trickle through her fingers. "Because I love you. Dirk," she answered. "I love to look at you."

"But—don't you ever think about anything except me? Is love all you ever think about?"

She raised her eyebrows a little, as if she were surprised. "Why, yes. What else should I think of? What else is there in life but love?"

"You're a strange woman, Miranda."

She took his hand and put it against her breast so he could feel the beating of her heart. "I'm not strange," she said earnestly. "Do you feel my heart beating? It beats because I love you. I'm a woman who . . . who was made to give and receive love."

Huygens looked at her and nodded. "Yes," he answered somberly.

The next night was nearly over when Huygens woke abruptly from sleep. He had been dreaming of Joan. For a moment he lay listening to Miranda's quiet breathing. Then he put out his hand to wake her. He had buried Joan two days ago. But in this moment he knew, with perfect and unshakable conviction, that Joan was not dead.

Miranda roused at his touch. She sat up, and even in the darkness he knew that she was smiling. "What is it, Dirk?"

"Where is Joan?"

She drew away from him. "She is dead. You . . . buried her yourself."

"She is not dead." He caught her wrist in a savage grip. "You know where she is. Tell me. If you won't, I'll make you tell."

"You're hurting me," Miranda said sadly. ". . . It wasn't enough, was it? I might have known. But you can't get her back, Dirk."

"Where is she?"

"In the place of shaping. Inside the mist."

He got to his feet. Miranda sprang up after him, in quick alarm. "You can't go after her. If you do, you will never come out."

"Even if that were true," he said quietly, "do you think I'd stay here? When Joan is still alive?"

Miranda said nothing more. She watched him silently while he made his simple preparations. Once he asked her, "What's it like, inside the mist?" and nodded indifferently when she answered, "I don't know."

She followed him to the place of shaping. He felt a moment of pity for her as she stood there, so quiet and lonely. "Goodbye," he said. Then he stepped over the line into the mist.

It was as if he had stepped into a roaring world of greenish glass. A current caught at him fiercely, and he felt himself toppling. He struggled against it, and it noosed itself treacherously about his knees and sent him sideways, up, about, down, and up again. His muscles flexed to fight it; then he remembered that Joan, somewhere within this glassy flux, must have been gripped by the current as he was. He ceased to resist.

Time passed, if there time had meaning. There were desperate eddies, whirlpools, watery precipices. Sometimes he seemed to be climbing shuddering crystal alps or leaping incredible crevasses. He toiled onward over a plain of vitreous volcanic rock. And always, mingled with his exertions, real or unreal, came the awareness that will and intelligence were leaving him. They ebbed away from him resistlessly, and a cold torpor took their place.

The motion slackened at last. He was borne almost gently on. He floated to a halt and stranded, as if whatever had carried him hither had abandoned him. Torpidly he felt that he had come to the dead center of things. Everything ended here, in sleep and uncreation, in the ambiguous twilight haze.

Joan was somewhere, needed him. He would not sleep. Desperately he roused himself and stared around the sad, dull-colored expanse. Fragments of creation floated by him—wraith-like faces, dim jewels, disarticulated limbs. And with these were stranger shapes and constructions, contours of which he could find no analogue and no name. Neither at this nor any other time did he see any sign of the Hands.

Joan came toward him, smiling, and another Joan after her and another. There were ten, twenty, a hundred. And still they seemed to form from the haze like bubbles and break as bubbles break. They stood about him smiling dimly, and he saw with dull eyes that for every Joan a phantom Dirk Huygens had sprung up and stood holding out his vague arms to her.

Lethargy weighed on him always more heavily. He tried to walk toward the wavering phantoms and found that his limbs were remote and disobedient as if in a dream. He sank to his knees and crawled a little way. Then he fell over on his side and sleep claimed him.

At the center of him something was groaning and crying out and striving to waken him, as a man might beat on a stone wall with ineffectual hands. He roused a little at last, and then more, as fear grew in him. The unsleeping sentinel in the depths of the mind told him clearly that if he slept again he would not wake. This was his last chance. He must find Joan now or lie sleeping on the dun-colored plain until time had come to an end. But his torpor was dreadful, like a crushing burden. He could scarcely breathe under it.

He sank his teeth into his lower lip with all his strength. The flesh broke. As the blood began to trickle his head cleared.

Where could Joan be? Had the myriad phantom Joans come from her? If the current that had floated him here had brought her too, she could not be far.

The horizon became ringed with voices. They spoke to him bodilessly out of the twilight. "Here . . . here . . ." they whispered, "here . . . here . . . here . . ." They were dim and remote as if the haze itself were speaking. But behind each impalpable susurrus, each toneless utterance, it seemed to Huygens that he caught the ghost of Joan's voice.

She could not be far. But near and far, in this ambiguous place, were all one. He looked around and thought he saw a low mound disturb the plane ahead. He plodded toward it. But when he reached it it was the body of a man, flattened by slumber, who might have been lying there for centuries while sleep silted over him. And Huygens' heavy eyes could make out no other mound against the dead level of the plain.

A leaden hopelessness came over him. He wanted to lie down beside the unknown man and let sleep drown him. To fight the desire, he ground his teeth into his already wounded lip. And as pain burned along his nerves he felt, for a moment only, the pointing of the compass in his head.

He gasped with relief. At a stumbling run he started toward the point to which it had directed him. And though he moved more and more slowly—it was as though the spot toward which he struggled was the source of the vast choking lethargy which lay on everything—he never stopped moving. He toiled through thickening cobwebs for a time that might have been centuries. And he came to Joan at last.

It was real Joan. She lay in a shallow depression into which she had drifted, and she was as wan and bloodless as the twilight around her. There was a jagged scar under her left breast, as if whatever wound she had received had healed distortedly. But she was alive.

He gathered her in his arms and kissed her. She stirred and opened drowned eyes to him. "Oh . . . Dirk . . . How alive you are! I dreamed of you. Have I been dead?"

"Get up, Joan," he said thickly. "We have to—to—" He could not remember the word.

"Go to sleep," she said, as if to a child. "This place hates us awake. We are too alive for it. Go back to sleep." She was sinking away from his embrace.

He dug his nails into her wrist. She gave a tiny cry, and he pulled her to her feet. "Wake up!" he said desperately. "Joan, wake up!"

"But why? We can never leave."

It was true, he saw. How could he push his way alone, much less cumbered with Joan, through the glassy torrent that had floated him here? Awake, Joan and he vexed this sad, dun-colored world; and it would cover them with layer upon layer of lethargy, as the oyster drowns the pricking grain of sand in layer after layer of pearl. They could never escape.

It did not much matter. But he had wanted her when he was awake. He would kiss her once more before sleep covered them.

He tipped her head up and put his lips to hers. And because it was Joan's mouth he touched, the contact was sweet to him.

She stirred and put her arms around his shoulders. "When you touch me," she said laboriously, "I feel more awake." She managed to smile at him.

More awake. Yes, it was as if between their two bodies they sheltered a tiny warmth of consciousness from the chill lethargy of this dead place. He kissed her again, embracing her tenderly, and before he had taken his lips from hers he felt a weak current fretting at his heels.

The current which had seized him when he stepped over the shining line into the place of shaping had been glassy and smooth, for all its violence. But even in its infancy this new force was as jagged and rough as if it flowed flint knives. Cross currents jarred and warred within it, and as its strength increased he felt his flesh wounded by it a thousand times.

The noise it made was a confused, painful screaming. Joan said almost inaudibly, ". . . to get rid of us." The sound of the flow rose to a rattling hysteria. Then Huygens clasped his wife in a rigid grip and the jagged torrent closed over them.

They were hurled head over heels with crazy violence. Dirk had hallucinated moments when he felt they were standing motionless on a broad plain while rocks beat up at them. He forced Joan's head down against his shoulder to protect her face, and as well as he could he sheltered her with his body and his limbs. There were times when the current would run smooth as glass, and he dreaded these times most, for then the numbing lethargy would come over him again. He knew that if his grip on Joan relaxed now she would be lost utterly, hopelessly.

They were dropping through jagged stars from a high, high cliff. The stars burned his flesh like fire, and he held Joan in a tighter grasp. They rose through a mesh of stinging fireflies, they sank into a pit whose stone sides rustled cruelly at them. No, they were still standing in the autumnal haze, embracing benumbedly. The current was beating against them bitterly, like hail. And suddenly

Dirk knew that its tormented force had brought them to the edge of its world, to the shining line.

There was some reason, Dirk knew, why he and Joan must get over it. Some reason . . . But he could not remember what the reason was. And who was Joan? Who was Dirk?

The current welled up in a glassy crescendo. Joan was half torn from his arms. He struggled wildly after her, caught her by one wrist. Still holding her, he fought upward through an excoriating rain. Though he had forgotten who he was, he knew that it was laid on him as a law to battle upward, never to let Joan go.

The moment tautened like a bow string. Dirk made a last, consuming effort. And then he and Joan were over the line.

They lay exhausted on the ground for many minutes, like people half-drowned. When Dirk's strength had come back a little, he went to the place where he and the others had camped on the first night, and brought back blankets and the aid kit. He smoothed ointment over Joan's bleeding limbs and covered her with the blankets. He looked toward the Hands, wondering at the difference between what seemed to be reality on this side of the line and on that. Then he lay down beside her and fell instantly into deep natural sleep.

It was nearly a day later when he awoke. Miranda was standing near him.

She looked at him and Joan. Her face was white. Slowly she said, "You brought her back, then, Dirk." Her voice was sweet as she said it, and for all her pallor Dirk thought he had never seen a woman as beautiful.

Joan stirred and sat up. She looked at Miranda and her eyes widened. She got to her feet. "You lived, then," she said.

Miranda laughed. "Sister—mother—" she answered, "why should I not live."

Dirk drew in his breath. He stared at their two faces, so uncannily alike. "What does she mean?" he asked his wife.

"That I made her," Joan said.

There was an instant's silence. The words he had just heard echoed meaninglessly in Dirk Huygens' brain. Then Joan said, "I made her, you see. When my plane crashed on the island, I was badly hurt.

I knew I had not long to live, and I knew what island this was. I didn't want to die.

"I went to the place of shaping. It was a hard trip for me. When I got there, I knelt by the line and put my hands into the mist. And I had the Hands shape Joan, shape my own self, for me.

"I didn't want to die, you see, Dirk, and I thought that if another Joan, a Joan just like me, lived on, I would not be really dead. But when Joan came out of the mist to me I knew that I had not made her well. Her face was vacant and strange, and she moved weakly, as if she were barely alive."

Dirk started. He looked at Miranda and knew by her expression that his surmise was right. "She did not live," he said to Joan. "She went back to the wreck of the plane and died there. I buried her."

Joan nodded. "It was wrong," she said, twisting her fingers. "I should not have done it. It was wrong.

"When I saw that the second Joan would not go on living, I tried again. I put my hands back into the mist—oh, how strong the current was, it pulled like death!—and had the Hands shape for me once more. And this time they shaped Miranda.

"Miranda, Dirk, is Joan as I always wanted her to be. When I made her I made myself after the pattern of a secret dream I had. She is more beautiful than I, taller, she has a sweeter voice. Even her name is different from mine. I never liked my name."

Comprehension was coming to Huygens. Miranda, then, was Joan's idealized picture of herself. Even the gem-set wedding ring on Miranda's hand—Joan had said once that she preferred gem-set bands to plain.

"I made her with all the strength and longing that was in me. I made her loving you, Dirk, because I was dying and was sick for you. And when she came out of the mist toward me I saw that she was well made and would live.

"I fainted then. The current swept me away with it. And after that there was nothing except sleep and heavy dreams, Dirk, until you came and woke me up. You brought me back to life." She turned to her husband. Dirk drew her to him and held her for a moment, embraced.

"You have won, real woman," Miranda said bitterly. "You have taken the real man from me, who am not quite real. Take him and have your desire of him, then. But I had him once." She put her hands over her eyes.

Joan took a step toward her. "Forgive me, Miranda," she said humbly. "I should never have shaped you. Forgive me for it." There were tears on her cheeks.

Miranda uncovered her face. She was as pale as death, but Dirk saw that she was dry-eyed. "You have done me no wrong," she said proudly. "Take your man and go. There are boats on the beach. I wish you joy of him. Goodbye." She turned away.

"What will you do, Miranda?" Joan asked, weeping. "What will become of you?"

"Oh, I?" Miranda said. She laughed. "I will go to the place of shaping and make Dirk for myself. I will shape him with all the love that is in me, and he will love me and be my desire. And if he is not quite real, why, neither am I quite real." She started through the trees.

Joan cried out in pity. She would have gone after Miranda, but Dirk held her back. "Let her go," he said, though he was deeply troubled. "We cannot help her. This is best for her."

For a moment he and Joan looked at Miranda as she walked away, her head high. Dirk knew that he would remember Miranda, her beauty and the love she had given him, to the end of his days. Then he and Joan started down to the beach, toward the sea and the boat that would take them away.

CONTINUED STORY

THE MARTIAN INVADER was still following him. Its slender, fantastically lacy outline had whisked back into the shadow of the garbage can on the corner only a minute before.

Milton Delisle drew a shuddering breath. The invader made him feel such intense, nervous apprehension that he wanted to scream or break into tears. But it stood to reason that the thing wouldn't try to follow him into the police station—it seemed to be shy about anyone seeing it except him and Marylin—and its broadcasts could reach only so far. And after he'd confessed he'd be safe because they'd put him in a cell. The cell would be nice and quiet. He hesitated a moment longer on the steps of the station. Then he went in.

The desk sergeant was a young, thickset man who loved criminology and privately thought his job the most fascinating in the world. He would rather have died than admit to anything but boredom in connection with it. He had a romantic temperament. When Milton entered, he put down the copy of *Psychiatry and the Criminal* he had been reading, and yawned cavernously. "Yeah?" he said.

"I want to give myself up."

The sergeant was instantly irascible. "Go on, get out," he said. "Who the hell do you think you're fooling? Get out."

"No, but listen. It's not a rib. I've been in here before. You can ask Fred Deeder in plainclothes—he knows me. He picked me up last year for petty theft. And I've really done something this time."

"Recidivist, eh?"

"Re—I guess so. Anyhow, I want to give myself up."

Deeder's name—a very sound man, interested in psychology—had soothed the sergeant. He said, "Well, what did you do?"

"I pilked three boxes of—toys, I guess you'd call them—from the toy shop in the seven hundred block on Fulton Street. Saturday night."

This time the sergeant really was angry. He got up from behind the desk. "What's the matter with you?" he demanded. "Get out before I throw you out. There's no toy shop in the seven hundred block on Fulton. I know. I live near there. Whatsa matter, you a masochist?"

Milt Delisle had begun to sweat. He pulled the neatly folded blue handkerchief with the corded border from his breast pocket and swabbed at his forehead with it. "Yeah, but *listen,*" he said pleadingly. "I know there's no toy shop there now. Marylin and I went back there on Monday and looked up and down both sides of the street for it, and we couldn't find it. But there was one there on Saturday night. There really was."

"Hunh. You must be junked."

"That's one thing I don't do and never did," Milt said virtuously. "You ask Deeder. He knows about me. Listen, why don't you just listen while I tell you about it? And then you can book me for theft." He looked over his shoulder nervously, toward the outside of the station. The Martian invader was neither broadcasting nor in sight.

"Pretty eager to get booked, aren't you?" the sergeant commented. But he sat down again.

Milton coughed and cleared his throat. "The toy store, the way it was on Saturday night, was a great big place," he said. "It was two or maybe three store fronts wide, and it was nothing but glass on the outside. Inside it was soft pink and pale blue and lavender lights, and lots of mirrors. Marylin said—"

"Who's Marylin?" the sergeant interrupted. "Dame ya shacked up with?"

"No," Delisle replied with a touch of coldness. "We're married, since last year. Seven bucks the license cost me."

"Oh. Sorry."

"Think nothing of it," Milt returned magnanimously. "We all make mistakes, That's why they got ink erasers. Well, as I was saying, Marylin said she didn't see how a swell-looking store like that could do enough business in the part of town where it was to keep going, and I said I thought so too. We looked in the window a while—there were all sorts of big dolls dressed in shiny stuff and stuffed animals as big as life, nearly, in funny colors, and sets of gold and blue building blocks—and then Marylin suggested we go in. She said some of the wire toys we couldn't figure out the way they worked looked interesting, and she thought there might be some good kits inside. Marylin loves kits."

"Mee-ows?" the sergeant asked.

"Naw, kits. You know, building kits. Last year we made a model airplane—-it flies good—and before we were married she made copper trays and leathercraft. That kind of kits.

"So we went in. The place was about three times as big inside as it looked from the outside. It was as big as a couple of barns. There was so much stuff we couldn't take it all in. But there was only one clerk.

"He was an ugly little sawed off guy with a big head, big pale eyes, and little bitty ears. He was dressed in a skinny green suit without any buttons. I don't know how he got in and out of it.

"Marylin and me sort of stopped when we saw him, because he was so funny looking. When he saw us, he smiled with his mouth tight. He didn't come up and start waiting on us, though—I guess he saw we wanted to look around. We liked that.

"You never saw so many kinds of different toys. A kid would just have gone crazy in there. There were building toys where you could make a whole funny big city in ten minutes, and toys to ride in with water around like submarines, and toys where you pressed a button and it made a lot of different shows—you could change the color and lighting and people by pressing other buttons—and toys so funny it made your head hurt to try to figure them out. In a way, all the toys were funny. I've got an idea about that stuff in the toy shop."

"What?" the sergeant demanded.

"Tell you later. When I get to it. Anyhow, there were all sorts of toys. The prices they wanted for the stuff were terrific, though. Off at the left there were three or four tables, big ones, with nothing but kits."

Milton ran his finger around the inside of his collar. "Now, I know I promised Deeder I wouldn't. I hated to break my promise. But you got to consider the prices they wanted for the stuff. Why, it was just robbery. Two or three hundred dollars for just a kit in a box. I knew I'd never be able to afford that kind of thing. Too rich for my blood."

"So you pinched the toys instead?" the sergeant asked sarcastically.

"Well—yes. I didn't feel too bad over it. With prices like that, they ought to be taught a lesson. And I knew the wife would get a bang out of the kits. I waited until she was over in a corner, looking at some puzzles made of glass, and the clerk was looking the other way. Then I lifted them.

"I knew Marylin would raise the roof if she thought I'd pilked. So I went and stood near the clerk for a while, like I might be buying something. Then I told her I'd picked out some stuff for us, for a surprise, and we could go. There wasn't any trouble. The clerk wasn't even looking at us."

"What did ya take?" the sergeant asked. "Some of the puzzles made of glass?"

Delisle shook his head. "No, they looked too hard. I pilked three kits I thought we could work. The first was just for Marylin. It was a box of makeup things, with maybe twenty-five or thirty packages and jars of make-up stuff inside and a made-up face on the cover. It was—it was a pretty face. But—" Milton ran his finger around his collar twice and swallowed. "I dunno. Even then it sort of scared me. I thought the kit was make-up for theatricals, and I thought Marylin would get a kick out of it, because she likes cosmetics and make-up stuff. But I dunno. I don't know who that kit could ever have been made for.

"The second kit was for a model—well, not exactly a model, more like a cast—of a scene on the moon. There was a package of powder in the kit and some heavy-looking stuff, like fixatif, to mix it with. There weren't any directions in the box, just the picture on the cover and the words 'Self-Setting Lunar Experience,' but I didn't think we'd get into any trouble with it. It looked easy to do."

"Lunar *experience?*" questioned the sergeant. Not landscape?"

"Yeah, that's right. It was spelled funny, but that's what it said.

"That kit was for me, because I've always been interested in the moon, but I thought Marylin would enjoy it too. The third one, the robot, was for both of us.

"It was a box with pieces inside like an erector set, only spindly and thinner, like black steel lace, and there was a diagram with numbers on the inside of the cover to show you how to put it together. When you got it done it was a robot. You know, a tin man. Only it was taller and lacier than robots usually are." Milt glanced back toward the street and licked his lips uneasily.

"You mean a rowbow," the sergeant corrected. "It's French. In French, you never say the last part of the words."

"Oh. Rowbow, then. When we got home we looked at our kits. Marylin was just crazy about her make-up box. She said she wanted to save it until Sunday, when she'd have plenty of time to fool around with it. So we decided to do the moon kit that night.

"Marylin got a mixing bowl and a pie plate from the cupboard— we got a room with a kitchenette—and I started to mix the powder with the liquid in the kit. It was as hard as pulling teeth to mix.

"The powder was a brownish putty colored stuff, full of lumps. The liquid was heavy and piled up on the powder and didn't want to get smooth. I had to stir so hard to mix it that the spatula that was in the kit got bent. But finally I got it done and we poured it out in the pie plate. Then we had to wait.

"For ten minutes or so nothing happened. Marylin got bored. She gave a couple of sighs. And then, all of a sudden, it began to set.

"It was a little like watching mush boiling. There were holes in it—craters—and splotches and rays going out from the craters. They changed while you watched for a while. Pretty soon the surface got hard and shiny and we thought that was going to be all. It looked like one of those big photographs of the moon, only close up.

"Marylin said, 'Gee, that was fun, Milt. You picked a swell surprise,' and I said, 'Glad you liked it, baby. We'll do—' And then I didn't say anything more, because I was down there on the moon."

"What do you mean, you were down there on the moon?" the desk sergeant demanded. "You mean you were up on the moon in the sky? Or you were down there in the pie dish? Which?"

"Both," Delisle said. "I mean, I was up on the moon in the sky—there wasn't any air and the sky was black and the light coming off the rocks and ground made my eyes hurt—and at the same time I knew it was the moon in the pie dish. Both."

"Well, go on."

I was wearing one of those space suits. I could breathe pretty well, but the air smelled like metal. When I walked, I made big duck leaps. I didn't seem to weigh much. And when I landed, my feet went down six or eight inches in the soft gray dust.

"I was scared. As soon as I knew I was on the moon, I got scared. Not because I was there, you understand—that might have been fun, in a way. It was other things. I knew somebody I couldn't see was watching me."

"From where?"

"From over my head. That was bad enough. But I knew that somebody else than that, somebody who was really there, was after me."

"There were two of them?" the sergeant asked.

"I guess so. One was the invisible one, who was just watching, curious and cold. The other was a man in a space suit, somebody who was down on the moon with me, and he was after my hide. I didn't know who he was or what he had against me, but I was sure of it. It was like I'd been on the moon a long time. And then a bullet—a red flash of light, really—went past my ear. I wasn't just imagining it.

"I reached down by the side of my suit and found I had a gun myself, a sort of pistol with a flaring mouth, in a holster. I got it out and fired at where I thought the red flash had come from. A piece of rock broke off. It took a long time to fall. And then another flash went past the side of my head.

"I dodged around behind a big gray rock and fired again. I couldn't see him at all. It was terrible. I've pilked stuff sometimes, sure, but I never hurt anybody, and I never did anything that would make anybody want to hurt me. And now this fellow I couldn't see was trying to kill me!" Milt shook his head sadly.

"We went on that way, dodging in and out among the rocks and shooting, for what seemed like hours. Now and then I'd hear somebody laugh. It was a nasty noise.

"I was getting tired, and my suit didn't have enough air. I knew if he ever hit the suit I'd die because the air would leave it. I thought he must be getting tired, too, though, and that cheered me up. Then I noticed that the light was leaving the rocks and I was having trouble seeing. And it came to me with an awful shock: it was getting dark.

"I'd thought I'd been scared before, but I hadn't. I was so scared my knees shook. I didn't see how I could stand being on the moon all night, with not enough air in my suit and another man in a suit trying to kill me. The worst of it was I had no idea how long the night would last. It might be only a few hours, or it might be a couple of weeks, or it might be a month. I just didn't know how night on the moon worked. But I was afraid it would last a month.

"Like I said, I didn't see how I could stand it. So I came out from behind the rock—it was still a little bit light—and started after him."

"Hunh ?"

"I was too scared to do anything else," Milt said simply. "I went hopping along toward him, taking as big jumps as I could, and he fired at me a couple of times. I don't know how he happened to miss. Then I was right on top of him and he fired once more. This time he got me in the right arm.

"I could feel the air leaving. I didn't care, so long as I could get rid of him. I got him by the neck—he was bigger than I was—and started choking. I could see spots and gray patches in front of my eyes, but I held on.

"The next thing I knew, Marylin was shaking me by the arms and saying, 'Wake up honey, do wake up' over and over again. She sounded scared. I opened my eyes and there I was in my chair, just the same as I'd been before I got down there on the moon.

"I looked at Marylin. She really was scared. I never saw her so white. She said I'd been sitting there for about ten minutes, my eyes fixed on the pie plate, like I was in a kind of a trance. She hadn't been able to get me to speak to her or anything.

"I asked her to get us some soda out of the ice box. We drank it, and I told her what had been happening. She didn't seem much surprised—she said she knew something was mighty queer. We threw the pie plate with the landscape in it in the garbage, and we decided we'd take the other two kits back to the toy store on Monday. She said we could get our money back. I told her I didn't care about that.

Sunday she kept opening her make-up kit and looking at it and putting it away again. It fascinated her, I guess. It really was an awfully interesting looking thing with all those little pots and boxes. Anyhow, on Monday we went back to Fulton where the store had been, and we couldn't find it. We looked up and down on both sides of the street for about three blocks. It just wasn't there. There was a package goods store and a fruit stand where it had been.

"We took the kits on back home. We passed a couple of trash cans on the way. Marylin said, 'We ought to throw those kits away right now,' and I said, 'Yeah. we ought.' But we didn't. Neither of us even slowed up. We just walked on past. I don't know why we didn't throw those kits away, when we knew we should."

"People don't always do what they ought to," the desk sergeant said sagely. "They got masochistic drives."

"I guess. Or maybe something wouldn't let us.

"When we got home Marylin got us some supper. All the time we were eating she seemed restless. I turned on the radio, but she made me shut it off. Pretty soon she said, 'Milt. I'm going to make up my face with some of the things in the kit.'

"I said, 'Honey, do you think you'd better? It might be dangerous, like the moon. How about my helping you with the dishes? And then we'll go take in a movie.'

"She gave me the darndest look. She never looked like that at me before, in all the time I've known her. 'You never want me to have anything I want, do you?' she answered. Her voice was bitter and hard. 'You're always against me. You grudge me every little thing.'

"I didn't say anything more. There wasn't anything I could say. I got the paper and sat there trying to read while she opened boxes and tubes and jars in the make-up kit. After a while—fixing her face the way she wanted it took her a long, long time—I got a bottle of whiskey from the cupboard and had myself a drink.

"I couldn't even taste it. It might just as well have been water. And I couldn't make myself pretend to read the paper any longer. I felt too tense. I folded up the paper and put it on the table and set the whiskey bottle down beside it. And I watched Marylin.

"She was sitting with her back to me, at the dressing table. I couldn't see her face except in the mirror, but she'd put on a cosmetic, lipstick or eyeshadow or something, look at it a minute, and then wipe it off again. With all the pains she was taking, she ought to have been as pretty as a picture, but she wasn't. I could only see her in the mirror, but I thought that each new thing she did to herself made her look—well—worse.

"The longer I waited for her, the more I got the jitters. Pretty soon I began to get the feeling I'd had when I was down on the moon, the feeling that somebody I couldn't see was watching us. I told myself that I was imagining it, that all there was in the room was me and Marylin, putting a lot of funny cosmetics on her face. It didn't help. I still felt it. That being watched by somebody you can't see is a nasty feeling to get.

"Finally, when I felt I'd go crazy if I had to wait any longer, Marylin turned round. 'Take a good look, Milt,' she said.

"The first thing that struck me was how *bright* her face was. It glittered all over as if she'd dipped it in diamond dust. From under her eyes there was a reddish sparkle, and her cheeks were a shiny fine pale green, but the rest of her face, including her lips, was a dead, dazzling blue-white. It was like she was wearing a mask set with hundreds of diamonds. Only her eyebrows were a flat, solid black.

"I sat there staring at her. She was horrible. She made me feel frozen right down to my feet. And yet I was crazy about her too. She was wonderful."

"Crazy?" the sergeant asked incredulously. "When she looked like that?"

"Yes. I didn't want her, I didn't like her, she wasn't Marylin. And yet there was a kind of lure coming out from her, a lure I just couldn't resist. If she'd told me to do anything, I'd have had to do it. If she'd said, 'Go over to the window and throw yourself out,' I'd have done it. I hated the way she made me feel. It was like being in love with a fish."

"Well, go on."

"We looked at each other for a minute. She was smiling a little. Then she laughed.

It was a perfectly normal laugh, just the way she always laughed, and yet it gave me the creeps almost worse than her face did or the way her face made me feel. There was something extra unnatural about her pretty, light laugh coming out of a face like that.

"She knew I was crazy about her, and hated her. She sat there smiling. She enjoyed it. In a smooth, soft voice she said, 'Milt, lie down on the floor.'

"I got down. I could hear my knees creaking—I got stiff joints—and the floor was draughty and hard. From where my head was I could see some rolls of dust under the studio bed. I was surprised that they were there. Marylin's a pretty good housekeeper.

"I heard her get up and walk over to the cupboard and open a drawer. She rummaged around in it. I knew she was getting out a knife. And I knew the person who was watching was getting real interested, almost excited. He was getting a bang out of this.

"It was worse than it had been on the moon. Lots worse. Because this was in my and Marylin's little apartment, and it was Marylin who was going to kill me as soon as she found a knife she liked the looks of. It was all going to be bad, but the moment I dreaded most would be when she stood over me wondering where to begin stabbing. I didn't think she'd do a good, quick job. And I wouldn't be able to do a thing to stop her as long as she was wearing the make-up mask.

"I was so scared I wondered my heart didn't stop beating. Looking up, I could see the edge of the table with the folded paper and the bottle of whiskey. It didn't mean anything for a minute. Then it gave me an idea.

"I raised up, trying to be quiet, and reached up for the bottle. She was clattering around in the drawer; I wondered which knife she'd pick. Then I lay down with the bottle in one hand. My fingers were so stiff I had trouble uncapping it.

"She came back. Her face was brighter than ever. She was holding one of the steak knives.

"When I looked at her, I didn't see how I could do it. She knelt down beside me, smiling with her dazzling blue-white mouth. I guess it was because I was so scared that I *could* do it. Anyhow, I raised my hand and threw the whiskey in her face.

"She gave a sort of whimper. I asked her afterwards, and she said it wasn't because the whiskey got in her eyes and stung. It was because wherever it hit her face it hurt and burned. Anyhow, her make-up began to drip and flow and run. It dripped down in big bright glittering drops on the front of her dress. She dropped the knife on the floor with a clatter. Her face puckered up. I could see her skin, pink, and irritated-looking, coming out from under the diamond-dust layer. She began to cry.

"I got up from the floor and put my arm around her. Now that her make-up was gone, I wasn't afraid of her, and she was crying. She was Marylin again. She'd tried to kill me, of course, but she hadn't really wanted to. I didn't hold it against her. I felt awfully sorry for her. She hung on to me and bawled and bawled.

"She was trembling all over. For a long time she couldn't stop crying. She'd say, 'Milt—Oh, Milt—' and gulp and shudder and begin bawling again. Finally she let go my shoulders and went in the bathroom and washed her face. When she came back her eyes were red and swollen, but her face was clean, and she'd combed her hair.

"We sat down on the studio couch. She didn't seem to want to talk about what had happened. Once she said, 'When I put that stuff on my face, it changed me all around. Like a mirror in a circus sideshow.' And I said, 'Yeah. Don't think about it any more, kid.' We sat there for quite a long time with my arm around her. Then—"

"Just a minute," the desk sergeant interrupted. "Was the invisible watcher looking at you all this time?"

Milt shook his head. "I don't think so. I think he stopped looking at us just about the time Marylin dropped the knife and began crying. He wasn't interested in us after that, you see. The story was over for him."

"Story?"

"Yeah. I'll tell you about that later. Anyhow, we sat there on the couch for quite a long time. Then, without saying a word about it to each other, we got up at the same time and began working on the rowbow kit."

"Hunh?"

"I know it was a crazy thing to do. Marylin and I both knew she'd tried to kill me, and had come within an inch of doing it. There was no reason to think the rowbow woudn't be as bad as the moon scene and the make-up kit had been. But we didn't even discuss it. We just got out the screwdriver and started working on it."

"Neurotic compulsion."

"Yeah. Somebody was making us.

"It went together fast. It must have been about nine when we started, and it was quite a bit before ten when the rowbow was done. We stood there holding hands and looking at it. My fingers were on Marylin's wrist, and I could feel that her heart was beating hard and fast.

"The rowbow was almost six feet tall. Neither Marylin or I is very tall, and it towered up over us. It was thin, though, and cobwebby, like black lace. Its face was pretty sketchy—just eyes and a little mouth. It didn't have any nose or ears.

"For a minute or two nothing happened. Then the robot— rowbow—said, in a high, twangy voice, 'I am an invader from Mars.' It walked over to the side of the room, where there was a straight chair, and sat down in it.

"Marylin giggled. It was a nervous giggle, I guess, and yet the invader had been funny. There was something about the stiff way it sat down that made you want to laugh.

"We waited. The invader just sat there, not even blinking. Finally Marylin said. 'I guess that's all. It's done its little trick. I'm hungry, Milt. Let's have something to eat.'

"I looked at the clock. It was after ten, and I felt as hollow as a drum inside. So I said—"

"Wait a minute," the sergeant broke in. "I got a couple of questions. Do you think it *was* an invader from Mars? And did you feel at this time that somebody was watching you?"

"Naw, it wasn't a real invader. That was just the name of the kit. About somebody watching me, that was about ten minutes later—

"Like I was saying, it was late, and we'd been through a lot. I said, 'I'm hungry too, kiddo. How about some fried egg sandwiches?' I and she both like fried eggs.

"She went to the cupboard and got eggs and bread and butter. While the eggs were frying, she broke off a little piece of bread and buttered it and ate it. She was bending over getting out some lettuce while she chewed. And I thought—I've never thought anything like this before, in all the time I've known her—I thought, 'If she keeps on eating all the time like that, she's going to be as fat as a hog in a couple of years.'

"Do you get what I mean?" Delisle looked at the sergeant earnestly. "It wasn't like me to have an idea like that."

"That's nothing. Lots of married men think the same thing."

"Yeah, but she's not fat. Just a little plump. On her, it's cute.

"It was just about then that I got the idea that somebody was watching me.

"I went on thinking while the eggs were frying. I thought, 'She's getting too fat. And she's bossy. What ailed me to marry a woman like that? In a couple of years I won't be able to call my soul my own. There must be some way of getting rid of her.' I looked over at the window. It was open. And it seemed to me it would be duck soup to call her over, pretending there was something I wanted to show her, and push her out."

"And did you?" the sergeant asked. "Try to push her out, I mean."

No, of course not. But I was scared. I looked at the rowbow. It wasn't doing anything, just sitting. But I was sure it was responsible for my thinking those thoughts. I could feel a—a sort of force, like a broadcast, coming toward me out of its head. And I had that nasty feeling of being watched.

"Now, I don't suppose I ought to have done it." Milton licked his lips. "Run out on her like that, I mean. I'll bet she was worried all night. But I knew she'd tried to kill me. And I knew that if the invader really put the heat on me, I wouldn't have a chance. I'd try to kill *her*.

"I couldn't think for a minute. I was so mad at myself for having helped make the invader that I wanted to go beat my head against the wall.

"I remembered there was a bunch of wires on the back of the thing, and I thought if I could get hold of those wires and rip them loose the invader wouldn't be able to broadcast any more. It was a good idea, but I just couldn't do it. I couldn't move a finger in the direction of the chair where the thing was sitting. It was like being paralyzed. I stood there sweating and trying to move, and I couldn't. They wouldn't let me end the story that way."

"Just a minute," the sergeant said. "That's the second time you've said something about a story. And before that you spoke about having an idea about the toys in the toy shop. Do you have some general theory about all this?"

"Well, yes." Milton Delisle shifted his weight from one foot to the other, and sighed. His arches were hurting him. "The things in the shop—they were pretty and bright colored and so on, but they weren't really *nice*. Do you know what I mean? The dolls had nice shiny dresses, but they had hateful expressions. The stuffed animals were nice and big, but they looked hard and lumpy. I don't know that they would have, but they looked like if a kid tried to play with them they'd give him an electric shock. The things in the shop, unh, looked like they were made by people who couldn't stop being mean and hateful even when they wanted to be nice and give a present. The shop was all like that."

"The toys were made by sadistic people. Um. You got any more ideas?"

"Well, I think the shop was from some other time, maybe the future, when everybody's going to be hateful and mean. And I think its being there on Saturday night was a sort of a trap."

"How? For whom?"

"For me and Marylin. I don't mean for us specially—I mean for anybody who came in the shop. I think that shop sometimes leaves its own time and comes into ours, to trap people. So there'll be a story for the people of that time to watch."

The sergeant looked baffled. "I don't get it," he said. "You've said a lot of funny things already, but they sort of hung together until now."

"Well, this hangs together too," Milt said with a flash of spirit. "What is a story, anyhow? It's getting the hero in a hole and then watching to see how he gets out, or maybe doesn't get out. I think the clerk in the store saw me pilking those kits and let me have them anyhow, because he knew they'd get me and Marylin in a jam. That's what the people we couldn't see were watching—how we'd act and what we'd do when we were in a bad jam.

"In a story, though, you want the hero to win, and these people didn't. They were just interested in seeing how we'd act when we were in trouble, threatened and scared."

"Sadistic interest," observed the sergeant. "Well, go on."

"Where was I? Oh, I was trying to get near the invader to rip the wires loose, and I couldn't.

"I stood there trying to think. I could smell the eggs frying, and they smelled good. I was hungry. But I didn't dare stay there for fear I'd do something to Marylin. So I just walked out."

"Without saying anything to your wife?"

"Oh, I called something like, 'Goodbye, kid, I'll be back.' I didn't have time to say much. She looked awfully surprised.

"You see, my idea was this. The invader was interested in me, not in Marylin. If I walked out, it would probably come after me.

She wouldn't be bothered. And I might be able to think of a way of getting rid of it."

"And did it? Come after you, I mean."

"Yeah. When I was about half-way down the second flight of stairs I heard it coming. It sort of rustles when it walks. I was almost running when I got to the foot of the stairs.

"It followed me all night, suggesting things. It doesn't want anybody to see it—whenever I got near people, it would hide. I didn't dare to go to a hotel, though, for fear it would come up in the elevator after me, or maybe climb up the side of the wall. I didn't think I could stand seeing its little black head coming up over the window sill. Or maybe it would get in the room with me, between me and the door. I'd have walked as long as my feet would hold up rather than be shut in a room with it."

"Claustrophobia," said the desk sergeant.

"I guess. Anyhow, I walked around all night. I went to the park, and down to the waterfront, and once I hired a taxi and had the man drive out beyond Twin Peaks. It didn't do any good—when I got out and paid him, there it was. It must have hung on to the car.

"It kept suggesting things. As it got later at night, the things got worse. I never had such ideas before in my life. It may not sound it, but having those ideas in my head was worse than having Marylin try to kill me, or being down on the moon with a man who was shooting at me. It was worse because it was in my *mind*."

"What were the things it suggested?"

"They were terrible."

"Yeah, but can't you give me an example?"

"When I passed a drinking fountain it suggested—listen, I'm not going to tell you. I got a right to some privacy. Just take it from me, they were terrible."

"Repressed scatological desires rising into consciousness," the sergeant said, as one who makes a long overdue diagnosis.

"I wish you'd stop talking like that," Milt answered irritably. "Why don't you talk English? I can't tell what you're driving at."

"Never mind. What happened after that?"

"Pretty soon it began to get light. I never was so glad to see anything in my life as I was to see the sun coming up. I was hungry and dead tired and I'd spent almost all my money on the taxi. I thought maybe when it was light the invader would stop following me. It didn't, but it stayed farther away from me, for fear people would see it, and its broadcasts weren't so bad. I sat down on a bench and rested, and I bought myself a hamburger.

"The trouble was, I didn't have any idea how to get rid of it. Then about ten o'clock I thought, maybe if I could go to jail—you see, there're always people hanging around a police station. It wouldn't follow me inside. And I'm hoping that after I've been in jail a few days it'll get tired of waiting for me and go away."

Delisle halted. He mopped his face with his handkerchief and gave a deep sigh.

"Go on," said the sergeant after a minute.

"That's all. There isn't anything more."

"Oh. Is the what you call it—invader—following you now?"

"It's outside, hiding behind a garbage can."

"Do you have that feeling of being watched at present?"

"Not since I came in the station."

"Pretty obvious," the sergeant commented. "Now that you're under the eye of a real representative of parental authority, the haunting, floating feeling of being watched has left you. Well, what do you want me to do?"

"Put me in jail. Like I said, I pilked the toys."

The sergeant deliberated, chewing his fleshy lower lip. He looked Delisle over slowly, frowning, while Milt, grown nervous, once more mopped at his face.

"I won't do it," the sergeant said abruptly.

"Hunh?"

"No, I won't. Lunar molds, diamond masks, Martian invaders! Why, I never heard of such rubbish in my life! Here." The sergeant drew a glass inkwell toward him, dipped a pen, and began to write. When he had done, he extended the note toward Milt.

"I've written a note to Dr. Zimberg, at city clinic," he explained to Delisle. "He's a very sound man, good Freudian, none of this

Adler stuff. I want you to take the note to him and let him look you over. For my book you need a thorough analysis, before something worse happens, but of course Dr. Zimberg will have to be the judge. Don't be ashamed to tell him *anything*. Here." He shook the note at Milt. "Come back in a couple of months and tell me how you're getting along."

At the sergeant's first refusal Milt had turned pale. He had listened with sagging hopes while he had spoken of Dr. Zimberg. But when he heard that he wasn't supposed to come back to the station for two months—two months of having the invader following him, rustling, suggesting—*two whole months*—he felt a shuddering panic. For a moment he stood gasping. Then his brain gave a decisive click. He picked up the inkwell and hurled it straight in the sergeant's face. . . .

The sergeant went off duty at five. Much scrubbing and Boraxo had got the ink stains off his face and neck, but his gray shirt front and the breast of his uniform still bore big blue-black spots. There was a large lump over his right eye where the inkwell had struck him. His head ached.

He walked downhill toward his streetcar, thinking. Now that Delisle was behind the bars, charged with assault, he felt a certain compunction. Of course the little punk—a pathological masochist, if the sergeant ever saw one—had dared him to do it, and a lot of officers wouldn't have been able to resist the temptation to sock him one, or at least give him a kick. But he, the sergeant, understood psychology, and he ought to have known better. No, he hadn't behaved any too well. He resolved that tomorrow he'd get Delisle to the clinic for Zimberg to look at if it took two hospital orderlies and an ambulance.

His car came. He swung aboard it and sat down in the back. It had been a bad day, but in police work you got bad days. And when he got home, Leona would have supper waiting for him. Baked ham, he'd said this morning, and apple pie. Leona was a darned good cook.

She was putting on weight, of course. Women always seemed to, after they were married. It wasn't becoming to her. But she still wasn't bad looking, and he was certainly fond of her. He considered that they'd adjusted to each other very satisfactorily.

His corner drew near. He pressed the button and got off the car. He had three blocks to walk, and then he'd be home.

It was too bad Leona was such a poor housekeeper. There were always rings in the bathtub, lint and hair on the carpet, dirty dishes in the sink. Nothing was ever put away or cared for properly. And it was just laziness, since they hadn't any kids.

She was lazy about her personal appearance, too. Her nose hadn't known the touch of powder for the last two years, her hair was dusty with dandruff, greasy and lank. What did she do all day while he was gone, lay on the couch and eat candy? And her temper was bad. She was always nagging. She was a shrew, a slut.

Her temper, her laziness, her dirt moved in his brain kalei-doscopically. He felt his mind contract in a paroxysm of disgusted hate. He loathed her, she sickened him. What in God's name had made him tie himself to a woman like that? And how in God's name could he get rid of her? There must be some way. He had a sudden, sharp, bright, voluptuous picture of his fingers fastening around her greasy throat.

He could, he would do it. That way or another. He— There was a rustle behind him. Startled, he turned.

Between him and the twilight skyline there stood a tall, fantastically slender shape of black steel lace.

Oh, no. Surely not. He wouldn't believe it. Delisle had been lying. Or were delusions catching? He looked around him wildly, hoping for relief, for escape. As a flood of hateful ideas poured in upon him, he clutched at his collar and licked his lips.

No, no, no. It mustn't. He wouldn't. He wouldn't be the next installment of the story.

It wasn't true. No.

From the vacancy above his head there came a high, pleased laugh.

BRENDA

BRENDA ALDEN WAS a product of that aseptic, faintly sadistic, school of child rearing that is already a little old-fashioned. The vacationing parents on Moss Island liked her, and held up her politeness and good manners as examples to their offspring, but the children themselves stayed away from her, scenting in her something waspish and irritable. She was tall for her age, and lanky, with limp blonde hair. She always wore slacks.

Monday began like all her days. She had breakfast, was told to keep her elbows off the table, helped with the dishes. Then she was told to go out and play. She sauntered slowly into the woods.

The woods on Moss Island were scattered clumps of birch and denser stands of conifers. There were places where Brenda, if she tried hard, could have the illusion of a forest, and she liked that. In the western part of the island there was a wide, deep excavation which people said had been a quarry. Nobody ever said what had been quarried out of it.

It was a little before noon when Brenda smelled the rotten smell. It was an intense, bitter rottenness, almost strangling, and when it first met her nose Brenda's face wrinkled up with distaste. But after a moment her face relaxed. She inhaled, not without eagerness. She decided to try to find the source of the smell. Sometimes she liked to smell and look at rotten things.

Sniffing, she wandered. The smell would be strong and then weak and then strong again. She was just about to give up and turn back—it was hot in the airless, piney pockets, under the sun—when she saw the man.

He was not a tramp, he was not one of the summer people. Brenda knew at once that he was not like any other man she had ever seen. His skin was not black, or brown, but of an inky grayness; his body was blobbish and irregular, as if it had been shaped out of the clots of soap and grease that stop up kitchen sinks. He held a dead bird in one crude hand. The rotten smell was welling out of him.

Brenda stared at him, her heart pounding. For a moment she was almost too frightened to move. She stood gasping and licking her lips. Then he extended an arm toward her. She turned and ran.

She heard the noise, she smelled the smell, as he came stumbling after her. Her lungs hurt. There was an ache in her side. She tripped over a root, fell to her knees, and was up again. She ran on. Only when she was almost too exhausted to go further did she look back.

He was more distant than she had hoped, though he was still coming. For a second she stood panting, her narrow sides going in and out. He was still separated from her by some fifty feet. She blinked. Then her lips curved in what was almost a smile. She turned to the right, in the direction of the quarry, and began running again, though more leisurely.

There was a thicket of poison oak; she skirted it. She stooped for a pine cone, and then another one, thrust them into the waistband of her slacks, and went on with her steady trotting. He was still following. The light seemed to hurt his eyes; his head hung forward almost on his chest. Then they were on the edge of the quarry, and Brenda must try her plan.

She was no longer afraid—or, at any rate, only a little so. Exertion had washed her sallow cheeks with an unaccustomed red. Carefully she tossed one of the pine cones over the steep quarry side so that it landed halfway toward the bottom and then rolled on down. With more force she threw the second cone; it hit well beyond the first and slid toward the bottom in a rattle of loose stones and dirt. Then, very quickly and lightly, Brenda ran to the left and crouched behind a tree.

The noise of the pine cones and stones had been not unlike that of a runner plunging over the quarry edge and down into the depths. Brenda's pursuer halted, turning his head from side to side blindly, and seeming to sniff the air. She felt a moment of anxiety. She felt almost sure he couldn't catch her, even if he started after her again. But—oh—he was so—

One of the pine cones slid a few feet further. He seemed to listen. Then he went over the edge after the sound of it.

Brenda's heart was shaking the flat bosom of her shirt. While the rotten-smelling man stumbled back and forth among the dusty rocks in the quarry bottom hunting her, she waited and listened. It took him a long time to abandon the search. But at last the moment for which Brenda had been waiting came. He left his hunting and began to struggle up the quarry side.

He slid back. Brenda leaned forward, tense and expectant. Her eyes were bright. He started up again. Once more he slid back.

It was clear to the watching child much sooner than it was to the man in the depths of the quarry that he was imprisoned. He kept starting up the sides clumsily, clawing at the loose handholds, and sliding back. But his blobbish limbs were extraordinarily inept and awkward. He always slid back.

At last he gave up and stood quiet. His head dropped. He made no sound. But the penetrating rottenness was welling out from him.

Brenda got to her feet and walked toward him. Her pale lips were curving in a grin. "Hi!" she called over the edge of the quarry. "Hi! You can't get out, can you?"

The mockery in her tone seemed to cut through to his dull senses. He raised his grayish head. There was a flash of teeth, very white against their inky background. But he couldn't get out. After a moment, Brenda laughed.

Brenda hugged her secret to herself all the rest of the day. She was reprimanded for being late to lunch; her father said she needed discipline. She was not bothered. That night she slept soundly and well.

Early next morning she went to see Charles. Charles was a year older than she, and tolerated her better than anyone else on Moss Island. Once he had given her a cast-off snake skin. She had kept it in the drawer with her handkerchiefs.

Today he was making a cloud chamber with rubbing alcohol, a jar, and a piece of dry ice. Brenda squatted down beside him and watched. After five minutes or so she said, "I know what's more fun that that."

"What?" Charles asked, without looking up from his manipulations.

"Something I found. Something funny. Scary. Queer."

The exchange continued. Brenda hinted. Charles was mildly curious. At last she said, "Come and see it, Chet. It's not like anything you ever saw before. Come on." She laid her hand on his arm.

Up until that moment, Charles might have accompanied her. The cloud chamber was not going well, and he did not actively dislike the girl. But the dryness and tensity of her touch on his—the touch of a person who has never received or given a pleasant physical contact—repelled him. He drew away from her hand. "I don't want to see it. It isn't anything anyway, just some sort of junk. I'm not interested," he said.

"But you'd like it! Please come and see."

"I told you, I'm not interested. I'm not going to go. Can't you take a hint? Go away."

When he used that tone, Brenda knew there was no use in arguing with him. She got up and walked off.

After lunch her father had her help him with the barbecue pit he was building. While she shoveled dirt and mixed concrete her thoughts were busy with the man in the quarry. Was he still standing motionless at the bottom, or was he once more stumbling back and forth hunting her? Or was he trying to clamber up the side again? He'd never make it, no matter how much he tried. But if he stayed there long enough, some of the other children might find him. Would they be more frightened than she had been? She didn't know. She couldn't form any mental picture of what might happen then.

When her father finished his work for the day, she lay down in the hammock. Her hands were sore and her back ached, but she couldn't relax. Finally, though it was almost supper time, she got up and walked off quickly toward the quarry.

He was still there. Brenda let out a deep breath of relief. The bitter, rotten smell hung strong in the air. She must have made a noise, for he raised his head and let it drop forward again on his chest. Other than that, he was motionless.

Charles wouldn't come to see him. So . . . Brenda looked around her. Farther along the edge of the quarry, twenty feet or so from where she was standing, were two long boards. She measured their length with her eyes.

It was thirty feet or more to the bottom of the quarry. The boards were not quite long enough. But the zone of loose, sliding stuff did not extend all the way up; once the man in the excavation was past it, he ought to be able to get up easily enough. Charles had said that what she had found wasn't anything. Just some junk. Brenda began to move the boards.

Her hands were sore, but the boards themselves were not heavy. In fifteen minutes or so she had laid a narrow path from the bottom of the quarry to within a few feet of the top. *He*—the man—had done nothing while she worked, not even watched her. But underneath her shirt Brenda's narrow body was trembling and wet with sweat. She had had to get closer to him than she had liked while she was putting down the second board.

She stood back. The man in the quarry did not move. Brenda felt a moment of anxious exasperation. Wasn't he going to do anything, after all her trouble? "Come on!" she said under her breath and then, more loudly. "Come on!"

The sun was beginning to decline toward the west. The shadows lengthened. The man below turned his head from side to side, as if the waning light had brought him a keener perception. One blobby gray hand went up. Then he started toward the boards.

Brenda waited until his uncertain feet were set upon the second of the lengths of wood. She could stand it no longer. She whirled about and ran as hard as she could toward home. She did not know whether or not he followed her.

Brenda did not go to the woods next morning. She stayed around the house until her mother sent her out to help her father, who sent her back, saying that he had got to a place in his construction where she could be only in the way. Brenda went to the kitchen and got herself a sandwich and a glass of milk. When she came back with them, her mother, pale and disturbed, was on the terrace outside the house talking to her father. Brenda went to the door and leaned her head against it.

"I don't see how it could be a tramp," her mother was saying. "Elizabeth said nothing had been taken. She was quite emphatic. Only the roast chicken. And even it hadn't been eaten, only torn into pieces." She hesitated. "She said there were spots of grayish slime all over it."

"Elizabeth exaggerates," Brenda's father answered. He gave the mortar he was smoothing an impatient pat. "What's her idea anyway, if it wasn't a tramp? Who else would break in her kitchen? There are only six families on Moss Island."

"I don't think she has any definite idea. Oh, Rick, I wish you could have heard her talking. She mentioned the dreadful smell over and over. She said she was phoning the other families to warn them. She sounded afraid."

"Probably hysterical," he answered contemptuously. His eye fell on Brenda, standing in the shadow of the door. "Go up to your room, Brenda," he said sharply. "Stay there. I won't have you listening behind doors."

"Yes, father."

Brenda did not resent the order. She was afraid. Would Charles remember her hints of yesterday, connect them with the raid on Mrs. Emsden's kitchen (the man from the quarry must be hungry—but he hadn't eaten the chicken), and tell on her? Or would something worse happen, she didn't know what?

She moved about her room restlessly. The bed was made, there was nothing for her to do. She could hear the rumble of her parents' voices indistinctly, a word now and then rising into prominence. For the first time she felt a sharp curiosity about the man who had been in the quarry, about the man himself.

She got out her diary and opened it. But it wouldn't do; the volume had no lock, and she knew her mother read it. She never wrote anything important in it.

She looked at the scribbled pages with dislike. It would be nice to be able to tear them out and crumble them up in the wastebasket.

But her mother would notice and ask her why she had destroyed her pretty book. No . . .

She hunted about the room until she found a box of note paper. Using the lid of the box as a desk, she printed carefully across the top of one of the narrow gray sheets: THE MAN.

She hesitated. Then she wrote: "1. Where did he come from?"

She licked her pencil. The idea was hard to put into words. But she wanted to see it written out on the paper. She began, erased, began again. Finally she wrote, "I think he came to Moss Island from the mainland. I think he came over one night last month when the tide was so low. I think he came here by acci—" She erased. "By mistake."

Brenda was ready for the second question "Why does he stay on the island?" she scribbled. She was writing faster now. "I think because he cannot swim. The water would—" she paused, conscious that the exact word she wanted was not in her vocabulary. At last she wrote, "would wash him away."

She got out another sheet of note paper. At the top she printed, "THE MAN—Page 2." She bit into the pencil shank judiciously. Then she wrote, "What kind of a man is he? I think he is not like other people. Not like us. He is a different kind of a man."

She had written the last words slowly. Now inspiration came. She scribbled, "He is not like us because he likes dead things to eat. Things that have been dead for much—" She erased. "For a long time. I think that is why he came to M.I. in the first place. Hunting. He is old. Has been the way he is for a long time."

She put the pencil down. She seemed to have finished. Her mother must have gone out; the noise of her parents' voices had ceased, and the house was perfectly quiet. Outside, she could hear the faint slap of her father's trowel as he worked on the concrete.

There was a long pause. Brenda sat motionless. Then she picked up the pencil again and wrote at the bottom of the page, very quickly, "I think he wants to be born."

She picked up what she had written and looked at it. Then she took the two pages and went with them into the bathroom. She tore them into small pieces and flushed them down the drain.

Supper that night was quiet. Once Brenda's mother started to say something about Elizabeth Emsden, and was stopped by her father's warning frown. Brenda helped with the dishes. Just before she went upstairs to bed, she slipped into her parents' bedroom, which was on the ground floor, and unlatched the window screens.

She had trouble getting to sleep, but slept soundly. She was aroused, when the night was well along, by the sound of voices. She stole out on the stair landing and listened, her heart beginning to thud.

The rotten smell was coming up in burning, bitter waves. The cottage seemed to rock under it. Brenda clung to the banister. He had come then, the man—her man—from the quarry. She was glad.

Brenda's father was speaking. "That smell is really incredible," he said in an abstracted voice. And then, to Brenda's mother, "Flora, call Elizabeth and tell her to have Jim come over. Hurry. I don't know how much longer I can keep him back with this thing. Have Jim bring his gun."

"Yes." Flora Alden giggled. "You said Elizabeth was hysterical, didn't you? For God's sake keep your voice down, Rick. I don't want Brenda to waken and see this. She'd be—I don't think she'd ever get over it." She moved toward the telephone.

Brenda's eyes widened. Were her parents really solicitous for her? Were they afraid she'd be afraid? She moved down two or three steps, very softly, and sat down on one of the treads. If they noticed her now, she could say their voices had awakened her. She peered out between the banisters.

Her father was standing in the hall, holding the man from the quarry impaled in the stabbing beam of an electric torch. *He*—oh, he was brave—he kept moving about and trying to rub the light out of his eyes. He made little rushes. But her father shifted the torch mercilessly, playing him in it, even though his hand shook.

Brenda's mother came back from the phone. "He's coming," she reported. "He didn't think the gun would do much good. He had another plan."

It took Jim Emsden long enough to get to the cottage for Brenda to have time enough to shiver and wish she had put on her bathrobe. She yawned nervously and curled herself up more tightly against the banister. But she never took her eyes from the tableau in the hall below.

Emsden came in by the side door. He was wearing an overcoat over his pajamas. He took a deep breath when he saw the gray, blobby shape in the light of the torch.

"Yes, it's the same man," he said in his rumbling voice. "Of course. Nobody could mistake that smell. I brought the gun, Rick, but I have a hunch it won't help. Not against a thing like that. Elizabeth got a glimpse of him, you know. I'll show you what I mean. Keep him in the torch."

He raised the .22 to his shoulder, clicked the bolt, and fired. Brenda's little scream went unheeded in the whoosh of the shot. But the man from the quarry made no sign of having received the impact. He did not even rock. The bullet might as well have spent its force in mud.

"You see?" Emsden demanded. "It wasn't any good."

Flora Alden was giggling gently. The beam of the torch moved in bobbing circles against the darkness. "What'll we do, Jim?" Rick asked. "I didn't know things like this could happen. What are we going to do?—I'm afraid I'm going to be sick."

"Steady, Rick. Why, there's one thing he'll be afraid of. Whatever he is. Fire."

He produced rags and a bottle of kerosene. With the improvised torch they drove him out of the cottage and into the night outside. Whenever he slowed and tried to face them, his head lowered, his teeth gleaming, they thrust the bundle of burning rags in his face.

He had to give ground. Brenda was chewing her wrist in her excitement. She heard her father's higher voice saying, "But what will we do with him, Jim? We can't just leave him outside the house," and Emsden's deeper, less distinct answering rumble, ". . . kill him. But we can shut him up." And then a confused roll of voices ending in the word "quarry." She could hear nothing more.

Next day an atmosphere of exhaustion and cold defeat hung over the house. Brenda's mother moved about her household tasks mechanically, hardly speaking to her daughter, her face white. Her father had not come back to the cottage until daybreak, and had left again after a few hours. It was not until nearly dusk that Brenda was able to slip out and try to find what had become of the man.

She made straight for the quarry. When she reached it, she looked about, bewildered. The sides were still sharp and square, but a great mound of rock had been piled up in the center. The men of Moss Island must have worked hard all day to pile up so much rock.

She slid down the sides and clambered up the heap in the center. What had become of him? Was he under the mound? She listened. She could hear nothing. After a moment she sat down and pressed her ear to the rock. It felt still warm from the heat of the sun.

She listened. She could hear only the beating of her heart. And then, far down, a long way off, a rustle within the heap like that made by a mole's soft paws.

After that, things changed. Brenda's father had to go back to the office, since his vacation was over. He could visit Moss Island only on weekends. Brenda's mother began to complain that Brenda was getting hard to handle, no longer obeyed.

The children who had rejected the girl now sought her out. They came to the cottage as soon as breakfast was over, asking for Brenda, and she went off with them at once, deaf to all that her mother could say. She would return only at dusk, pale with exhaustion, but still blazing with frantic energy.

Her new energy seemed inexhaustible. The physical feats that had once repelled her drew her irresistibly. She tumbled, climbed, dove, chinned herself, did splits and cartwheels. The other children watched her admiringly and applauded. For the first time in her life she tasted the pleasure of leadership.

If that had been all, only Brenda's parents would have complained. But she drew her new followers after her into piece upon piece of mischief. They were destructive, wanton, irrepressible. By the end of the summer everyone on Moss Island was saying that Brenda Alden needed disciplining. Her parents complained bitterly that she was impossible to control. They sent her off ahead of time to school.

There the events of the late summer were repeated. Brenda's school-mates accepted her blindly. The teachers punished and threatened.

Her grades, for the first time in her life, were bad. She was within an inch of being expelled.

The year passed. Spring came, and summer. The Aldens, fearing more trouble, left Brenda at school after the school year was over. She did not get back to Moss Island until late July.

The last few months had changed Brenda physically. Her narrow body had rounded and grown more womanly. Under her shirt—she still wore slacks and a shirt—her breasts had begun to swell and lift. She seemed to have outgrown her tomboy ways. Her parents began to congratulate themselves.

She did not go at once to the cairn in the quarry. She often thought of it. But she felt a sweet reluctance, an almost tender disinclination toward going. It could wait. August was well advanced before she visited the mound.

The day was warm. She was winded after the walk through the woods. She let herself down the side of the quarry delicately, paused for breath, and went up the mound with long, slipping steps. When she got to the top she sat down.

Was there, in the hot air, the faint hint of rottenness? She inhaled doubtfully. Then, as she had done last year, she pressed her ear to the mound.

There was silence. Was he—but of course, he couldn't be dead. "Hi," she called softly, her lips against the rock. "Hi. I've come back. It's me."

The scrabble began far down and seemed to come nearer. But there was too much rock in the way. Brenda sighed. "Poor old thing," she said. Her tone was rueful. "You want to be born, don't you? And you can't get out. It's too bad."

The scrabbling continued. Brenda, after a moment, stretched herself out against the rock. The sun was warm, the heat from the stones beat up lullingly against her body. She lay in drowsy contentment for a long time, listening to the noises within the mound.

The sun began to wester. The cool of evening roused her. She sat up.

The air was utterly silent. There were no bird calls anywhere. The only sounds came from within the mound.

Brenda leaned forward quickly, so that her long hair fell over her face. "I love you," she said softly to the rock. "I'll always love you. You're the only one I could ever love."

She halted. The scrabbling within had risen to a crescendo. She laughed. Then she drew a long wavering sigh. "Be patient," she said. "Someday I'll let you out. I promise. We'll be born together, you and I."

STAWDUST

"Are you doing it?" Miss Abernathy demanded.

"Are you?" he countered. His neat, prettily arched eyebrows had gone up.

"Certainly not."

"Don't be too sure. You might not be conscious of it. And it's exactly the sort of thing a woman *would* do." He looked at her with such concentrated disgust that Miss Abernathy thought: he's real all right. Not like the others. But he's not exactly a man.

She turned her gaze from him toward the flat blue water of the swimming pool. She had liked the swimming pool the best of anything on board the *S.S. Vindemiatrix,* but today there was neither inspiration nor solace in it. "But what are we going to do?" she asked, looking at Mr. Faxon again.

"Wait and find out, I suppose," he answered. "It's about all we *can* do. Whichever of us doesn't change—"

"Is the one who's been doing it," she finished.

"Exactly." He turned his back on her and began to walk away, threading his way lissomely through the dummies that crowded around the pool. Mr. Pooley, Miss Davis, Mr. Elginbrod, Mr. Harris, Miss Raylor—what a lot of them there were! Not to mention the captain and the first mate in the dining salon and all the others who, transformed privately, were sitting or standing woodenly within the confines of their cabins. Twenty-five or thirty people, all dummies, all neatly stuffed with sawdust, all with sleek kidskin skins.

Miss Abernathy's mind moved back to her fourth day on board the *Vindemiatrix* and the first of the transformations. She had been standing by the side of the plunge, talking to Mr. Pooley. "This is a nice pool," she had said.

"Yes, nice," he had answered.

"And the color of the water—that's nice, too."

"Yes. It's nice." Had a spark of something autonomous flickered behind Mr. Pooley's beautiful eyes? At any rate, he had gone on to add an original observation. "The color of the light from above—I like that too. It's nice."

"Oh, do you?" An imp of the perverse had moved in Miss Abernathy. "Don't you think it would be prettier if it were a brighter yellow? A little more like sunshine?" It was true, the diffused lighting over the pool had a sullen, smoky tinge, like the sandy glare of a dust storm. The robot who had designed it had slipped up.

Mr. Pooley seemed not to have heard her. "It's nice," he had repeated blandly, as if she had never spoken at all.

Miss Abernathy had turned from him with a throb of disgust. What a dummy he was! They were all dummies, every one of them. All they could do, men and women alike, was to repeat "nice" or "interesting," and think they'd said something. And speaking of dummies—what a fool she'd been, to think that the passengers on a space ship would be an improvement over the people in her office. Romantic space travellers, indeed. They were worse, if anything.

Where were the men who did things and made things? All gone? Surely the men who designed the machines. . . . But the machines designed themselves now. They were better at it than any human being could have been.

She had turned from Mr. Pooley and slipped into the turquoise water of the plunge. She swam its length twice. Then she had clambered out of the water and come back to Mr. Pooley.

He was standing exactly where he had been when she had left him. When she got up close to him, she saw why he hadn't moved. He'd never move again. He was . . . he was. . . .

Oh, no. Miss Abernathy's jaw had dropped. There must be some mistake. They'd introduced her to him, only a couple of days ago. They wouldn't have introduced her to a dummy, would they?

She had looked around herself almost distractedly. Nobody had been looking toward them, nobody had been paying any attention. Delicately she had put out her fingers and touched Mr. Pooley on the arm. He felt cool and smooth and creamy, like a good grade of kid.

The bell for tea had rung. People had begun to get out of the water. Miss Abernathy had gone with the others. At the door of the plunge she had looked back. Mr. Pooley was still standing there.

The second transformation had occured at the dinner hour. The captain—they all sat at the captain's table—had been talking in his nice, interesting voice. Miss Abernathy had found herself listening with pleasure. The captain was more the sort of man she had been hoping to meet. He knew things. He did things. He had ideas. No doubt he was married already. But—well—she didn't care. Anything would be better than being married to one of the usual dummies, like Mr. Pooley. She didn't care if he was married. She could be his concubine.

"We are going through an unusually interesting region of space just now," the captain had said. "We are skirting the fringes of an enormous cloud of hydrogen gas and tiny particles of dust. Though by earthly standards the cloud of gas is thin indeed—it contains about ten hydrogen atoms per cubic centimeter—its density is ten or a hundred times that at its center. The cloud is highly magnetized. Actually, it is considerably elongated in the direction of the interstellar lines of magnetic force. Sometimes interesting phenomena occur."

"Is it dangerous?" Miss Abernathy had wanted to know, leaning forward hopefully.

"Not at all. Merely interesting. We are skirting the fringes of an enormous cloud of hydrogen gas and tiny particles of dust. Though by earthly standards the cloud of gas is thin indeed—it contains about ten hydrogen atoms per cubic centimeter—its density. . . ."

He was, Miss Abernathy had perceived, repeating himself all over again. He didn't know anything more, or have any more ideas, than the others. He'd probably memorized the whole speech from a printed tape one of the news machines had given him.

Concubine, indeed. She felt a pang of self-disgust. What had been the matter with her?

". . . elongated in the direction of the interstellar lines of magnetic force," the captain was finishing. "Sometimes extremely interest—"

He had stopped in mid-word. Miss Abernathy had bent toward him in a sort of guilty prescience. While she watched, a dribble of sawdust had trickled down from the side of his nose.

Surely the others had drawn away a little. Hadn't there been a movement, a voiceless rustle, away from the captain and her? Hadn't there been the slightest of pauses in the conversation at the table, if only for a fraction of a second? But they had gone on again almost immediately, talking, saying that things were nice, interesting, good. When dinner was over they had all got up and left the captain sitting there.

He had been sitting there in his place at the next meal, breakfast. Miss Abernathy, slipping back to the dining salon later, had found one of the robot servitors dusting him.

There had been a lot of transformations after that. It was after the sixth, or perhaps it was the seventh, that the committee had been formed.

Mr. Elginbrod had been the chairman. He had, he said, been in space a dozen times before, and nothing like this had ever happened. There must be something wrong with the servo-mechanisms. They ought to complain.

"Yes," echoed Miss Davis. "We ought to complain to the captain."

Miss Abernathy had raised her eyebrows a little. "To the *captain*?"

"Well, then, to the first mate. To someone in authority. There's no telling where this will stop. Any of us might be next."

"Absolutely," boomed Mr. Elginbrod. His expression was just as fatuous as ever, but his eyes had a wild, glassy glare. "Miss Davis is right. Something must be done. I ag—"

He stopped. Miss Abernathy, peering at him in the yellowish light, saw that his eyes had become, literally, glass.

The others had looked at him. They began to back away. When they were a reasonable distance off, they turned and ran. A little later, Miss Abernathy had heard a series of slams from their cabin doors.

That had been the end of the committee. Miss Davis hadn't been able to get back to her cabin before she had succumbed. And Miss

Abernathy, making the rounds of the cabins a couple of days later with a master key she had taken from the robot chambermaid, had found that the rest of them had succumbed too. Their taking refuge in their cabins hadn't done them any good. Now they all had kidskin bodies, sawdust stuffing, and glass eyes.

Was being turned into a dummy painful? Apparently not, since none of them had cried out in the moment of transformation. Still, it was a nasty idea. And who was doing it? Was it she? Was it Mr. Faxon? Or was it just something that happened in the part of space where the *Vindemiatrix* now was? There was nobody to ask, no way of finding out. She and Mr. Faxon were the only human beings left on the ship.

Miss Abernathy sighed. She looked toward the door through which Mr. Faxon had vanished. Where had he gone? To the snack bar, for something to eat? He was fond of eating. Or to the gym, to have one of the robots massage him? He spent most of his time eating or trying to work off the results of eating. Still, he wasn't so bad. There was more to him, in a way, than there had been to the other men.

The next few days were less difficult than Miss Abernathy had feared they would be. The dummies around the swimming pool and in the dining salon were a surprising amount of company. She went swimming several times, and enjoyed it. At meals she and Mr. Faxon sat at opposite ends of the dining table, with the dummies in between, and the robots waited on them punctiliously. It wasn't very different, really, from what it had been before the other passengers were transformed.

All the same, she was sleeping badly. She went to the iatric robot and got a box of sleeping pills. They helped, but she wakened feeling depressed. Was it the thought of all the dummies waiting woodenly in the cabins around her, or was she personally frightened? It didn't seem to be either of these. Suddenly she knew what it was. She was lonesome.

Yes, lonesome. She and Mr. Faxon were the only living people left on the ship, and yet they never exchanged a word, not even good morning. He kept his nose stuck in a book most of the time they were at table. Something ought to be done. Perhaps she'd misjudged him. His mannerisms were peculiar, certainly. But. . . .

She dressed for dinner that evening with unusual care: her washed-gold lamé dress with the bouffant waist and the little gold lamé panties, three layers of color in her hair, the appropriate perfumes, and shimmer wristlets and anklets.

It took her a long time to be satisfied. She kept making the robot maid do her hair over again. When she entered the dining salon, the second gong for dinner had already been rung.

Mr. Faxon didn't look up from his book. Well, she hadn't thought he would. It was not until the robots were serving coffee with the dessert that she got up courage enough to speak to him.

"Could I trouble you for the sugar?" she asked. Her voice sounded unnatural in her ears.

Without looking up, he gave the sugar bowl a shove that sent it flying along the cloth to her place, "And the cream, please?" she said.

This time he did look up. He gave her a scathing glance. "The cream jug's right by your elbow," he said ungraciously.

"Oh . . . thanks." She swallowed. "Are you . . . I thought . . . if . . . perhaps we might dance a little this evening. If you're not too busy, that is. The orchestra would be glad to play."

"Sorry, no. When I was a dancing instructor, I got enough of women walking on my feet to last me the rest of my life."

Once more Miss Abernathy swallowed. "Or . . . we might play some bezarique. Or we could see what records there are in the library for the stereo."

"No, thanks. Frankly, Miss Abernathy, I don't want to do anything at all in company with you."

It was almost with relief that she laid the weapons of allurement aside. "Why not?" she demanded.

"Two reasons. In the first place, I think you're dangerous. Darned dangerous, though you probably don't know it. In the second place, I just don't like you very well."

For a moment he twisted the bangles on his wrist thoughtfully. He seemed about to say something more. He didn't. He shut his book with a bang, pushed his chair back, and walked out.

Miss Abernathy stared after him. Her eyes felt hot. So. If that was the way it was . . . Why, he sounded as if he thought it was either him or her! As if they were enemies. She hadn't known he disliked her so. But perhaps he was right. Yes, perhaps he was.

She had to take three sleeping pills that night. When she woke, though, she felt alert and rested, not at all depressed.

She dressed slowly and thoughtfully, stopping often to examine her fingernails, or arrange her toilet things. She might just as well wear that quiet little brown dress and put plain, instead of shimmer, gold dust on her hair. When you were going to war (Was she? Her hands were awfully cold), there was no point in getting all dressed up.

She entered the dining salon with her head held high. Mr. Faxon was already eating—porridge with butter and sugar and cream. Through the transparent cover of the platter beside him, she could see the next course he had selected: three plump hot cakes, garnished with bacon, sausage, ham, and eggs. No wonder he was getting a double chin.

She drank her fruit juice. Really, she felt terrible. She didn't know whether she could go through with it. But she couldn't go on like this either. If Mr. Faxon was wrong, it didn't much matter. If he was right, she might as well find out.

"Mr. Faxon," she said loudly and deliberately, "after breakfast, you and I are going to play a nice game of bezarique."

He looked up sharply from his dish of porridge. His face was savage with annoyance. (If he thinks I'm so darned dangerous, Miss Abernathy thought, he's an awful fool to antagonize me.) "What? Play bezarique with you? You're crazy. Of course not. I told you so before."

Their glances met. Miss Abernathy had a sense of profoundly exerting herself. She was trembling all over. She had to . . . if she didn't . . . he . . . oh . . . he. . . .

Suddenly it happened. There was a sort of plop in the air between them, and Mr. Faxon's eyes grew glazed. His body took on the familiar slickness and rigidity. He was a dummy too. She'd done it again.

He didn't look quite like the other ones. Miss Abernathy got up from her place and walked around the dummies to where he was sitting. She examined him closely. The stitches in the kidskin of his right forearm seemed a little loose. She worked at them with her fingernail until she got a hole started.

Um-hum. It was just as she had thought. He *wasn't* like the others. He was stuffed with fluffy pink cotton. It smelled of violets.

She was shaking all over. She got back to her chair somehow and sat down in it. It was awful, terrible; she supposed she was responsible, but she hadn't really meant it to happen. Not exactly. And now she was the only living thing left on the ship.

What should she do now? She didn't know whether to laugh or to cry. It was like wanting to sneeze and hiccough at the same time. And no matter what she did, it wouldn't make any difference. She was the only living thing left—No. No, she wasn't. There *was* another person left alive. The astrogator. He must still be carrying on his duties; his lonely, high-minded, all-important duties. The astrogator! Of course, of course!

Miss Abernathy's trembling had stopped. It wasn't too odd, really, that she hadn't thought of the astrogator. Out of sight, out of mind; and everybody knew that astrogators were too absorbed by their weighty duties to appear in public. Did that mean she oughtn't to go call on him?

She hesitated. But she did so want to see him—and she'd be careful. After all, Mr. Faxon might have been wrong. The captain had said that odd things happened in this part of space.

Almost running, she started toward the part of the ship where the astrogator's quarters must be. At the end of the recreation area there was a bolted door and a sign saying, "No Admittance." She pulled the bolt back and went through.

It was noisier here. The corridor was not so well carpeted, and the hum of machinery filled the air. Nervously, still eagerly, Miss Abernathy hurried on.

There were more doors, more signs reading, variously. "No Admittance," "Entrance Forbidden," "Keep Out." Miss Abernathy, brows puckered, disregarded them all. At last she came to the door

of doors. The sign on it read, "ASTROGATOR. ENTRANCE
EXPRESSLY DENIED. KEEP OUT."

She tried the door. It was unlocked. She faltered. Then she rapped
softly on it.

"C'mon in," said a husky male voice.

Miss Abernathy stepped inside. She could not repress a gasp.

Throughout the rest of the *Vindemiatrix,* every attempt had
been made to fence out awareness of the vastness of space. The
idea had been to make the passengers feel that they were spending
two pleasant months in a superior luxury hotel. Only in the main
lounge, inconspicuously placed, were there two small indirect viewers
through which passengers could look out at what surrounded them.
Nobody had ever used the viewers much. But here, in the astrogator's
cubicle, one realized abruptly where the *Vindemiatrix* was.

The whole forward end of the room was a huge indirect viewing
plate. It was flanked by a curving double tier of enigmatic instruments
and gauges. And all around the room, from ceiling to floor and back
to ceiling again, there ran a broad, broad belt, a zodiac, of direct
viewers. The reddish light of the ionized hydrogen shone through
it. The cubicle seemed to be girdled with misty fire.

Except for the red glow of the gas, the only light in the room came
from a small green-shaded lamp over the astrogator's lonely seat.

It was an awesome room. The astrogator himself lay face downward
in his bunk, while a robot servant gave him a body massage.

Miss Abernathy advanced timidly. Almost under her feet, in the
direct viewers, an enormous blue star burned through the reddish
haze with a steady, baleful glare. "Are you the astrogator?" she
asked.

"Yessum," he answered languidly. He turned his head toward
her. "Sit down, ma'am, and I'll have the robot bring you a drink."

"Thank you." She seated herself on the edge of a chair. "I'm not
thirsty now." She paused for a moment. "So you're the astrogator.
It must be an awfully responsible job."

"Oh, it's not so bad." He yawned. "Robbie, here, does most of
the work." He indicated a tall, vaguely humanoid mechanism that
stood to the left of the tier of instruments.

"Oh. I thought you astrogators had to do a lot of figuring." She relaxed a bit.

"Used to be that way. Not any more. I just punch a button at the beginning of the trip, and the machines bring us on in. It's up to them to do the work."

Once more he yawned. "Wouldn't you like a drink, ma'am?" he asked a little wistfully. "They make nice drinks."

"No, thank you." Miss Abernathy groped after her illusions. "But . . . supposing you wanted to take the ship somewhere besides to Sirius? Wouldn't you have a lot to do then? A new course to compute, all sorts of calculations?"

"Naw. See that wheel?" He pointed. "It's got a list of all the major stars on it. You just set the wheel for the right star. It's duck soup."

"I think . . . I will have a drink now," said Miss Abernathy. While the drink was being brought, she asked, "Don't you get lonesome, though? I'd think you would."

"Nope." He rolled over on his back, exposing his beautifully muscled chest and half his handsome face. "I sleep a lot. I don't mind it."

"Then you mean you don't really do any work at all?"

Some of the indignation she felt must have shown in her voice. The astrogator giggled. "Aw, ma'am," he said soothingly, "you don't want to take it so hard. It's just one of those things."

One of those things. . . . Miss Abernathy felt a flood of uncontrollable disgust. He was worse than any of them—worse than the captain, worse than Mr. Elginbrod, worse than Mr. Faxon. He was worse than the dumbest of the passengers. He lay in his bed, and the machines steered the *Vindemiatrix,* and it was just one of those things. What a fool he was!

She was not in the least surprised, she was, rather, gratified, when the one of his eyes she could see took on a glassy stare.

She finished her drink and then went over to his bunk. His skin was kid, like that of the others, but he looked much lumpier, and slackly stuffed. She squeezed him. There was a crunkle. Was he filled with straw? No, it was probably excelsior.

She set the empty glass down on the floor beside him. Through the band of viewers the cloud of gas still burned redly. There was no use in letting the ship go on to Sirius: everyone said that Sirius' planet, which had been colonized by Earthmen, was just like being on Earth. She wouldn't find what she was looking for there.

Well, then. . . . She walked over to the wheel the astrogator had indicated. She studied the list of stars for a moment. Aldebaran. The list said it had a planet, and the name had a lucky sound. It would take a long time to get there, but she had plenty of food. She could wait. Aldebaran.

She moved the pointer on the wheel from Sirius to the new name. Then she began to turn the wheel so the notch in it would correspond.

The wheel turned easily. Eagerly she watched the star fields in the indirect viewer. In a moment they would begin to swing and shift as the ship set on its new course.

The moments passed. The star fields in the viewer continued rock steady. Slowly Miss Abernathy began to feel frightened. Still no change in course, only the steady movement ahead.

She turned on the overhead lights in the room. Now she could see the wheel better. Its connections seemed to be a little loose. She knelt down and followed the cord back with her fingers.

No. It wasn't connected on to anything. It never had been. It just came to an end. The star wheel . . . was a dummy wheel.

She got back to the passengers' quarters somehow. For a while she wandered among her dummies, touching their kidskin bodies and shivering. On impulse she pitched Mr. Elginbrod into the swimming pool, and then shivered worse than ever.

The ship would arrive at Sirius' planet on schedule. (If there was some way of making the machines take the *Vindemiatrix* to Aldebaran, she'd never be able to find it.) The landing would be made just as competently, just as purposefully, as if she weren't the only living thing left on board.

There wouldn't be any trouble about the transformations. People would look the other way and ignore the whole subject. Even if she'd killed everybody on board with arsenic, instead of transforming them accidentally while the ship was going through a cloud of magnetized hydrogen, there wouldn't have been any trouble. People were too dumb to care. It would just be considered one of those things.

She began to cry. Dimly, far forward in the ship, she could hear the usual happy, impersonal hum of the machinery, inexorably carrying the ship toward Sirius. It made her cry harder than ever. A robot servant glided up and gently put a fresh white handkerchief in her hand.

THE INVESTED LIBIDO

DENTAUTASEN HAS A rather dubious reputation even in Martian psycho-pharmacology. Conservative medical opinion frowns on its use except in the desperate cases, for people who already feel so bad that any change one can produce in them is an improvement. The drug's action is drastic and unpredictable. But, Mars being Mars, there are no restrictions on its exportation from the planet. And the short-sighted skullduggery Mars runs to has been known to result in its being substituted for senta beans, which it somewhat resembles.

It was the irony of fate, perhaps, that Wilmer Bellows, who was loaded to the gills with psychiatric drugs already, should have bought a bottle of it thinking it was a simple cathartic.

Wilmer's psycho-therapist was on vacation, or Wilmer would have asked him about the syrup before taking it. As it was, Wilmer swallowed a tablespoonful of the syrup, took four neuroquel tablets and a deutapromazine capsule, and got into bed. He got out again immediately. He had forgotten to practice libidinal investment with his machine.

The therapist had diagnosed Wilmer's difficulty, which he referred to as "depersonalization," as proceeding from Wilmer's lack of libidinal investment in Wilmer's own self. What Wilmer experienced was a feeling of being entirely detached from his person and personality.

His ego seemed to hover impersonally over his body and watch it, clockwork-wise, going through its daily tricks; he would look at his hand and wonder whose hand it was, or speculate numbly as to who the person was who sat in Wilmer's chair. It was a horrid feeling, though only intermittent, and Wilmer had spent a lot of time and money trying to get rid of it. He had not had much success.

The machine for practicing libidinal investment was something like a stroboscope. Discs rotated, slots shot in and out across them, lights flashed. Wilmer looked in at the eyehole and tried to feel libidinally involved with himself.

After fifteen minutes of eyestrain, he was ready for bed. He got between the sheets. The neuroquel and the deutapromazine made him sleepy; the dentautasen opposed their action. Wilmer felt feverish. When he got to sleep, he dreamed about Dr. Adams, his therapist.

He woke, however, feeling much better. He had none of the hideous moments of depersonalization while he was shaving, his breakfast tasted pretty good. He decided he would visit the city aquarium after breakfast. Looking at marine life was one of the few things he enjoyed.

It was a fine sunny day. He *did* feel better. Maybe the therapy was beginning to help at last. He walked toward the aquarium feeling positively benevolent toward life. It wasn't such a bad world, after all—if only they'd put muzzles on those god-damned big snakes on the street corners,

Snakes? Wilmer stopped walking so suddenly that the man behind him bumped into him. What was the matter with him? Was he going psycho? And yet for a moment he'd had the definite impression that big snakes had been gliding effortlessly along the curbing. He hadn't been particularly afraid of them.

He was sweating. He looked about himself wildly. For a moment his ego seemed to hover bee-like in the air above him—above the little girl with the pink parasol, above the brown paper parcel the brisk old lady was carrying, above the wide furry dog who was irrigating a lamp post. He was all of them, he was none of them. Who was he?

His eye fell on a manure bun in the street, relic of one of the horse-drawn carriages that were currently fashionable. No. No. Not it. He wasn't, he wouldn't. He recalled himself into his body desperately. He was Wilmer Bellows, that's who he was. Wilmer

Bellows. He made the rest of the distance to the aquarium almost at a run.

The echoing, wet-smelling building soothed him. Early as it was, there were quite a few people looking into the greenish light of the cases, and that soothed him too.

He looked at a case with sea horses, sea stars, and a lobster. He looked at a case with sea roses and sea anemones. He looked at a case with a flat fish and two ugly, poisonous Scorpaena. He looked at a case wi—

Suddenly the hovering depersonalization descended on him crashingly. Descended? No, he was being sucked up into it. He was being drawn up a varnished staircase into a hideous vacuum, a spiral of emptiness.

He had to stop somewhere, he couldn't go on. The little girl, the parcel, the dog, the manure bun? He must be one of them, he must be somebody, he—

His eyes were fixed wildly on the glass of the tank before him. His hand had gone to the knot of his tie. He didn't know who he was any longer, but he was aware of sweat pouring down his back. If he had had enough ego left for prayer, he would have prayed.

Lib—invest—if he could lov— There was a sort of click and a feeling of pressure released in his ears.

He drew a long, shaky breath. A weak smile of gratitude spread over his face. He knew who he was at last, at last he loved himself. It was the squid in the tank before him. He loved the squid. Because he *was* the squid.

The green water slid over his back. He sucked in deliciously salty water, pushed it on out, and jetted backward silkily. A frond of tentacles moved to his beak and then away again. He jetted backward exuberantly once more.

How much of his new sensations was hallucinatory and how much was a genuine empathy cannot be decided. The action of dentautasen is very obscure. Wilmer, at any rate, was happy. He had never felt this good before.

He hung over the tank lovingly. Though he felt that he *was* the squid, some physical limitations remained. He could feel identified with it only when he could see it. He knew intuitively that he would feel depersonalized again when he was no longer near his "self."

The keeper fed him around four. The food was delicious; he was angry at the keeper, though, because he was so stingy with it.

The aquarium closed at five-thirty. Wilmer left reluctantly, with many a backward glance. On the way home he realized that somebody, probably a sort of Wilmer, was hungry. He stopped at a hash house on the corner and had two bowls of clam chowder. As he spooned it up, he wondered whether enough fresh water was coming into his tank.

When he got back to his apartment, he stood for a long time in the middle of the living room, thinking. Of water, of the taste of salt, of sun. At last he roused himself to undress. In the bathroom he took his usual assortment of psychiatric drugs. And the syrup of senta beans.

He woke about two in the morning, feeling utterly miserable. His head hurt, his throat ached, the air in the room was hot and dry. Worst of all was his longing for his absent person. He knew now who he was—Wilmer Bellows, who was a squid in a tank at the municipal aquarium. He wanted to get back to himself.

He started to dress. Then he checked himself. He couldn't possibly get into the aquarium building at this hour. If he tried, he'd only set off a burglar alarm. But he wouldn't go through another night like this one. Tomorrow he'd hide in the aquarium when it came closing time.

He sluiced his face and neck with water, and lay down on the chesterfield in the living room. He turned and twitched until daybreak. Then he took a long cold shower. For breakfast, he unzipped a plastic package of sardines.

Once he was back in the aquarium, his malaise disappeared. He seemed in fine shape, with his tank properly aerated and plenty of clean salt water bubbling in. Glub-glub. Life was good.

As the day progressed, Wilmer began to fear that he had attracted the attention of the guard. He'd tried to stay away from his tank, but it hadn't been easy, when he was so deeply attracted to himself.

All the same, he managed to hide at closing time, dodging adroitly from the visiphone booth to the men's room and back to another visi booth, and when the building was quiet, he came tiptoeing out again.

He shone his flashlight on himself. Yes, he was fine. Well, now. They might have a little snack.

He would have liked to feed him some fish meal, but he was afraid that if he went into the passages behind the tanks he'd get caught. He had to settle for some seaweed crackers and a thermos of clam broth. He didn't know when he'd enjoyed a feed so much.

The night wore on. Wilmer grew sleepy. He leaned up against the glass of his tank in drowsy contentment, dreaming softly of rock pools and gentle tides. When the nightwatchman made his third round, at one-fifteen, Wilmer was asleep on his feet.

The watchman saw him, of course. He hesitated. He was a big man, and Wilmer was slight; he could probably have overpowered him easily. On the other hand, an aquarium is a poor place for a scuffle. And something in the pose of the man by the squid tank alarmed the watchman. It didn't seem natural.

The watchman went to his office and vizzed the cops. He added that he thought it would be a good idea if they brought a doctor along.

Wilmer awoke from his dreams of pelagic bliss to find himself impaled on the beams of three flashlights. Before he had time to get alarmed and jet backward, the fourth man stepped forward and spoke.

"My name is Dr. Roebuck," he said in a deep, therapeutic voice. "I assume that you have some good reason for being where you are now. Perhaps you would like to share that reason with me."

Wilmer's hesitation was brief. Years of psychotherapy had accustomed him to unburdening himself to the medical profession. "Come over by the sea horses," he said. "I don't want the others to hear."

Briefly—since his throat was sore—he explained the situation to Dr. Roebuck. "So now I'm a squid," he ended.

"Um." Dr. Roebuck rubbed his nose. He had had some psychiatric training, and Wilmer did not seem particularly crazy to him. Besides, he was aware that a patient who is aggressive, anxious, and disoriented may actually be in better psychological shape than a person who is quiet and cooperative. Wilmer wasn't anxious or aggressive, but he was certainly disoriented.

"When's your doctor coming back?" he asked.

"Week from next Friday."

"Well, we might wait until then. You can't stay here, though. Could you afford a few days in a nursing home?"

Wilmer made a sort of gobbling noise.

"What's the matter?" asked Roebuck.

"Don't know. Air's dry. Throat hurts."

"Let me look at it."

With one of the cops' flashlights, Roebuck examined Wilmer's throat. "Good lord," he said after a moment. "Good lord."

"Matter?"

"Why, you've got—" it had been a long time since Roebuck had taken his course in comparative anatomy. Still, there was no mistaking it. "Why, man, you've got gills!"

"Have?" Wilmer asked uncertainly.

"Yes. Well, I don't suppose that makes much difference. Can you afford a nursing home?"

"Got 'nuff money. Can't go."

"Why not?"

"Live *here*. In tank."

"Nonsense," answered Roebuck, who could be stern on occasion. "You can't stay here."

". . . not?"

"Because it would annoy the other fish."

Against the cogency of this argument, Wilmer was helpless. He submitted to being led out to the police 'copter and flown to the Restwell Nursing Home. Roebuck saw him into a bathtub of salty water, and promised to come back next day.

Wilmer was still in the bath next morning.

"Where am I?" he asked as Roebuck came in.

"Why, in the Restwell Nursing Home." Roebuck sat down on the corner of the tub.

"No, no. Where am I?"

"Oh. Still in a tank at the Municipal Aquarium, I suppose."

"I want back."

"Impossible."

Wilmer began to weep. As he wept, he kept ducking his neck under the water to hydrate his gills.

"Let me look at those gills," said Roebuck, after the third duck. "H'um. They're more prominent than they were."

". . . I want my squid."

"You can't have it. I'm sorry. You'll just have to put up with this until Dr. Adams gets back."

"So long to wait," said Wilmer wistfully. "Want squid."

He continued to ask for his squid on Roebuck's next two visits, but on the fourth day the doctor found him sitting up in a chair, wearing a faded pink bathrobe.

"Out of the water, I see," said Roebuck. "How are you feeling today?"

"Okay," Wilmer answered in a high-pitched, listless voice. "Joints hurt, though." There was the hint of a lisp in his speech.

"Joints? Could be caused by staying in the water so long.

"Move over by the light. . . . You know, this is most unusual. Your gills seem to be going away." Roebuck frowned.

"Gillth?" Wilmer giggled. "What are you talking about, you funny man? Jointh hurt. And boneth. Fix it, Mither Man."

Roebuck frowned a little longer. Then, on a hunch, he ordered a series of skeletal x-rays. They showed an unusually large amount of cartilage for an adult skeleton, and a pelvis that was definitely gynecoid.

Roebuck was astonished. He knew how powerful psychosomatic effects can be; he would not have found it inconceivable that Wilmer's libidinal identification with the squid would finally have resulted in Wilmer's becoming completely aquaticized. But now the man's gills were atrophying, and his skeleton was becoming that of an immature female! It wasn't reasonable. Some remarkable psychic changes must be taking place.

What was happening, of course, was that Wilmer's libido, balked of its primary object, the squid, was ranging back over the other objects it had almost identified with, trying to find a stable one. It was an unconscious process, and Wilmer couldn't have told Roebuck about it even if the doctor had asked him. Roebuck didn't ask him.

On Roebuck's next visit, Wilmer wasn't talking at all. His skin had become a flat, lusterless tan, and he crunkled when he moved. That phase lasted for two days, and then Wilmer took to standing on one leg and barking. The barking phase was succeeded by . . .

The trouble with these surrogate libidinal identifications, as Wilmer realized on a sub-sub-unconscious plane, was that each of the objects had existed in relation to somebody else. The little girl had had her mama and her pink parasol. The furry dog had had its owner and the lamp post. Even the brown paper parcel had been carried by the old lady. But the manure bun—

Only the manure bun had been orbed, isolated, alone, splendidly itself.

On the day of Roebuck's final visit, the day before Adams was due back, Wilmer did not bark or crunkle or lisp. He merely sat in the armchair, spread-out, shiny and corpulent, exhaling a faintly ammoniacal smell that Roebuck, who had had a city boyhood, could not identify.

Early next morning Roebuck got Adams on the visiphone. They had a long conversation about Wilmer. Both of them were a little on the defensive about the way the case had turned out. Adams called at the Restwell Home, but he couldn't get Wilmer to speak to him. The psycho-therapist was just as much baffled by the symptomatology as Roebuck was.

Wilmer stayed on at the nursing home for a few days, both doctors watching him. There were no more changes. He had reached his nadir, his point of no return. There is nothing ahead for a man who has made a libidinal identification with a manure bun. Absolutely nothing.

When it became plain that nothing more was going to happen, he was removed to a state institution. He is still there. He still just sits, spread-out, shiny and corpulent, giving off an obsolete smell.

Whether he is happy or not is a question for philosophers. On the one hand, he has invested his libido in a thoroughly unworthy object. On the other hand, he has unquestionably invested it in *something*.

After Wilmer's commitment, his apartment was cleaned out and redecorated. The building superintendent was a frugal-minded woman who disliked wasting things. She latched on to the bottle of Syrup of Senta Beans.

She took the syrup for a couple of nights and then, since she couldn't see it had any effect, threw the bottle into the garbage reducer. She does not connect the "grand old Martian remedy" with the disembodied voices she has begun to hear.

THE AUTUMN AFTER NEXT

THE SPELL THE Free'l were casting ought to have drawn the moon down from the heavens, made water run uphill, and inverted the order of the seasons. But, since they had got broor's blood instead of newt's, were using alganon instead of vervet juice, and were three days later than the solstice anyhow, nothing happened.

Neeshan watched their antics with a bitter smile.

He'd tried hard with them. The Free'l were really a challenge to evangelical wizardry. They had some natural talent for magic, as was evinced by the frequent attempts they made to perform it, and they were interested in what he told them about its capacities. But they simply wouldn't take the trouble to do it right.

How long had they been stamping around in their circle, anyhow? Since early moonset, and it was now almost dawn. No doubt they would go on stamping all next day, if not interrupted. It was time to call a halt.

Neeshan strode into the middle of the circle. Rhn, the village chief, looked up from his drumming.

"Go away," he said. "You'll spoil the charm."

"What charm? Can't you see by now, Rhn, that it isn't going to work?"

"Of course it will. It just takes time."

"Hell it will. Hell it does. Watch."

Neeshan pushed Rhn to one side and squatted down in the center of the circle. From the pockets of his black robe he produced stylus, dragon's blood, oil of anointing, and salt.

He drew a design on the ground with the stylus, dropped dragon's blood at the corners of the parallelogram, and touched the inner cusps with the oil. Then, sighting carefully at the double red and white sun, which was just coming up, he touched the *outer* cusps with salt. An intense smoke sprang up.

When the smoke died away, a small lizardlike creature was visible in the parallelogram.

"Tell the demon what you want," Neeshan ordered the Free'l.

The Free'l hesitated. They had few wants, after all, which was one of the things that made teaching them magic difficult.

"Two big dyla melons," one of the younger ones said at last.

"A new andana necklace," said another.

"A tooter like the one you have," said Rhn, who was ambitious.

"Straw for a new roof on my hut," said one of the older females.

"That's enough for now," Neeshan interrupted. "The demon can't bring you a tooter, Rhn—you have to ask another sort of demon for that. The other things he can get. Sammel, to work!"

The lizard in the parallelogram twitched its tail. It disappeared, and returned almost immediately with melons, a handsome necklace, and an enormous heap of straw.

"Can I go now?" it asked.

"Yes." Neeshan turned to the Free'l, who were sharing the dyla melons out around their circle. "You see? *That's* how it ought to be. You cast a spell. You're careful with it. And it works. Right away."

"When you do it, it works," Rhn answered.

"Magic works when *anybody* does it. But you have to do it right."

Rhn raised his mud-plastered shoulders in a shrug. "It's such a lot of dreeze, doing it that way. Magic ought to be fun." He walked away, munching on a slice of the melon the demon had brought.

Neeshan stared after him, his eyes hot. "Dreeze" was a Free'l word that referred originally to the nasal drip that accompanied that race's virulent head colds. It had been extended to mean almost anything annoying. The Free'l, who spent much of their time sitting in the rain, had a lot of colds in the head.

Wasn't there anything to be done with these people? Even the simplest spell was too dreezish for them to bother with.

He was getting a headache. He'd better perform a headache-removing spell.

He retired to the hut the Free'l had assigned to him. The spell worked, of course, but it left him feeling soggy and dispirited. He was still standing in the hut, wondering what he should do next, when his big black-and-gold tooter in the corner gave a faint "woof." That meant headquarters wanted to communicate with him.

Neeshan carefully aligned the tooter, which is basically a sort of lens for focusing neural force, with the rising double suns. He moved his couch out into a parallel position and lay down on it. In a minute or two he was deep in a cataleptic trance.

The message from headquarters was long, circuitous, and couched in the elaborate, ego-caressing ceremonial of high magic, but its gist was clear enough.

"Your report received," it boiled down to. "We are glad to hear that you are keeping on with the Free'l. We do not expect you to succeed with them—none of the other magical missionaries we have sent out ever has. But if you *should* succeed, by any chance, you would get your senior warlock's rating immediately. It would be no exaggeration, in fact, to say that the highest offices in the Brotherhood would be open to you."

Neeshan came out of his trance. His eyes were round with wonder and cupidity. His senior warlock's rating—why, he wasn't due to get that for nearly four more six hundred-and-five-day years. And the higest offices in the Brotherhood—that could mean anything. Anything! He hadn't realized the Brotherhood set such store on converting the Free'l. Well, now, a reward like that was worth going to some trouble for.

Neeshan sat down on his couch, his elbows on his knees, his fists pressed against his forehead, and tried to think.

The Free'l liked magic, but they were lazy. Anything that involved accuracy impressed them as dreezish. And they didn't want anything.

That was the biggest difficulty. Magic had nothing to offer them. He had never, Neeshan thought, heard one of the Free'l express a want.

Wait, though. There was Rhn.

He had shown a definite interest in Neeshan's tooter. Something in its intricate, florid black-and-gold curves seemed to fascinate him. True, he hadn't been interested in it for its legitimate uses, which were to extend and develop a magician's spiritual power. He probably thought that having it would give him more prestige and influence among his people. But for one of the Free'l to say "I wish I had that" about anything whatever meant that he could be worked on. Could the tooter be used as a bribe?

Neeshan sighed heavily. Getting a tooter was painful and laborious. A tooter was carefully fitted to an individual magician's personality; in a sense, it was a part of his personality, and if Neeshan let Rhn have his tooter, he would be letting him have a part of himself. But the stakes were enormous.

Neeshan got up from his couch. It had begun to rain, but he didn't want to spend time performing a rain-repelling spell. He wanted to find Rhn.

Rhn was standing at the edge of the swamp, luxuriating in the downpour. The mud had washed from his shoulders, and he was already sniffling. Neeshan came to the point directly.

"I'll give you my tooter," he said, almost choking over the words, "if you'll do a spell—a simple spell, mind you—exactly right."

Rhn hesitated. Neeshan felt an impulse to kick him. Then he said, "Well . . ."

Neeshan began his instructions. It wouldn't do for him to help Rhn too directly, but he was willing to do everything reasonable. Rhn listened, scratching himself in the armpits and sneezing from time to time.

After Neeshan had been through the directions twice, Rhn stopped him. "No, don't bother telling me again—it's just more dreeze. Give me the materials and I'll show you. Don't forget, you're giving me the tooter for this."

He started off, Neeshan after him, to the latter's hut. While Neeshan looked on tensely, Rhn began going through the actions Neeshan had told him. Halfway through the first decad, he forgot. He inverted the order of the hand-passes, sprinkled salt on the wrong point, and mispronounced the names in the invocation. When he pulled his hands apart at the end, only a tiny yellow flame sprang up.

Neeshan cursed bitterly. Rhn, however, was delighted. "Look at that, will you!" he exclaimed, clapping his chapped, scabby little hands together. "It worked! I'll take the tooter home with me now."

"The tooter? For *that*? You didn't do the spell right."

Rhn stared at him indignantly. "You mean, you're not going to give me the tooter after all the trouble I went to? I only did it as a favor, really. Neeshan, I think it's very mean of you."

"Try the spell again."

"Oh, dreeze. You're too impatient. You never give anything time to work."

He got up and walked off.

For the next few days, everybody in the village avoided Neeshan. They all felt sorry for Rhn, who'd worked so hard, done everything he was told to, and been cheated out of his tooter by Neeshan. In the end the magician, cursing his own weakness, surrendered the tooter to Rhn. The accusatory atmosphere in the normally indifferent Free'l was intolerable.

But now what was he to do? He'd given up his tooter—he had to ask Rhn to lend it to him when he wanted to contact headquarters—and the senior rating was no nearer than before. His head ached constantly, and all the spells he performed to cure the pain left him feeling wretchedly tired out.

Magic, however, is an art of many resources, not all of them savory. Neeshan, in his desperation, began to invoke demons more disreputable than those he would ordinarily have consulted. In effect, he turned for help to the magical underworld.

His thuggish informants were none too consistent. One demon told him one thing, another something else. The consensus, though, was that while there was nothing the Free'l actually wanted enough to go to any trouble for it (they didn't even want to get rid of their nasal drip, for example—in a perverse way they were proud of it), there *was* one thing they disliked intensely—Neeshan himself.

The Free'l thought, the demons reported, that he was inconsiderate, tactless, officious, and a crashing bore. They regarded him as the psychological equivalent of the worst case of dreeze ever known, carried to the nth power. They wished he'd drop dead or hang himself.

Neeshan dismissed the last of the demons. His eyes had begun to shine. The Free'l thought he was a nuisance, did they? They thought he was the most annoying thing they'd encountered in the course of their racial history? Good. Fine. Splendid. Then he'd *really* annoy them.

He'd have to watch out for poison, of course. But in the end, they'd turn to magic to get rid of him. They'd have to. And then he'd have them. They'd be caught.

One act of communal magic that really worked and they'd be sold on magic. He'd be sure of his senior rating.

Neeshan began his campaign immediately. Where the Free'l were, there was he. He was always on hand with unwanted explanations, hypercritical objections, and maddening "wouldn't-it-be-betters."

Whereas earlier in his evangelical mission he had confined himself to pointing out how much easier magic would make life for the Free'l, he now counciled and advised them on every phase of their daily routine, from mud-smearing to rain-sitting, and from the time they got up until they went to bed. He even pursued them with advice *after* they got into bed, and told them how to run their sex lives—advice which the Free'l, who set quite as much store by their sex lives as anybody does, resented passionately.

But most of all he harped on their folly in putting up with nasal drip, and instructed them over and over again in the details of a charm—a quite simple charm—for getting rid of it. The charm would, he informed them, work equally well against anything—*or person*—that they found annoying.

The food the Free'l brought him began to have a highly peculiar taste. Neeshan grinned and hung a theriacal charm, a first-class antidote to poison, around his neck. The Free'l's distaste for him bothered him, naturally, but he could stand it. When he had repeated the anti-annoyance charm to a group of Free'l last night, he had noticed that Rhn was listening eagerly. It wouldn't be much longer now.

On the morning of the day before the equinox, Neeshan was awakened from sleep by an odd prickling sensation in his ears. It was a sensation he'd experienced only once before in his life, during his novitiate, and it took him a moment to identify it. Then he realized what it was. Somebody was casting a spell against him.

At last! At last! It had worked!

Neeshan put on his robe and hurried to the door of the hut. The day seemed remarkably overcast, almost like night, but that was caused by the spell. This one happened to involve the optic nerves.

He began to grope his way cautiously toward the village center. He didn't want the Free'l to see him and get suspicious, but he did want to have the pleasure of seeing them cast their first accurate spell. (He was well protected against wind-damage from it, of course.) When he was almost at the center, he took cover behind a hut. He peered out.

They were doing it *right*. Oh, what a satisfaction! Neeshan felt his chest expand with pride. And when the spell worked, when the big wind swooped down and blew him away, the Free'l would certainly receive a second magical missionary more kindly. Neeshan might even come back, well disguised, himself.

The ritual went on. The dancers made three circles to the left, three circles to the right. Cross over, and all sprinkle salt on the interstices of the star Rhn had traced on the ground with the point of a knife. Back to the circle. One to the left, one to right, while Rhn, in the center of the circle, dusted over the salt with— with *what*?

"Hey!" Neeshan yelled in sudden alarm. "Not brimstone! Watch out! You're not doing it ri—"

His chest contracted suddenly, as if a large, stony hand had seized his thorax above the waist. He couldn't breathe, he couldn't think, he couldn't even say "Ouch!" It felt as if his chest—no, his whole body—was being compressed in on itself and turning into something as hard as stone.

He tried to wave his tiny, heavy arms in a counter-charm; he couldn't even inhale. The last emotion he experienced was one of bitterness. He might have *known* the Free'l couldn't get anything right.

The Free'l take a dim view of the small stone image that now stands in the center of their village. It is much too heavy for them to move, and while it is not nearly so much of a nuisance as Neeshan was when he was alive, it inconveniences them. They have to make a detour around it when they do their magic dances.

They still hope, though, that the spells they are casting to get rid of him will work eventually. If he doesn't go away this autumn, he will the autumn after next. They have a good deal of faith in magic, when you come right down to it. And patience is their long suit.

THE SORROWS OF WITCHES

WHO CARES FOR the joys or sorrows of witches? In both they are set apart from ordinary humanity. If witches are glad, it is because they have purchased joys beyond the common at the cost of their souls. And if they suffer in ways that we cannot know, when their dark lords desert them, it is no more than the wicked things deserve. Yet they are women, with the hearts of women, for all that.

Morganor was a queen of Enbatana, one of the great Enbatanid line of necromantic queens. From her earliest years she had studied the mantic arts with her grandmother, her mother being dead; and by the time she was twenty she had attained an unheard-of mastery of unholy things. Those of her subjects who hated her—and there were a few—swore that she had her power from the rotting mummy of a monkey that she fed in abominable ways at the dark of the moon, and that she was attended always by the writhing spirits of two men whom she had slain in torture. It was certain that no wizard of her time or before it could approach her in invocation, the lore of philtres, and the power to summon up and dismiss.

But for all her necromantics she was a wise queen, and the land throve under her. The faïence of the workmen of Enbatana went wherever white-winged ships could sail; the webs of the women of Enbatana brought a great price in any marketplace. No child in Enbatana went hungry, no old man or woman thought with dread of what the morrow might bring.

Morganor had many lovers. They were won, it was said, not so much by the glamour of her queenship or the power of her philtres as by the wonderful beauty of her person and the sweetness of her voice, which was like the notes of a golden lyre. She tired of her lovers quickly, and left them, and they were forbidden to feel jealousy.

But in the queen's twenty-third year there came an embassy to her court from the land of the burnt faces. Among the soldiers who attended the embassy was a captain named Llwdres, a huge man like a lion, with a bronzed face. And Morganor, as if her stars had enjoined it on her, fell desperately in love with him.

She wooed him shyly at first, with gifts of fruit and little presents. Then, when she met no response, she showed him favor openly and sent him queenly gifts.

Morganor could scarcely believe it when he continued cold and averse. She bit her lips in vexation and set herself to brew a sovereign philtre, and this philtre she gave him to drink as he sat at table by her side. With kindling eyes she saw him put the golden cup down empty from his lips. But Llwdres might have drunk clear water for all the good she had from him.

Then indeed was Morganor desperate. She rose hastily and went to her apartments. Up and down she paced, gnawing her white wrists and tearing her dark hair. Remember, from her birth until this moment no wish of hers, possible or impossible, had gone ungratified. Llwdres' stubborn refusal seemed to her out of the order of things, perverse, unnatural, intolerable.

At last she called the chief of the palace guard to her and gave him orders. Llwdres was to be taken to a dungeon and whipped. He had ignored her soft words, her smile and her love-presents, had he? She would see what physical pain could do. Then she threw herself down on a long divan and wept.

The minutes went by—so many that Morganor, who had ordered but twenty lashes, grew afraid. She had risen to her feet and started to the door when a terrified servant, beating the ground before her with his head, stammered out that Llwdres had been put to death.

Morganor felt that her heart would stop beating. She ran through the palace like a madwoman. When she reached the dungeon she saw by the winking light of the torches that Llwdres' limbs had been severed from his body; he had died painfully. And she saw, without understanding it, that another body was dangling by a noose from a crenation in the dungeon walls, the body of the chief of her palace guard. He had hanged himself.

Morganor realized then, too late, that she had given Llwdres for punishment to a man who had been her lover for a pair of nights. He had trembled and turned white when she had told him she wanted no more of him. Why had she not seen how jealous he was? Unbearable jealousy had driven him to kill Llwdres. And after that he had hanged himself.

Morganor knelt by the body of her beloved and gathered the severed limbs to herself, like Isis in search for dead Osiris. She covered them with tears and kisses. Then she had them lifted up carefully and borne to her apartments. And after that, for many days and nights, she wept.

She wept until her hair was sodden with weeping. She could have put out the coals of a great fire had she shaken her hair over it. But at last her old nurse came to her, a book of enchantments in one hand and in the other Morganor's rings and bracelets of sorcery, and she said in a quavering voice, "Queen of the Enbatanians, how long will you weep for your beloved and lament? Have you forgotten that you are the daughter of queens and the mistress of all mantic arts?"

Morganor was as if deaf at first, but at last she roused herself. She called her maids, and they bathed and anointed her. She purified herself with incense and put on garments of virgin samite. She donned her rings and bracelets, her pectorals of sorcery. And she opened many volumes from her shelves of books.

Nonetheless, it was a dreadful task she had set herself. To rouse the dead after a fashion is not difficult; it lies within the province of any hedgerow sorcerer. False life may be infused into them, and they may be set to striding about stiffly with unseeing eyes. Or demons, great strange spirits may be made to enter and animate them. But Morganor would have none of this. Llwdres must live again as he had been in very life. And this goal, Morganor knew, lay at the very limits of sorcery.

She labored for many days, and without success. She had arrested decay in Llwdres' body by a great spell, but for the rest he was mere lifeless flesh. She stopped for a day, waiting out an inauspicious aspect of her stars, and during this time she sent a dire enchantment against the soul of the slayer of her beloved. Wherever he was, in whatever dim after-world, he should pay for it, he should pay! Then Morganor returned once more to her work.

On the twenty-sixth night, as she stood in a triple circle and the palace lights burned blue, a mighty spirit appeared to her. He proposed a bargain to her. If she would surrender much of her mantic power—nay, the greater part—it could be done, and Llwdres could live again. There was also another sacrifice—but the demon would not name what.

Morganor turned pale, but she nodded. She erased the circle around her, and gave to the spirit all her symbols and arcana of power save for two elementary volumes and a simple gold amulet. The mighty spirit, free from the constraint Morganor had put on him and his whole tribe, beat his wings together in a paroxysm of delight and darted like a river of fire through the roof. And Llwdres, lying on his bier, stirred.

He stirred and mumbled words. After a moment he sat up and looked at her. And he smiled.

For, whether the necromancy of the mighty spirit had changed Llwdres' nature, or whether, as Morganor thought, be had only refused her before from country pride and fear to be ruled by a woman as great as Morganor was, this time he loved her with all the strength and ardor of a man. They met in an embrace like the coupling of eagles. And Morganor had such joy at the fulfillment of her love that she anointed the posts of her bed with nard from Punt, and kissed the bed covers. Joy shone in her face as if a lamp had been lit within the flesh.

She kept her resurrected love with her for a month, and all those days were to her as one day. With each embrace he gave her, her love for him grew. She dreamed of setting him beside her on the throne of Enbatana as king, but she knew this was impossible. Her people were proud in a perverse way of their necromantic queen, but they were a stiff-necked and narrow-minded folk. If she set a dead man over them as lord—and there were certain inescapable signs that Llwdres, though he lived now, had once been dead—some of them would rise against her, and some would be true. There would be war within Enbatana then, and all the bitterness of civil strife. Already gossip, though wide of the mark, was beginning to seep through the palace and out into the streets.

On the thirty-first day, therefore, Llwdres consenting, Morganor cast him into a deep sleep most like that sleep of death from which he had arisen recently. For his bed he had a massive chest wrought and inlaid with gold, and this chest Morganor kept always in her bedchamber. Whenever it seemed to her safe, she would rouse her captain, using what remained to her, of her mantic art, and they would hold love dalliance. And this unhallowed commerce wrapped her senses in such a blaze of sweetness that she had eyes for no other man.

But always her councillors urged on her to wed. They presented her with petitions written on velum, respectful in phraseology but peremptory in tone, in which they spoke of her daughterless state, and the evils which befall the kingdom left without a queen. When Morganor cursed them royally, the councillors bowed to the ground and drew up new petitions to present to her. At last Morganor, acknowledging the justice of what they said, gave in.

She told the council to pick what mate for her they pleased. Puffed with self-importance, they went fussily to their task, and pitched at last on a neighboring princeling named Fabius, a man famed for his virtue (here Morganor laughed), and his piety. From the picture they showed her, he was well-enough made, with a girlish, small-featured face.

The marriage was celebrated with more rejoicing among the people than there was in Morganor's heart. She but endured her new consort for the sake of her realm, though he was a well-intentioned man. To her he was a small flame bleached by Llwdres' lordly sun.

In time a child was born to Morganor. It was certainly the child of her consort, since those who have been dead, however ardent they are, can kindle no new life. But Morganor, in the unfailing sweetness of her love for Llwdres, felt that her womb had been enchanted and that her child was begotten by her own true love and none else. She was happy in her motherhood. Then Enbatana was afflicted by two dry years.

The drought in itself would not have harmed the land. The vast granaries which Morganor's mother's mother's mother had built, Morganor herself had consolidated and enlarged. Enbatana might have suffered a dozen worse years and known no dearth. But the nomads to the north of Enbatana, always on the edge of starvation, saw their scanty pasturage dry up and the sands begin to blow. Soon they were in motion like a deadly storm sweeping onward from the desert's heart.

Morganor, wise queen, hated war. She tried to treat with the nomads, to settle them on the marshes of her land as husbandmen. But they broke treaty after treaty, and Morganor saw at last that they were fierce and faithless men who despised the tasks of husbandry and civic life. Their only art was to destroy what others had built, to turn fruitful land to desert under the hungry jaws of their sheep and goats. They gathered on the borders of Enbatana as many as locusts, and their sunken eyes were dark with battle lust and hate.

Morganor assembled her council and asked for plans. One said one thing and one another; all trembled and uttered doleful prophesies. Fabius, the virtuous Fabius, advised prayer and fasting and sacrifice. So Morganor once more roused her lover, this time for counsel, not dalliance. And Llwdres proved himself as skillful and brave in war as he had been in love.

He told Morganor to levy armies with the grain tithe lists ranging battle plans. Then, the armies being assembled, the as base. He told her how to judge her generals and captains, which to trust and which to dismiss, and how to lay long-queen and her dead leman rose out at their head.*

While the do-nothing king hugged the capital and prayed and fasted, there were many battles. The terror of the times had relaxed all ordinary rules of conduct, and Morganor spent many a brief, alarm-broken night in her lover's arms. The men of Enbatana, for all their lack of practice in war, fought with desperate bravery. Morganor herself was wounded once, in her right thigh. And it was

---

* Ed.: The text of this paragraph matches the original source material.

said in aftertimes by grave historians that Enbatana was saved in her darkest hour by a dead man and an accursed necromantic queen.

There was one great battle, a nightmare of confusion and blood and dust. Llwdres bore the royal standard in it and fought as a lion fights. When the battle was over, nearly half the men of Enbatana were dead. But the nomads had died to the last man.

Morganor remembered prudence then. She cast Llwdres once more into the sleep that was so like death and, giving out that he had died of wounds received in battle, had him placed in state on a bier in her train. When they reached the capital he was conveyed secretly to her apartments and placed once more in the gold-wrought chest.

But Fabius, like a virtuous man, was jealous of his honor. Rumors reached him. He conceived suspicions. One night, when Morganor had been long asleep and Llwdres slept unbreathing in the chest, he came to her apartments with his bodyguard.

"Accursed witch!" he shouted at her as she blinked up at him with sleep-dazzled eyes. "Where is the man with whom you defile my bed?"

Morganor was for a moment utterly puzzled. Fabius had never been real to her. She did not know what he meant. "I have never defiled it," she said in a sleep-roughened voice.

"No?" He strode stiffly about her bedchamber, looked under draperies and pulling out hangings with his sword. At last he said to his attendants, "The dog must be here. We will drive him out. Fire the room."

One of his men touched a torch to a length of drapery that hung beside Llwdres' chest. Flame shot up instantly and spread over the ceiling in a gush. And Morganor screamed.

She sprang from her bed and darted toward the shelf that held her last tools of the mantic art. In her mind was only one thought, to put out the fire by magic before it could fasten on Llwdres' enchanted limbs. She feared not merely his death but some horror which should transgress the bounds of the possible. The mighty spirit had warned her of another sacrifice. But two of Fabius' guards caught her and held her, for all her struggles and imperious cursing she could not get free.

Then Morganor, turning to her consort, said, "Let me go and I will confess it. Let me go, and I will swear never to defile your bed again."

Fabius looked at her narrowly. His face was flushed with his poor triumph. "Do you swear it on your royal honor?" he demanded. The flames were already licking around the chest.

"I swear it," Morganor said.

"Release her," Fabius ordered his men.

They let go the queen's wrists. The room was full of smoke and fire. Morganor ran through it, choking, and seized her books and amulet desperately. She gasped out a spell, traced figures in the air, cast a powder toward the fire. And the flames died down sullenly.

Morganor saw that the chest, though charred, was unhurt. She ran to it and cast her arms about it, sinking on her knees. Except for that, she was too spent to move.

Fabius came toward her, naked sword in hand. "So that was where the dog was, was it?" he said bitterly. "Out of the way, witch. I am going to kill him now."

Morganor got slowly to her feet. "Consort of the queen of Enbatana," she said in a clear voice, "do you hope to sit again on the lower throne by my side?"

Fabius wavered. Then he recovered himself. "I avenge my honor," he said.

"Your honor will not avail you when my people tear you in pieces," Morganor said. "They remember who saved them in battle, and who fasted and prayed. Therefore I charge you solemnly as you hope to consort with me and beget other children on me: do not open the chest." This she said because she knew that if Fabius saw who slept in the chest there would be civil war.

Their eyes met. His eyes were hawk's eyes, but Morganor's were the eyes of an eagle. At last he said, "So be it. But remember, my queen, your royal oath."

"I remember," Morganor said.

When he and his men had gone she went over to a window and stood looking out. The sky was paling; it would not be long before dawn. She saw the greater infortune regarding her malevolently from her tenth house, and she thought of the configurations of the stars and the varied fortunes of men. Then she went to the chest and, for the last time, awakened her love.

They sat for some hours together, talking quietly, their hands joined. There could be no love between them, because of Morganor's great oath. Only, before she lulled him into sleep again, Llwdres gave the last of many kisses to his queen's lips. Then Morganor went out to her lawful consort, and thenceforward day and night were alike to her, and both wearied her.

But the body of her beloved she had conveyed by those she trusted most to a great mountain to the east of her domain, a mountain at whose heart there was a chamber cut out of solid rock. The attendants left Llwdres in the chamber, as the queen had ordered them, and sealed it with masonry. And there the captain lies in his enchanted slumber until a greater necromantic queen or a more fortunate of Morganor's line shall come to awaken him.